NOTHING PERSONAL

A ROMANTIC COMEDY

KARINA HALLE

METAL BLONDE BOOKS

For anyone who needs a bit of love, laughter and light right now

WARNING: Just in case you're sensitive to foul-mouthed heroines and heroes, graphic sex, raunchy humour and other silliness and shenanigans, this book has a fuckton of it.

Therefore, Reader Discretion is strongly advised.

CHAPTER ONE

NOVA

SEINFELD.

My life has officially turned into an episode of Seinfeld.

To be specific, the "Vegetable Lasagna" one where Elaine and Puddy go to Europe, break up, get back together on the plane and then break up again.

That awkward plane ride full of bickering, all to the discomfort of the passenger next to them (aka Vegetable Lasagna), is pretty much what I'm going through right now as we come back from our Vegas vacation.

Except Roger doesn't really bicker, which is a good thing since he has this problem controlling the volume of his voice. We might be at a romantic restaurant and he'll say, "you look ravishing tonight" (yeah, he uses ravishing, which should have been a red flag), and someone across the restaurant will say, "thank you." That's how loud he is. Even when he whispers, he's trying to rupture your eardrum.

No, Roger doesn't bicker but he also doesn't do much of anything.

Everyone was surprised when we started dating five

months ago. Roger is very much the opposite of the guys I usually date and I figured that was a good thing since the guys I usually date are rat-bastards. Handsome rat-bastards, but rat-bastards all the same.

Turns out Roger is a rat-bastard too, and one I didn't see coming, which has really given my pride a kick in the ass. I went out with Roger because he was a supposed nice guy. I went out with him because he was a dependable and financially stable banker. I went out with him because he looked like a potato with long legs. All of those things were supposed to mean that Roger was a safe choice.

It turns out that when a guy refers to himself as "a nice guy," they usually aren't. That when they have a boring job and dull attitude, they might go looking for excitement elsewhere. And just because they have a big fat balding potato head and tend to shout lyrics to songs instead of singing them, doesn't mean they won't think they're god's gift to women.

I found that out two days ago when I decided I'd had enough and went to bed early, and he went out to get a lap dance on the Strip and well, I guess those dancers can spot a sucker a mile away, because a lap dance led to a blow job, and a blow job led to who knows what else was on the menu and that dancer turned out to be a hooker.

And how do I know all of this?

Because at four a.m. he came stumbling into the room and went straight to the shower, crying his damn eyes out. When I asked him what was wrong (I thought maybe he was mugged at gunpoint) he told me everything that happened. Okay, not everything—I stopped him at the blow job part.

I appreciated his honesty and all, but that was officially the end of us.

Then the next day, when he'd sobered up and slept off the skank and the shame, he acted like nothing happened. Back to yelling ("I didn't know she was a prostitute! I thought she was being nice!") over coffee and wondering if I wanted to see David Copperfield (yet another red flag).

I did what any sensible person would do—I got another room.

In another hotel.

Immediately.

Then I proceeded to get drunk.

By myself.

Immediately.

The only thing I couldn't fix were the flights back to Honolulu. They were all booked solid which isn't surprising for November. If you've ever wondered where the people who live in Hawaii go on vacation, it's Las Vegas. The money, the glamour, the lights, the chaos, the dry, desert air —it's pretty much everything you start craving when you've been in Hawaii too long.

Which is why Roger and I decided to go to Vegas, taking our first vacation together.

Of course, it also ended up being our last.

The most annoying thing about all of this *isn't* that we couldn't find anyone to switch seats with us for this six-hour plane ride from hell, but I'd specifically chosen Roger to date to avoid all this sort of stupidity.

Roger is currently trying to adjust his seat-back, much to the annoyance of the person behind him. He can't even do anything subtly or gently, he's just this long-legged, potato-headed clumsy oaf who sleeps with hookers and cries about it. You can how imagine how the sex between us was. I'd felt like I was being mauled by a mule, lots of accidental kicking, big teeth where there shouldn't be big teeth, and the occasional braying noise.

I look at him, fixing him with a hard stare, both hating him for being such a loser and myself for dating him to begin with. I need to get my high standards back.

"What?" he asks defensively, after I've been glaring at him for a good minute. Did I mention he's also kind of dense?

"Do you mind not doing that?" I tell him.

"My back hurts," he grumbles, loud enough for everyone on the plane to hear. "And these seats are made for children. Why didn't we fly first class again?"

Seat goes back, seat goes up, seat goes back.

"Because you wanted to save your money...probably so you could spend it all on that hooker."

The woman next to me stiffens. That's our Vegetable Lasagna. She's been trapped here with us for five hours now, pressed up against the window as if she's wiling it to suck her out. This is the first time I've brought up the hooker.

It won't be the last.

"Don't you dare mention *her* in public again," he says, shoving up his glasses. "I told you, I thought she was just a stripper."

And of course, because he's so damn dense, he has no idea that the whole plane can hear him talking about this now, too.

But as much as I would love to argue loudly with him about the blow jobs, and the fact that it doesn't even matter if she was a hooker or not—hello, he cheated on me—I decide it's not worth it. He's embarrassing himself enough as it is.

The only silver lining in this whole thing is that I didn't love him.

I liked him but I convinced myself I liked him more than I did.

That was it.

So my heart is staying intact, it's only my pride that's taken a tumble, and the fact that I feel like I've wasted months of my life sleeping with a mule (who was *definitely* not hung like one).

On the heartbreak scale, Roger is about a one.

And believe me, I've had my heart broken at level-ten on the scale before, so anything less than ten is a blessing. That's something I wouldn't wish on my worst enemy.

It's ironic that my worst enemy is the man who did that level ten heartbreak.

I sigh, partly in relief that I can feel the plane start to descend, partly because even though bygones are bygones, some people can really do a number on you.

Thank god Roger won't be one of them.

THERE's something strangely intimidating about your first day back at work after a vacation. Even though I'd only been gone for just over a week, and I've been working at my job for five years, I still feel like I'm the new kid during first day of high school. Even the commute from my house, over the Koolau Mountains to downtown Honolulu, feels like I'm going a new route and my fingers can't stop tapping anxiously on the steering wheel.

It probably has a lot to do with the fact that I haven't taken a vacation in a really long time. I visited my parents in Washington state for Christmas last year, but that was anything but relaxing. Before that, I was in Seattle for my sister's funeral. As you can imagine, that wasn't a vacation either.

I shake the thought out of my head—despite the familiar pang in my chest, like a septic wound that will never actually heal—and stay focused on the day ahead.

Even when I pull into my reserved parking spot, something I'd fought hard for when I became the Brand Marketing Director for Kahuna Hotels, I still feel like it belongs to someone else.

I turn off the car and rest my head on the steering wheel. When I left for Vegas, everyone told me to go completely off the grid, to enjoy being with Roger (insert eye roll here). To get drunk, have fun, let loose. I was forbidden from checking my emails and, even though I did check my emails nearly every day anyway, no one sent me anything. It's like the whole office conspired to let me take a break.

Now it feels like I didn't take a break at all, I was just on sabbatical, forced to let the rest of the world do my job.

But when the elevator pops me out on the tenth floor and I stride into the lobby, I feel like I'm shrugging on my armor again, ready to battle. It feels good to be back.

"Welcome back," Kate, the receptionist, says, as I stroll over to her desk. "You look well-rested." She's a recent transplant from the island of Kauai after her old workplace, a hotel, closed due to the massive flooding they've had. She's sarcastic, honest and fun—my kind of people.

Except, despite the cheery greeting, there's a look of trepidation on her well-groomed brows.

"You know, when you go to Vegas, the whole point is to *not* rest," I remind her, leaning on the edge of her station.

Her computer screen is showing Facebook, which she knows to not bother hiding from me.

"So, it was a good trip?" she asks, uneasily tucking her straight black hair behind her ear.

"Actually it was the trip from hell, but I won't get into that right now," I tell her. "Are you okay? You seem a bit...cagey."

Her eyes dart over to the rest of the office. Since we take up the whole floor, it's a circular design with the reception area and lobby, elevators, break room and washrooms all in the center, cubicles fanning out in a radius toward the windows where the executive offices and boardrooms are. I'm early for work—I usually am—so the office is still a bit quiet.

"We all promised we wouldn't tell you," she says in a hush. "I mean, I wanted to text you, but Desiree said she'd have my head on a stick, and I believe her. Did you know she teaches Tae Kwon Do on the weekends?"

"Tell me what?" I ask. Oh my god, did they find someone better to do my job while I was gone? Is it my assistant, Mahina? She's always so nice and such a go-getter, but I knew she was secretly gunning for my position.

"Mike is gone," she says.

"He's dead!?" I yell.

"Shhh," she says harshly and we both look over to see Wallis from accounting peering over his partition at us. "He's not dead. If he was dead, do you think I'd so casually drop it like that?"

"I don't know, you're a casual kind of person, you once told me about the time you got your butthole bleached when we were discussing where to eat for lunch, and I'd only known you for a week. So, if he's not dead, what do you mean *gone*?"

"He quit."

"Quit!?"

Kate shushes me again, Wallis's head is poking up again, like an aggravated groundhog. He makes a show of putting on his headphones to drown us out.

"Stop shushing me, Wallis chose his cubicle life. Is it supposed to be a secret?"

"No, everyone knows now," she says with a sigh.

"Except for me." Totally irked about that. "Why did he quit? Is he okay?"

Mike is...*was*...my superior, my boss, even though I thought of him more as an equal. He held the title of the Senior VP of Sales, Marketing and Revenue, the position I've been building myself up to take over.

"He's fine," she says, and lowers her voice again. "He fell in love."

"In love?"

She nods just as the elevator dings. "He fell hard."

"With who? Who quits their job because they fell in love?"

Now she's biting back a smile. "You won't believe it if I tell you."

"Do I know her?"

"I doubt it, but you could surprise me."

I don't even know what that means.

"And this all happened while I was gone?"

She nods and then quickly clicks away her Facebook browser as the CEO, George Proctor, and Desiree Wakatsuki, the Senior Vice President of Human Resources, walk over to us from the elevators.

"Nova Lane," George says heartily. "I was starting to think you might not ever come back. How was Vegas, did you get lucky? Did you bet sixteen red like I told you? Hope you didn't have too many of those drinks in the big cups, those things are deadly."

If you haven't already guessed, the CEO is a giant dork. If you looked up "giant dork" in the dictionary, you'd see his face, right next to Bill Gates and Carlton from *The Fresh Prince of Bel Air*. I used to think George had some hidden ruthless side of him, because how else do you get to the top of a company without stepping on a few heads, but he's honestly just a nice guy.

"Sixteen red, I remembered," I tell him, because you always suck up to the big boss. "And you won twenty dollars."

He makes a horrible awkward fist pump. "Awesome. Have that Andrew Jackson turn into some ramen from Lucky Belly and we'll call it even."

I feign a smile. I barely gambled in Vegas, so the whole betting on red sixteen was a lie and now I have to buy him lunch.

"I hope you enjoyed the time off," Desiree says in a measured voice. She's a half-Japanese woman in her sixties, always so cool and calm, perfectly choosing her words and intonation. No wonder she's a master of Tae Kwon Do. "Do you want to pop by my office at eleven? There's something I need to discuss with you."

"Of course," I tell her as they walk off.

"She wants to fill you in about Mike but they aren't going to tell you the real dirt," Kate says, when they're out of earshot.

I'm tempted to ask about the real dirt, because so far his reason for quitting is crazy. Mike Epson was the most even-keeled man you could imagine. He wore the same thing every single day, the ugliest, craziest Hawaiian shirt you could imagine, and in a city full of Hawaiian shirts as corporate wear, his made your eyes bleed. It was his way of being exciting, since his life consisted of watching the NHL, avoiding the sun, and bowling on Friday nights.

Suffice it to say, the fact that the shy middle-aged perpetual bachelor found love and quit his very prestigious and well-paid job over it, is completely out of character.

And while I loved Mike as a boss and always wanted the best for him, the fact that he's gone means his job is now vacant.

His job that I've spent the last two years actively working toward.

Yeah, maybe I work a lot because that's all I know how to do, but I'm very goal-oriented and competitive and if I'm not moving up, I'm not going anywhere.

This has been in my line of sight for a long time.

That job should be *mine*.

"Has she said anything about filling the position?" I ask Kate bluntly.

She shrugs. "Not to me. Maybe that's what she wants to talk to you about."

I'm this close to doing an embarrassing happy dance in front of her, which I know resembles Snoopy dancing on top of Schroeder's piano, but I manage to rein it in. I don't want to put the cart before the horse, even though what I really want to do is get on that pony and ride it all the way to Promotionville.

"Do you want to do lunch today?" she asks. "We could go to Lucky Belly and get George's ramen and you can fill me in on your sexy vacay."

I roll my eyes. "Lunch sounds good. We might not get a lot of eating done because I have a lot to tell you. And no... it's not what you think."

Although knowing Kate, she probably factored hookers

somewhere in the equation.

The next two hours fly by as I await the meeting with Desiree. There's a lot of work to catch up on and, even though my assistant Mahina has done a really good job managing it (a little too good), most of the stuff only I can do. I'm hit with a lot of post-vacation guilt and my mind starts to run away on me.

If I hadn't gone away, I wouldn't be so behind on everything.

If I hadn't gone away, maybe I'd already have Mike's job.

My mother always told me that there was no use worrying over something that's already happened since it can't change a thing. But the thing is, I always thought worrying could change something. I thought it worked like a prayer. I thought it bought you insurance so that when the worst happened, you wouldn't be caught blindsided.

But both of us knew that worrying about my sister wouldn't change anything and we did it anyway.

At ten past eleven, Desiree calls me and tells me to come into her office. With the call coming ten minutes later than expected, I've already given my pineapple-shaped stress ball a real workout and I'm practically flying out the door. I give a quick wave to Teef, our IT guy in the office next door, and hurry around the other side.

The door to Desiree's office is open slightly so I poke my head in. "I'm here," I tell her.

"Come on in," she says. "Shut the door, please."

Desiree's office has sweeping views of the harbor and you can even see a bit of Diamond Head peeking out from between high-rises. Today the water looks extra nice, sparkling in lines of deep blue and turquoise. The office next door to hers is...*was* Mike's and I would kill for this view. My office faces another building with only a glimpse of the green mountains behind. There's one guy across from me who spends his lunch hour doing yoga in his underwear on top of his desk.

I shut the door and take a seat across from her.

She has a folder in her hands but she pushes it to the side. It has a name on it that I can't quite read and I don't want to be obvious that I'm trying to.

"So, I take it you had a nice time," Desiree says, folding her hands in front of her.

This is where it gets tricky. Do I just pretend everything is fine or do I tell her the truth? Before I got to the office, I was all prepared to vent to everyone since my co-workers are my only family here. But now that this whole Mike quitting thing has reared its head, I'm not sure if the distraction is a good idea.

"It was very dry and busy and hot," I tell her with a quick smile. "So, what did you want to speak to me about? Did something happen while I was gone?"

She frowns for a moment. I'm usually not so blunt.

"As it happens," she slowly goes on with a sad look in her eyes, "something did happen while you were gone. We didn't want to bother you about it until you got back but Mike quit unexpectedly."

I try to act shocked. "Oh my god," I say in a hushed voice, my hand at my chest.

Her lips quirk up. "So, I take it Kate already told you," she says dryly.

"Am I that bad of an actor?"

She laughs. "Yes. You are. So what did Kate say?"

"She didn't say much except that Mike fell in love."

"That's pretty much it," she says with a sigh. "I don't understand it myself, but he met this woman who was here on vacation, I guess she'd gone to his bowling alley, and the next thing I know I get his resignation letter saying he was going to go live in Thailand with her."

"Thailand?! Are you sure she's a woman?"

She shrugs. "Oh, she's a woman all right. I guess Kate didn't tell you the part where this woman happens to be a quasi-famous...adult film actress."

"He ran away with a porn star?"

This is getting weirder.

She winces at the thought. "Yes." Then she shakes her head, as if trying to shed a mental image. "So that's the story as far as we know. He's already gone. No two-week notice either. So we're scrambling to try and fill his position."

Oh my god.

Here it comes.

My promotion.

I try to keep from squirming in my seat, pressing my lips together so I'm not prematurely smiling.

She goes on. "As you know, you've been working for Mike pretty much since you got here. You've learned a lot from him. And you know we've been talking to him to see who he'd recommend for his spot."

Here it comes, here it comes...

"But as adamant as Mike was, we just couldn't be sure. There's so much pressure right now to fill this role and we want to do it right."

"Uh, huh," I manage to say, getting confused.

"It's a bit unorthodox to ask someone to uproot their lives for a three-month temp position but we figured it would be the best thing to do, considering your history together."

I blink at her. "My what? My history?"

For some reason, anytime anyone mentions some sort of

dubious history, I always think back to the time I got taken in by the cops when I was fifteen for tipping cows in a neighbor's field.

"This isn't about the cows is it?" I add.

She frowns. "No," she says slowly. "This is about your work history. Mike knew you worked together for a few years and because of that we thought we'd run it by you. Though I do hope it's not a problem, because he's waiting in the lobby."

Hold the phones. What the hell is going on here?

Does this mean I'm *not* getting the job?

Who is *he*?

"I'm sorry Desiree, maybe it's the jet lag, but what on earth are you talking about? What history? Who is in the lobby?"

"The man who Mike recommended for the job. He's been working at one of our rival chains for the last few years, same position as you. And before that, you both worked for us in Palm Desert." She picks up the folder and tosses it to me.

It lands face up with a splat.

The name glaring up at me as if it were carved from a dagger.

Kessler Rocha.

My ex-coworker.

My ex-lover.

My level-ten heartbreaker.

"Kate," Desiree says, pressing the intercom button on her phone. "Can you show Mr. Rocha into my office now? Mahalo."

OH.

MY.

GOD.

CHAPTER TWO

KESSLER

"FIRST DAY AT WORK, little buddy. You going to wish me luck?" I ask Hunter while I fiddle with my tie in the mirror.

When I don't get an answer, I glance over my shoulder at him.

He's hanging out in the doorway, one finger up his nose, shirtless, even though I just saw the nanny put his shirt on a minute ago.

"I'm afraid of leprechauns," he says in a quiet voice. I've gotten used to having to lean in and really listen because he's just so quiet but I'm still not sure I heard him right.

"What leprechauns?" I ask carefully.

"The leprechauns who hang out with the pot of gold in the toilet and wishes you luck."

Ah. I see.

Sorta.

"Well let's just ignore all that for now. You going to be good while I'm gone?"

He stares at me for a moment with his big blue eyes and as usual I'm struck with the strangest combination of love and fear. Love for him because he's my child, and that's becoming more and more apparent every day.

Fear because I have no clue in hell what I'm doing and I don't think I'm ever going to get any better.

He doesn't answer. Getting him to talk is like pulling teeth, something I'm trying not to take personally. It's not *me* he doesn't want to talk to, it's everyone, and I should just understand that he's quiet for a three-year-old.

"Loan," I call out, and she appears right behind him, silent as snow. "Hey Loan," I say, giving her my biggest, most charming smile, the smile that appeared on many sports calendars back in the day.

Loan nods her greeting but doesn't smile back. I met her only three days ago and she hasn't smiled once. She rarely talks either, even though I know she speaks fluent English. She and Hunter seem to be well-paired.

"So you think you'll be okay for the day? I won't even be there that long. Just a couple of hours to get my office set-up and get myself oriented."

She stares at me like it's annoying her that I've already asked her this a million times. Is this what it's like to become a helicopter parent? I barely know what it is to be a parent as it is.

"Okay then, good talk," I tell her. Hunter runs away from the door and over to my leg, wrapping his arms around it and hugging it.

Well, fuck.

I'm not used to a lot of affection from the little guy either, and this is breaking my heart. "Hey, hey, hey," I say softly, crouching down so we're at eye level. "I'm going to miss you buddy. But I'll be right back."

"Don't go," he says. "I don't want to be with the leprechauns."

I really wish I knew where he was getting all of this from.

"You're safe from the leprechauns," I tell him, messing up his hair. "Miss Pham will take very good care of you, don't you worry. She's a bona-fide leprechaun hunter, isn't that right?" I glance up at her, and upon seeing her stone-faced expression, immediately look back to Hunter. "And when I get back from work, I'll bring you a present."

He swallows as he thinks that over. "Will you bring me a present every every day you go to work?"

"Um, yes," I say, knowing I walked right into that one. "Every every day."

He seems to consider this thoughtfully, then he nods.

Whew. Meltdown averted. Even though Hunter is quiet, he can throw a tantrum that rivals Steven Tyler's vocals.

Now that he's calmed down, it's time for me to do the same.

I may look like the picture of serenity in my tailored blue-grey suit and shiny new Audi, but I'm anything but. For one, I've only walked down the driveway and I'm already sweating like a criminal. I know that people in Hawaii like to keep it casual and don't usually wear full suits, even in the corporate world, but since I'm needing to make the right impression, I'm sticking with it.

Just as my shirt is sticking to me.

And then there's my car, which is pretty sweet, but I'm only leasing her for three months.

That's all the guaranteed time I have here.

Three months.

Three months that I was only aware of five days ago.

In a life that completely changed six months ago.

I glance back at the house and see Hunter at the window with Loan standing behind him, and for a second I'm reminded of some scene from *The Omen* of Damian with his nanny. This is what fatherhood is doing to me. I raise my hand in a wave and Hunter wiggles his fingers back at me. At least he wasn't crying for his mother this morning —it was good to feel wanted for a change.

And frankly, feeling wanted was the reason I packed up our lives and moved us out here for three months. I felt like my career at the Rockstar Collection was stalling. It didn't matter the work that I was putting into it, once the novelty of who I was wore off, I was watching promotions pass me by.

I needed the pay raise. I was getting on just fine with checks coming in from the NHL and sponsors, even though those had dried up to nearly nothing over the years. But once Hunter was in my custody, I knew that it wouldn't cut it anymore.

Then I got the call that changed everything.

My old buddy Mike Epson said he did something crazy and he needed help.

Specifically, he quit his job unexpectedly and felt bad about it and thought I would be the right person to replace him.

In a way I can't believe I said yes. I wanted a new opportunity but to go back to working for Kahuna Hotels after all this time wasn't the one I was thinking of, plus uprooting Hunter and I from San Francisco and transplanting us to Hawaii looked too big for us to handle.

We'll see how we do, though with Hunter's age and all the changes and moves he's been through lately, he's taken to Hawaii better than I have.

A lot better.

Look, I grew up in the Yukon. I may have worked in Palm Desert for a few years but that's a totally different beast than a tropical island in the Pacific. I know everyone would be chomping at the bit to have the chance to move to Hawaii for a job, but honestly I'm approaching this with a lot of caution. I prefer rain and gloom and cold and things that keep to a schedule. Plus, I doubt there's a single hockey rink on this sweltering rock and, despite everything, hockey is still my number one hobby.

Thankfully, the drive from the house to the office isn't that long and GPS gets me to downtown Honolulu on time. For a moment I'm almost tricked to thinking I'm back in San Francisco as I stare up at all the high-rises with Korean, Japanese, and Vietnamese restaurants dotted in between. But if I look a little closer, the abundance of shorts, Hawaiian shirts, shaved ice signs and lush foliage remind me that I'm not in Kansas anymore.

It isn't until I've parked my car in the parking garage and wiped a bunch of sweat off my forehead en route to the elevator that I start to get nervous.

Now, I don't usually get nervous. Playing for the NHL for that one year had me wishing for a pair of heavy duty Depends before every game, and after a while my body just learned how to obliterate those nerves (or risk spending the game on the toilet).

But...I am nervous now.

Just a smidge.

Enough that I'm not sure if it's the incessant humidity that's making me sweat or that I'm about to start my first day on a job that's essentially just a trial period.

Who am I kidding? It's both those things, but it's also the fact that I'm going to see Nova Lane again.

The moment Mike called and said he was putting my name down for a job, the first thing I thought about was Nova.

Gorgeous, ambitious, closed-off, slightly neurotic Nova.

She was the girl that got away.

Okay, so she was the girl that I cut loose once I realized I didn't want any commitment from her and that things would be better for us as co-workers if we just stopped having all that hot sex.

Big, big mistake.

It feels like it's been so long since I've been laid, I've forgotten what sex is, let alone hot sex. Like it's the tastiest dish on a menu in a restaurant I've been shunned from, probably because I used to treat it as an all-you-can-eat buffet, cutting in line and hogging all the roast beef.

Or so analogies go.

Naturally, things between Nova and I became strained after that. She went from liking me, a lot, to hating me...a lot.

Soon she was switching jobs, being transferred from the hotel in Palm Desert to the corporate office in Honolulu, in what felt like the snap of her fingers. Once she was gone, she cut me out of the rest her life. Instantly removed from Facebook and Instagram, emails bounced, phone number was switched. It's like she never existed when she was making sure that *I* never existed.

And yet here I am, existing, barely, about to start a new job of sorts in the same office where she works. Hopefully five years was enough for her to forget me so that we can start over.

The Kahuna Hotels corporate office takes up the entire tenth floor of the high-rise. It's interesting to finally be able to see where these people work. When I used to work for them in Palm Desert, I always pictured the head office as some zany loosey-goosey zoo on the beach, with the CEO surfing the waves in-between taking conference calls. Even though it was corporate and the head of the company, things seemed to run a little slower on their end.

But now that I'm here, it looks clean and modern, lots of white with faded watercolor art on the walls, and the occasional teak furnishings.

The receptionist, however, is only borderline professional. When I give her my name and tell her who I'm here to see, she eyes me up and down, very slowly, pausing at every corner of my body. It's both flattering and unnerving, especially the way she raises her brows at the end. I can't tell if she's impressed or disappointed but it's something.

Then, when I sit down in the lobby to wait, she spends the whole time staring at me, deadpan, even as she's typing something. I have the sneaking suspicion she's typing something about me but I'm not sure what it is.

Finally, she answers a call and after she hangs up, says, "Mr. Rocha? Desiree will see you now. Office just down there to the right."

I get up quickly, happy to get out of there, and take stock over my sweat situation. The AC in here is helping but a few strands of my hair are sticking to my damp forehead. The receptionist was probably tweeting about the sweaty monster in a suit she now has to work with.

I head down the hall to the door and then take in a deep breath.

You got this, I tell myself. *No different than the start of any game.*

I knock.

"Come in," says a voice.

I open the door, my smile already plastered on my face as I finally meet Desiree.

Except that there are two people in the office.

Desiree, the tiny, older Japanese woman with a flower clipped in her hair, and Nova Lane.

God, even her name in my head sounds sexy.

It doesn't help that she's only gotten even sexier over the years.

Nova is still stunning and completely unique to any woman I've ever met. Her mother is Bahamian (or was it Barbadian?), her father Northern European, so she has high cheekbones and the roundest, cutest cheeks you'll ever see on a woman. Then she has these pouty lips that I know for a fact are expert at sucking dick (specifically, my dick) and these dark, beguiling bedroom eyes that tempt you with all the dirty things she wants to do to you. Her body is both lush and strong and oh so soft. I once told her she had skin like mocha cream but that resulted with her hitting me upside the head for how inappropriate it is to compare her skin tone to food, but I do have to say her skin still positively glows.

And she's here.

Sitting right in front of me, dressed in a sleeveless black dress and sandals, staring at me with total condemnation.

Something tells me five years weren't enough.

"Mr. Rocha," Desiree says, getting to her feet and extending her hand across her desk. "It's so nice to finally meet you."

"Likewise," I tell her, and wince when I realize my palm is sweaty. "Sorry, it's really hot here."

Desiree laughs and luckily doesn't look put out that she shook hands with a wet orangutan in a suit. "You'll get used to it," she says, then nods to my clothes. "And you'll learn pretty fast to leave your blazers in the closet. Please sit."

All this time I'm both trying to look at Nova and also avoid the dripping disapproval in her eyes. She visibly stiffens as I sit next to her.

"Now, I take it you two know each other," Desiree says, looking back and forth between us with a gentle smile on her lips, obviously clueless. "So we don't have to get into the introductions. But perhaps you should get me caught up." She looks at me. "Kessler, Mike spoke very highly of you and insisted you were the best person to take over his job."

Only because he's a huge hockey fan, I think. But of course I wouldn't dare tell them that.

"Considering our circumstances, we didn't have a lot of time to figure this out," she continues. "Of course we would take Mike's word and recommendation but there's a lot we need to work out, hence why this position is just for three months. Already I really appreciate the fact that you were able to pack up and move here on such an unbelievably short notice, especially when you have a son."

"You have a son?" Nova squeaks, brows raised to the ceiling. It's the first thing she's said to me and I can't blame her for looking so shocked. When we were having our affair, I was very adamant how against marriage and children I was.

Times, do they fucking change.

"I was happy for the opportunity," I tell Desiree, ignoring Nova because I'm not about to open that can of worms right here. "And Hunter is very adaptable."

Nova's eyes go wider, as if the mention of his name made him real. She folds her arms and sits forward, eyes focused on the wall. She's done acknowledging me.

"That's excellent," Desiree says. "But of course, you

ended up leaving Kahuna Hotels in Palm Desert not too long after Nova did. You went to work with the Rockstar Collection, which, as you know, are our competitors. What prompted that change?"

I shrug, feeling a trickle of sweat at the back of my neck. "I wanted to challenge myself."

Desiree goes on, prompting me to talk more about my role over there, what I did, what I wanted for myself. I answer her questions but I'm incredibly aware that Nova is sitting next to me this whole time, making my answers sound a bit stiff and formal.

I'm starting to wonder why she's in this meeting at all when Desiree says, "Nova reported to Mike when he was here, so in this situation she'll be doing the same to you, Kessler. I assume that won't be a problem. It was like that back in Palm Desert, wasn't it?"

"No," Nova says quickly, her tone sharp and steady. "Kessler and I were *equals*."

"Ah," Desiree says, and I do the same inside my head.

Ah.

I think I know why Nova still hates me so much, and it might not have anything to do with our little tryst back in the day or me breaking it off because of my commitment issues.

I think I might have just stolen her potential job out from under her.

I turn my head and give Nova an apologetic smile, realizing that if I don't try and smooth things out now and really empathize with her, the next three months might just be a living hell.

But she takes one look at my smile, then another look at the sweat on my forehead, and her eyes narrow into a look I know all too well.

The look that tells me I'm dead to her.

Okay. So it looks like the next three months are going to be a living hell after all.

It's definitely fucking hot enough.

CHAPTER THREE

NOVA

"OKAY, we're out of ear-shot now," Kate says, looking over her shoulder as we hurry down the street. "Can you please tell me what the fuck is going on with you?"

I look behind us as well, as if I expect to see Kessler or Desiree, or, hell, Roger, following me. There's so much going on right now in my head I'm not even sure what to process.

But no, it's Kessler Fucking Rocha taking up the most space in my frontal cortex.

"I don't even know where to begin," I mutter as we take a right down the street toward Lucky Belly. "Do I tell you about how Roger slept with a hooker while we were in Vegas?"

She gasps and slaps me across the shoulder, her dark hair flying. "Shut. Up!"

"Suffice to say, we broke up. But then I find out that not only did my beloved boss quit on me, leaving me totally unmoored, but that I'm not getting his position."

"Oh fuck nuts," she swears. "I'm sorry, I totally thought you were going to get it."

"Uh-huh. And there's more fuck nuts to come. That tall, burly sweaty dude you saw in reception? He's the guy who stole my promotion."

"I knew he was too sweaty for his own good," she says, squinting. "Though if he invited me to have a naked sweat session with him, I definitely wouldn't turn him down. If you know what I mean."

"I always know what you mean, Kate. And you might take that back in a few minutes...actually, no, it's you, you never take anything back."

"No takesies backsies," she says with a nod, opening the door to the restaurant for me. "Whatever I give, the world is free to keep."

"Right," I say, stepping inside. As usual, there is a huge lineup for lunch. Originally I was just going to get George's ramen to go and get something along with it, but I'm in no hurry to go back to the office. "We're eating here now, by the way."

Kate shrugs. Linda, the office manager, handles the phones while Kate is at lunch and Kate has no problems coming back late. She says Linda always takes *two* pieces of cake during any office birthday celebration and apparently Kate considers that to mean war.

"So is that all?" she asks as we're seated at a booth.

"No." I sigh noisily and rest my head down on the menu, closing my eyes. "That tall sweaty burly man..." I pause. "Is..."

"What?"

"My..."

"*Yes?*"

"Ex-boyfriend."

"What?!" she screeches.

I sit right up. "Calm down."

She frowns at me. "I'll calm down when you remove that noodle from your forehead."

I swipe away at my forehead until a noodle dislodges and plops back on the table. I swipe it away onto the floor.

"He's your ex-boyfriend?" she says, and her voice is still so high that only dogs can hear her now.

"He's my ex...whatever we were," I tell her, pressing my hands into the table as I lean forward to look her in the eye. "You have to promise me, you can't tell a soul."

Kate looks like I slapped her. "Why? Why would you do this to me? You know I can't keep a secret. At all."

"You're going to have to try," I plead. "It's only going to make things worse if people know, especially since he's my fucking boss now. Argh!"

"You need some fucking alcohol, stat," she says, after watching me for a moment. She flags down the waitress and puts in an order for a mai tai for me and a beer for her.

"A mai tai? Really?" I ask.

"You love them and there's no shame in it. Plus all that booze will only make things better. So, before we discuss the whole Roger and the hooker thing, you're going to have to take me back further and explain...just how the hell Mr. Almond Roca was your boyfriend?"

I flinch. "Don't act like he's out of my league."

She rolls her eyes. "Come on, hot stuff. No one is ever out of your league. Was he always that sweaty?"

"It was a dry heat in Palm Desert."

"Okay, so you *worked* with him?"

I nod, take in a deep breath, and then launch into it.

"I was fresh out of an internship at a hotel in Seattle. I'd just gotten hired, I was green, I was eager, I was happy to move down to California for a million reasons. About a year after I started work as a marketing assistant, Kessler came on board. At first he was an assistant to the executives, then he moved to the marketing team. He pissed me off right from the get-go."

"Because he's so handsome and you hate that?"

I roll my eyes, though she's kind of right. "He didn't have any experience." I practically spit the words out. "You know, my dad had a motel growing up, we lived there. I grew up knowing how to run one. I went to school for it. I worked my ass off. Then he just shows up with no degree and no experience, looking to get into the hotel business because he's bored or something and within no time he has the same job as me."

The waitress stops by with our drinks and while Kate orders our food, I'm sucking back that mai tai through the metal straw, as if the booze will obliterate all memories of Kessler immediately. I barely take a breath to place my order for George's soup to-go and a chicken karage sandwich for myself.

"That's men for you," Kate mutters. "We do all the work, they take all the credit."

"Well that's Kessler, especially. And really it's all because he was in the NHL."

If she had ears on the top of her head, they'd be perking up right now. "Really?"

"He doesn't look all big and burly by accident. He's straight from the Yukon, forged of ice and maple syrup, with legs like Douglas firs."

"Are his legs the only thing in the shape of a Douglas fir?" she asks, before sipping coquettishly on her drink.

I raise my hand. "I don't want to get into it."

She grins at me. "You don't have to. You're blushing."

"I do *not* blush."

"You do and you are and okay so now we know that Kessler has a penis that belongs in an old growth forest. What else can you tell me? Was he good in bed?" Before I can even give her a dirty look, she goes on. "It could go either way, you know, it's either he's never had to work for pussy a day in life and he has this massive dick, so he doesn't know shit about pleasing a woman. Or, because he's so blessed in the looks department, both above and below, he's found it his calling in life to make women come, much like Mozart was called to the piano."

"You are the worst," I tell her, feeling the rum start to swirl through me. I don't make it a habit of drinking during my lunch hour, and now with Kessler here I really should be sharp and clear-headed, but fuck it.

"Guilty," she says. "I just don't get what being an NHL star has to do with the hotel business."

"It doesn't have anything to do with it, it just buys interest and favors from the CEOs and what not. Anyway, so Kessler and I pretty much worked together for a good few years."

"When did he start impaling you with his tree trunk?"

"It took a while. I mean, I was only twenty-four."

"Only twenty-four? That's the prime hook-up stage of your life. If you're not getting laid, you're doing something wrong."

"Says you. Anyway, I was getting laid and it was wrong."

"Yes all that good sex with the sweaty big-dick beast must have been terrible."

The thing that I don't want to admit to Kate, because as much as I like her and trust her, she's not exactly emotionally vulnerable, is that I used to be head over heels in love with Kessler.

I was from the moment we started working together.

I knew I shouldn't have been so easily charmed by his looks and his effervescent humor and the way he made me feel, but I was swept off my feet. By the time he made a move on me at our Christmas office party, I would have done anything he said. I was completely his in heart and soul, and soon my body belonged to him. We had a passionate and secret affair for three months and during those three months I had fallen deeper in love with him than I had with anyone before, deeper than I had ever thought possible.

And then, one day, he wanted to call it off. Didn't want us getting too serious. Said he didn't want to complicate things at work, didn't want a girlfriend at the moment, didn't really believe in marriage, never wanted children. Just a whole mess of things thrown at me, as if they'd all make it easier to fall out of love with him.

I never told him how I felt and that's my greatest possession. He never knew just what he did to me, the way he broke my heart. He never knew what he meant to me, and that's something I hope he never finds out.

Which is why I can't tell Kate. I am sure at some point our security guard, Bradah Ed, will know that Kessler and I were an item back in the day so I sure as hell won't let her know the truth.

Kessler was the man I never quite got over.

My level-ten heartbreaker.

And he's now my motherfucking boss.

"It's going to be okay," Kate says, reading whatever horrid expression I have on my face. She puts her hand on top of mine and then winces as she picks a noodle up. "Do they not wipe down these booths?"

"How is it going to be okay?" I ask her, as she flicks the noodle onto the floor where it lands with the other noodle. "I thought I escaped him. I moved all the way here, I transferred jobs. I've been happy for the last five years, moving toward something and suddenly I discover there is no something. I've had the wool over my eyes, Kate. And now, now he's here and he's taken what's mine. I can't let this happen."

"I hate to be all adult and responsible because believe me, I'm usually down for inter-office espionage, but maybe you should have a talk with Desiree about it. Tell her what happened with you guys. Let her know you're not comfortable."

I sigh just as the waitress comes by with my sandwich and Kate's soup. My appetite is suddenly gone so I order another mai tai. "I don't want to do that. It's not over yet. The job might still be mine and I'm not about to show any vulnerability, not now. I can tell Desiree isn't one-hundred-percent sold on him. She's still super pissed abut Mike. Hence why he's here on a three-month probation."

"Hmmm." She slurps her soup noisily. "It's a gamble to move all the way here for three months when you might not even get the job in the long run."

"Especially since he has a son."

She stops, dead slurp, noodle dangling from her mouth. Slowly she sucks it in. "I'm sorry, you said he has a son? Oh my god, it's not yours is it?"

I frown. "What? No, Kate. No. That's not how things work. I never knew he had a son until today."

"So he's married," she says. "Bummer."

"Not a bummer, and I don't know if he's married or not. The point is—"

"He's a DILFOAH," she says, poking a mushroom in her vegan soup with a chopstick. "Daddy I'd Like to Fuck Often and Hard. And Sweaty. With Your Tree Trunk Dick." I can tell she's trying to make the abbreviation in her head. "Mr. Almond Roca."

I'm about to tell her to stop when something, maybe instinct, brings my attention to the front door of the restaurant.

Kessler has just walked in, and he's scanning the restaurant like he's the T-1000.

"Oh shit," I swear under my breath.

The waitress took my menu away, so I have no way to hide unless I hold up my chicken sandwich.

Before I even know what I'm doing, I'm ducking down and sinking under the table.

"What are you doing?" Kate hisses, as I'm on my hands and knees underneath, the top of my head bumping against the bottom of the table.

"He's here," I whisper harshly up at her.

"Who?"

"Who do you think? Pretend I'm not here. God, it's so fucking gross under here!"

"Damn, hot stuff, it's like you're acting out one of my fantasies right now," Kate says.

"Are you talking to me or him?"

"You of course," she says, and then I see a pair of male legs stop right beside our table.

"You're the receptionist, right?" Kessler's voice booms. He's always had an obnoxiously sexy voice, that kind of gravelly low sex voice that ignites you in seconds flat.

Thank god I'm surrounded by used noodles and who

knows what, so he doesn't have that effect on me anymore. I focus on his shoes, shiny, expensive Italian ones and then his dark grey-blue tailored pants and I hate that even his style has improved over the years.

"That would be correct. And you're Mr. Almond Roca," Kate says, and I delight in how absolutely bored she sounds.

"Can't say I haven't heard that before."

"It's a popular candy around the holidays," she says dryly.

"Yes. I know. It's actually Portuguese."

"Almond Roca is Portuguese?"

"No. My last name is."

"Oh."

"What's your last name?"

Oh god. Really Kess? This is your small talk now?

She sighs and nearly kicks me under the table as she uncrosses her legs. "It's Kim."

"Kate Kim?"

"Yeah, it's Korean."

"Are you from Korea?"

"I'm from San Francisco," she says with an edge to her voice.

"Well, so am I."

"*Oh no*. Does that mean we have to be best friends now?"

"Uh, no..."

"You're from the Yukon, anyway."

"How did you know that?"

Long pause. I don't even have to see their faces to know their expressions.

"HR file," Kate says smoothly. "As receptionist, it's my job to know everything. And I do mean *everything*."

Kessler's feet pivot in my direction. "Listen, I'm not interrupting anything am I? Seems like you're not dining alone. Someone must really love mai tais."

"Those are my mai tais."

"And the beer?"

"Being a receptionist is stressful."

"And you have both the soup and the sandwich?"

"I like to eat. Don't food shame me."

At that she crosses her legs and manages to kick me right in the jaw.

"*Ahhhh,*" I cry out, cupping my chin in pain.

Fucking shit, Kate and her killer feet.

"What the hell?" Kessler says and the next thing I know he's bending down to look at me under the table. "Nova? Is that you? What are you doing under there?"

There's only one way out of this. In a panic, I pretend to be looking for something "*Ahhh,* here it is," I say, trying to blend it in with my cry of pain. I quickly pop up the other end of the table and get to my feet, holding a noodle.

"I was looking for this," I say, smiling and waving the noodle at him. "Here you go, Kate."

I drop the noodle right in her soup.

She stares at it for a moment and then slowly pushes her bowl of soup away from her.

"Listen," Kessler says after a moment, staring at the soup and then back to me. "I was wondering if I could have a moment to talk to you. Alone."

Kate stares up at me expectantly. "You go ahead, Nova," she says. "I'll bring the soup back to George. I could use the extra brownie points with the head honcho. Or, the big Kahuna, as we say here."

Kessler manages a tight smile. "Right." He looks to me, brows raised, and I'm struck by how good age has been to him. He has to be now, what, thirty-four? Thirty-five? And he's just the right amount of youth and manliness combined. The baby fat is gone from his face, leaving chiseled cheeks and a jaw sharper than a hockey skate. The crinkles at the corners of his teal eyes hint at fun life lived and the pepper of grey in his dark hair makes him look distinguished. Then there's his actual hair. It was curlier back in the day, but it's still wavy and somehow thicker, like he's got male pattern baldness in reverse.

What a dick.

"Do you mind?" Kessler asks. "I don't want to interrupt your lunch."

"Our lunch was already interrupted when Nova decided to hunt down that wayward noodle," Kate says before she has a slow sip of her beer, her focus now on the crotch of Kessler's pants and never wavering. If she dared to look at me, she'd see all the seven circles of hell in my glare.

And I do mind, of course. He's the damn reason I went under the table and he knows it. I'm just so blindsided by him, by today, by this week, that I can't get a handle on anything and I'm bound to say the wrong thing, do the wrong thing. For example, hiding under the table like I'm a thirteen-year-old that just spotted her crush. But the last thing I want is for Kessler to think he has some upper hand, as petty as that sounds. Even if it's kind of true.

Faking a smile, faking everything, I say, "Sure. That's fine, I have a few minutes to spare on the way back to the office."

"Great," he says, and I hate his smile, stupid perfect veneers. Why can't he be like most hockey players and have a mouth like a broken piano?

I grab my purse and give Kate one last glare, which she won't acknowledge, before marching out of the restaurant.

"Seems like a cool spot, do you come here often?" Kessler calls after me as he exits out onto the street. "I have to say, Honolulu is nothing what I expected."

Don't say it, don't say it, don't say it.

I make it about half a block before I stop and turn to him.

"Why the hell are you here?"

He stops, stepping out of the way as a group of lost tourists wander past. "Excuse me?"

"Why are you here?" I repeat, wishing I could play it cooler than this. "You're the last person I ever expected to see again."

"I thought I was the last person you ever *wanted* to see again," he says, shoving his hands in his pockets. He looks all cool and comfortable, but I can see the sweat starting to break out on his forehead.

"What makes you say that?"

"What makes me say that?" he repeats. "Uh, I don't know. How about the fact that after we stopped sleeping together, you fucking ghosted. And when you ghost, Nova, you're gone. You changed jobs and came here within weeks. Half-way across the Pacific Ocean. You cut me out of social media, you changed your number, you never answered any emails."

I fold my arms, tapping my foot impatiently. "What's your point?"

"My point?" he repeats, and then wipes the sweat off his forehead with the back of his hand. "Fucking hell, is it ever not a million degrees outside?"

"You're the one wearing a suit," I point out. "And I'll have you know it's only eighty degrees. I think San Francisco broke you."

He makes a face but he's still handsome somehow.

"Anyway, I just...I don't know what happened between us back then, but I just want to make things right. And I know that's going to be difficult now that I'm your boss."

My eyes narrow venomously. "You're only my boss for three months. Anything can happen after that. Which brings me to my original question: why the hell are you here? You have a child now? I'm assuming a wife or baby mama? Why were things so bad at your old job that you were willing to throw it all away and move here for a chance. Don't tell me you've secretly harbored dreams about living in Hawaii because I know you Kess, and you're not that type."

Now it's time for his eyes to narrow. "You don't know me, Supernova." I roll my eyes at the mention of my old nickname. "If you did, you'd know I'm not married, nor do I have a baby mama."

Somehow the fact that he's not with anyone makes things worse.

"Then where did the kid come from?"

"The *kid*," he says patiently, "came from a night of poorly planned sex. I was drunk, she was...a sexy Russian model. We met at a party at Kirk Hammett's house." There he is with the name-dropping again. "Anyway, long story short, she's in jail and I have custody of Hunter."

I stare at him blankly. "I'm sorry. Back up. You can't just long story short that part. What happened?"

He sighs and runs his hand down his face, staring up at the sky scrapers. "Look. Her name is Natalia. She was a legit model. Seventy-five-percent of her was just vagina and legs." I scrunch up my nose. "She got pregnant. She lived in LA and I said I'd support her anyway that I could—money, time. I'd be as involved as she needed."

This should surprise me but it doesn't. Kessler was anti-marriage, anti-children, but he's also a got a good heart beneath that burly, sweaty facade. I'd seen it enough to know he's at least coming from a genuine place in wanting to do the right thing.

"But," he continues, "she was adamant she be on her own. I talked to her when I could, she seemed fine. She gave birth. I wasn't there for it, though now I really wish I was. I wanted to be..." he trails off and his expression turns wistful. "Anyway, Hunter was born and I saw him only a handful of times. Then she moved to New York. Then she moved to Chicago. Then she was arrested for fraud and I learned that Natalia was never her name anyway and she had dozens of them and was in the business of fleecing rich men, stealing identities, and credit card theft." He shrugs. "Maybe that's why she never wanted me very close. Either way, I got the call and I was the father and it was either I take Hunter or he goes into foster care. He had no other family."

"Oh my god."

Do you ever know how to pick 'em, Kess.

He nods. "Yeah. Obviously I wanted him. He's my son. So, there you have it. This only happened six months ago."

Damn. "You've only had him for six months?"

He gives me a wry smile. "I'm learning as I go. And I can really use the extra help. So when Mike called and said there was this job and that I could stay in his house and that he would arrange a nanny for Hunter, I jumped at the idea. The last six months have been rough. I thought maybe this would be a good way for Hunter and I to start fresh."

Hmmm. For all the reasons for Kessler to come here, it seems like a good one.

Just a major inconvenience for me.

"So why is Mike doing all of this for you? You get to have his job, stay in his house, he hires you a nanny?"

"I guess love can really change a person."

Yeah. Love can also shatter them.

"It's nothing to do with Mike being a giant hockey fan and you being an ex-NHLer?"

He tilts his head. "It still really bugs you, doesn't it?"

"What?"

"The whole hockey thing. Back in the desert, you could never let it go. How I got a job. How I moved ahead. You always blamed it on the hockey."

I raise my brows. *Your point?*

"I was in the NHL for one year before I was injured. You really think I have that much sway? I'm nobody, Nova. And it's fine. I got all the jobs I got because I work hard and I'm smart. I know that's hard for you to believe."

Kessler is smart but more than that, he can be conniving. Which is a dangerous quality to have when you're working with someone who may or may not be on your team.

"You're smart. I'm secure enough with myself to admit that," I tell him, raising my chin. "But if you're going to tell me that you worked hard for all of this, you have another thing coming. I'm the one who grew up in a motel, I—"

"Yes, I know," he cuts me off quickly. "You went to college. You did internships. You worked your way up the ranks. Now you're here and you're probably still busting your ass trying to get ahead. Has anyone ever told you that maybe you try a little too hard?"

I reach out and poke him in the chest. His very firm, sculpted chest. "I only try hard because people like *you* don't have to try at all."

"NHL players?"

"Men!"

He rolls his eyes. "Oh my god, here we go, she's about to go Supernova on us."

"Don't pretend it's not true, it'll be 2019 in a month. You could at least acknowledge your privilege as a rich white man."

He snorts. "Rich? Oh, you have no idea."

"I see those shoes," I tell him, kicking the tips of them, hoping to scuff that leather.

"Haven't you heard of dressing for success?" he says, moving his feet out of the way. "Besides, I may have money but I still have to work, especially now that I have a son in my life. You know, responsibility. Caring for another human being. Or do you still not know anything about that?"

Oh my god. And he's just standing there, sweating, waiting for me to tell him that I have a husband or a boyfriend or a child or a fucking pet and I've got nothing.

Five years and I've got *nothing*.

For a moment I think I'll just resurrect potato-head Roger from the dead but I think that lie would get the best of me.

So instead I just say, "Fuck you," before spinning around on my heel and storming off toward the office.

"Hey, that's not a nice way to speak to your boss!" he calls after me.

I just stick my middle finger up in the air and keep walking.

CHAPTER FOUR

KESSLER

IT'S BEEN five days since I started work at Kahuna Hotels corporate office as their new, possibly temporary, Senior VP of Sales, Marketing and Revenue.

Five days in which I still feel completely clueless as a father (Hunter's happiness can only be bought with daily presents and the promise of leprechaun eradication).

Five days in which I don't have a handle on my new job at all (I made a major blunder when I proposed we change our logo from a pineapple to a banana, since we're all about going for a younger, sexier audience now).

And five days in which I've barely talked to Nova at all.

The major problem with that is I *need* to talk to her. I mean, if I'm being honest with myself, she really should have taken over my job to begin with. I'll never let her know that because that would be the end of me, but it's true. She knows everything and I'm floundering, and when I do have the courage to reach out, I have to deal with her through her assistant, Mahina. Otherwise I'm given the cold shoulder which I can feel through the walls.

Or maybe that's the AC. The only good thing about this week so far is that I've managed to get my sweating under control with the art of blasting the air conditioner to Yukon-esque temperatures and keeping my blazers in the office.

At the moment I'm sorting out all the pineapple-shaped shit on my desk. I've got a pineapple stress ball and a pineapple pencil-holder and pineapple note papers and a pineapple mouse pad and my whole office looks like a pineapple threw up in here. That's probably why they didn't like my banana logo idea, they're fully committed to the Kahuna Hotels pineapple merch and can't afford to switch.

I glance up at the pineapple clock on the wall. It's almost six-thirty at night and I'm assuming the office is empty by now. I've been staying late the last few days, wanting the extra time to keep learning so I can stay on top of things. I feel bad because I should be rushing home right after work to have dinner with Hunter, but Loan has assured me that she's got it under control. At least that's the gist of what I've got from the few things she says to me.

I'm staring at the stress ball, wondering if it would suffice as a present for Hunter (I brought him a pineapple pillow the other day, which he immediately started to color all over) when I hear a strange sound from out in the office, almost like a ravaged cry.

I get up and open the door, poking my head out. It's silent.

I decide I should probably use the bathroom anyway and while I'm heading over there I pass by Nova's office. Her door is slightly ajar and I can hear her typing.

I think better of it and then slowly push it open wider.

She's got her noise-canceling headphones on and her laser eyes spear me as she looks up over her computer.

I know she can't hear me, so I do the annoying thing of gesturing for her to take hers off, which she does so very begrudgingly.

"What?" she asks sharply.

"You weren't just crying, were you?" I ask.

She frowns. "No. Have you checked in with Teef? Sometimes he does a podcast after work."

"Teef has a podcast?" I ask. Teef is a good guy with a strange name. I mean, he has a lot of teeth so maybe that's it. He's our IT guy so I'm assuming his podcast is about boring technical stuff.

"He lives with like ten people, so he says this is the only place he gets any peace and quiet."

"And does he normally cry during podcasts?"

"Not that I know of. But who knows what makes those nerds upset."

I smile at her. This feels good, the fact that for once she's relaxed, just a little, and that gorgeous, sunshiny part of her is coming through. This was the way she used to be, it's why I was so attracted to her, what made me want to be around her all the time. There's fun and adventure and this raw sensuality inside her, something real and spirited.

Except that little glimpse of the old Nova disappears in an instant, like the clouds blocking the sun. She's changed. The walls she's put up now seem unsurmountable. She's still sexy as hell in her pale yellow sleeveless top and I can't stop staring at her mouth, even when it turns into a sneer, but she might not be the girl I once knew. The girl whose body I knew like the back of my hand.

"Is that all?" she asks hastily, as if she can read the lust starting to build in my eyes.

I swallow hard, hating how this whole bitch-hot thing is starting to get me going.

"You're working late," I manage to say, my voice coming out coarse. Dear god, am I getting a fucking hard-on right now?

She cocks a single brow. "So are you."

I nod. "Good talk."

"See ya," she says dismissively, slipping her headphones back on, her attention going back to the computer.

I back out of her office before she can notice my half-hard cock, and then proceed to head directly to the men's washroom, passing by Teef's empty office on the way.

Seems like Nova and I are the only ones here.

Which is good because the last thing she's going to do is walk in on me while I'm taking care of myself.

Now, I don't make it a habit to jerk off at work. I do believe some things should be done at home and in private (okay, well I'm willing to share with certain people). But there's no one here and she's got me riled up in ways I can't even explain.

Maybe because I know how well we fit together. Our bodies spoke their own language when we were in the same bed, she knew exactly what to give me and I knew exactly what to give her.

Actually, in hindsight, I was a fucking idiot to break it off with her. Had I not grown so scared of committing to her, who knows where my life would have gone? I don't believe in regrets, at all, but if I had stuck it out, I would have gotten to know her on levels I was never able to. Even though we connected in sweaty sex sessions, she still kept herself tucked away.

But none of that matters in a fantasy, and the one I have right now needs to be addressed.

I march right into the bathroom, head for the first stall

and bring my cock out of my pants, immediately stroking it from balls to tip.

My fantasy leaps right into high gear.

There's no time for foreplay, no time to stretch it out.

It's just Nova.

On her desk, on all fours, her skirt hiked up to her waist, leaving her round and luscious ass out and open and begging for me.

I've missed your cock, she says to me, biting her lip. *I've needed it, so bad. Fuck me, Kessler. Fuck my tight little hole with your big fat dick.*

Jesus.

I'm stroking faster now, the precum sliding down the rigid length of my shaft, the tension building deep inside my balls, begging for release.

I imagine grabbing Nova by her tiny waist, my big rough hands encompassing her soft skin as I yank her back into my cock, right into her ass. I've fucked her up the ass once before and as much as she pretended it was dirty, she fucking loved it. I conjure up all the ways she cried out and called my name, her breathy little moans as she arched her back and pushed herself back into me, my cock sliding in to the hilt, the way I reached down and found her cunt all wet and gushing for me and...

I'm so close to coming now.

Everything tightens.

My grip gets harder.

My stance firmer.

My pants slip down to my ankles.

I...

Have the strangest feeling I'm being watched.

Just before I'm about to blow my load, I glance up to my left.

And meet a pair of round yellow eyes.

It's a motherfucking *chicken*.

I open my mouth to scream when the rooster leaps off the top of the stall and flies at me, wings flapping, beak open, letting loose a battle cry which was what I'd probably heard earlier, only ten-fold as it's coming to peck my eyes out.

I lift up my arms in defense, the chicken's claws going into my shirt, and now I'm shrieking, screaming, yelping, flailing back and forth in the bathroom stall while the bird beast starts climbing up into my hair, squawking hellishly.

Somehow I manage to spin out of the stall, the door flying open until I'm slammed up against the wall and the chicken loses it's grip enough for me to open the washroom door and take off screeching down the hallway, trying not to fall down as I run while struggling to pull up my pants.

Just then Nova steps out of her office.

Sees me with my disheveled hair and my hands clutching my waistband, my cock hanging out.

I can't imagine the expression on my face but it makes her stop dead in her tracks, ripping off her wireless headphones.

"Kessler, what the fuck?" she cries out, her eyes darting between my face and my dick. "Are you...okay?" Before I can even try to form words she frowns at my dick again. "Why do you have a hard-on?"

"This isn't the cock we have to worry about," I yell, yanking the rest of my pants up before pointing frantically down the hall. "It's the cock in the washroom."

Her forehead creases. "A cock...in the washroom. Is it... Teef's?" I can see she's getting all sorts of bizzare ideas in her head.

"Teef isn't even here!" I yell at her. "It's that mother-fucking chicken."

Her mouth opens, trying to find words, just as the afore-mentioned cock lets out another warrior battle cry that rings through the office.

"What the hell was that?" she cries out.

"That's the motherfucking chicken!" I zip up my fly and do up my belt, beckoning for her to follow me. "Don't believe me, I'll show you."

She doesn't move. "I've already seen one cock today, I don't need to see another."

She's disarmingly blasé, although I can see she's starting to bite back a smile.

"This isn't funny," I tell her. "That thing is dangerous. It wanted to peck my eyes out."

"Really caught you with your pants down, huh."

"Well what the hell is a chicken doing in the washroom? Doesn't that surprise you?"

She shrugs. "It happens."

"It happens?" I repeat. "Since when? I know Oahu has a feral chicken problem but we're on the tenth floor."

"Chickens can fly, people leave windows open. Maybe they're using the service elevator."

"You do think this is funny."

Finally she cracks a grin and shrugs one shoulder. "It's at least a little bit funny. Now if you'll excuse me, I have to go."

It's only then after all the commotion that I realize she's got her purse on her arm and her car keys in her hand. "Well what am I supposed to do about it? I can't leave it here until tomorrow."

"The cleaners will take care of it later. Or you can call up Bradah Ed from security, but I do recall him telling me he has a phobia of birds, so I'm not sure how much help he'll be."

"Well I can't work here knowing he's in there."

"Kess," she says, and for a moment I bask in the way she's said my name, like we're old friends, "it's just a chicken. Deal with it. Go grab a hockey stick if you have to and have some target practice. I really have to go." She moves past me.

Against my better judgement I reach out and grab her arm, holding her in place. "Where are you going?"

She eyes my grip on her bicep. "Why?"

"I'm just curious," I tell her. "Are you afraid I'm going to follow you?"

She holds my stare for a moment and I wish I could read the myriad of thoughts that are running behind her eyes.

Just give me an inch, I plead.

"I'm doing volunteer work," she says with a sigh, relaxing into my grip slightly. I'd forgotten how good it felt to hold her, even just like this, my fingertips on the warmth of her skin.

"Where?"

She rubs her lips together for a moment, thinking. "It's for Honolulu Mental Health Services. Sometimes I work the call center, sometimes the front desk."

"That's what you do on Friday nights?"

"That's the busiest night. Drugs, alcohol, payday for some. Least I can do is put in a couple of hours."

"What made you want to volunteer there?" It's not that Nova is heartless. Even though she never quite opened up to me outside the bedroom, I knew she cared a great deal about many things in her life. Her parents, her sister, rescue animals, pollution.

But as I thought, she doesn't let me in.

"Just want to make a difference," she says, shrugging out of my hold. "I'll see you on Monday."

And just like that, she leaves, not giving a second glance back to me or the chicken squawking in the washroom.

IT's dark when I pull into Mike's driveway.

Funny, I should start calling it home already. Even when I'm in a hotel room for long enough, I start calling it home. But even though Mike is running on the beaches of Southeast Asia with a porn star, this is still Mike's house.

You can feel him in every inch of the walls, because he's covered every inch of the walls with hockey paraphernalia, from framed photos of him posing along various hockey stars like Sidney Crosby, Roberto Luongo, and even Wayne Gretzky, to a clashing mix of signed jerseys and replica Stanley Cups. As an ex-NHL player, I find it a little creepy and I have every reason to suspect that Mike never brought the porn star back here, unless she happened to have a hockey fetish. Which, you never know. There are many uses for hockey sticks.

It's a dark and damp place, too. It's way up in the hills behind the city and even though it's surrounded by other suburban houses, there's this general feeling of uneasiness, like there are things in the house that don't want us there. I'm guessing the fungal spores in mold.

I try to ignore it though and get out of the car, getting inside just as the skies open up with a deluge of spontaneous rain.

"You're home," Hunter says, appearing at the end of the hall by the kitchen. I can hear Loan doing the dishes.

"I am," I tell him, taking out the pineapple stress ball from my pocket. "And I brought you a present."

He gingerly takes it from me, staring at it. "Another pine-abble?"

"It's where Sponge Bob lives."

I wait for him to have some sort of issue with it, but I guess the mention of Sponge Bob helps because he clutches it to his chest. "Pine-abble under the sea," he says and then runs off to his toy chest in the living room that's already overflowing with Kahuna Hotels *pine-abbles*.

I poke my head in the kitchen.

"Hey Loan," I say.

She glances at me over her shoulder and gives a nod. "Hello Mr. Rocha." Then she goes back to doing the dishes.

"You know it's been a week, Loan," I tell her, leaning against the doorway to the kitchen. "You can call me Kessler."

"I prefer Mr. Rocha," she says.

"Well if it's what you prefer," I tell her, happy that she's talking at least this much. What's with the women in my life barely giving me anything? "How was the kiddo?"

"Good. He napped. We went to the park." She pauses. "He won't go to the washroom."

Uh oh. "What do you mean won't go to the washroom? Is he constipated?"

She stops what she's doing and turns to face me, shaking her head. "No I don't think so. He says he's afraid of the bathroom. Says the leprechauns live in there."

"These damn leprechauns," I say. "Do you know what he's talking about?"

She shrugs. "No. He's been okay otherwise. Hasn't cried much. Said he misses you."

My heart thaws into a puddle. "So if he hasn't been going to the bathroom..."

"He won't go alone, I have to go with him."

I nod. "I see. Well, I'll have a talk with him and maybe get to the bottom of it."

I head over to the living room where Hunter is playing with the stress ball and a stuffed chicken I bought him at the airport. I'm already shuddering at the sight. I left the office with a note on the door for the custodians to beware of the cock in the washroom.

"Hey buddy," I say to him, easing myself down to the floor so I'm sitting beside him. "How was your day?"

He doesn't say anything. It's like he doesn't hear me.

"Hunter?"

He looks at me. "It was fine."

"Just fine?"

"I saw a bird at the park."

"It wasn't a chicken, was it?" I ask sharply. I'll be damned if they start coming after my child too.

He shakes his head. "It was a white bird. Miss Loan said it was a tractor bird because they drive tractors."

"That's pretty neat," I tell him. "Hey, speaking of Miss Loan...you like her, right?"

He nods.

"Good. Just wanted to make sure she was nice to you."

"I'm very nice!" Loan yells from the kitchen.

Sheesh talk about supersonic hearing.

"She's very nice," Hunter repeats. "She knows a lot about fish."

"Good, great. Look, Hunter, she mentioned that you're afraid of the bathroom now. Because of the leprechauns."

"That's where they live," he says. "And under the bed."

"Did you want to show me?" I ask, hoping that if I play along, I can act like the leprechauns are our friends.

"I caught one earlier," he says.

"Oh really. Can I see?" I hold out my hand.

"Yup," he says, twisting around to reach into his toy box.

Okay, when he shows it to you, there will be nothing there, so just pretend it's something special and magical and rare. Like, he's a famous leprechaun hunter now for catching it. Oh wait, work in the fact that his name is Hunter, like it was meant to be. Hunter the Leprechaun Hunter.

While these thoughts are going through my head, Hunter twists around to face me and plunks something in my hand.

That's when I know something is wrong.

That he put *something* in my hand.

I look at what it is.

A giant fucking cockroach.

Right there in my palm.

"Oh my god!" I yell, throwing the cockroach across the room and scrambling to my feet.

Hunter starts yelling with me.

Loan comes running in.

"What happened?" she asks, eyes wide.

"Cockroach!" I yell. "Hunter just gave me a cockroach."

"Was it dead?"

"I don't know. Hunter, did you kill it?"

But Hunter is staring at us wide-eyed and on the verge of tears, so I know I have to step up and be a motherfucking man for once. "It doesn't matter Hunter, I'm very proud of you. You said that's the leprechaun?"

He nods, pinching his lips together.

"Okay, great," I say then look at Loan. "Want to keep an eye on him while I check out the bathroom?"

"Yes but cockroaches are common here," she says, grabbing Hunter's hand and leading him over to the couch.

"How common?" I ask, as I step inside the downstairs bathroom, the one that Hunter uses most often. Loan and I both have our own upstairs.

"You'll see one occasionally," she says.

I enter the bathroom but I don't turn on the light as I would normally. Instead I bring out my phone's flashlight and shine it on the floor near the toilet where I figure they would be.

I only see them for a second before they hide but it's enough.

"Fuck," I mutter.

"Bad word!" Hunter yells from the living room. He seems to have picked up Loan's crazy hearing.

I step in further and crouch down in front of the cabinet beneath the sink. Other than putting in toilet paper, I haven't been in this bathroom yet so I have no idea what I'll find.

I open the doors.

Shudder at the sight.

Double fuck.

I close the doors.

"Hey Loan," I call out to her. "I think we have a major problem."

CHAPTER FIVE

NOVA

"ARE you sure you don't want to visit?" I ask my mom while pulling my Civic onto Queen Emma Street downtown. "I promise I can afford to fly you both. I have a big house and you know there is plenty of room for both of you. If you're sick of dad, you can even have your own bedroom each."

My mother chuckles on the speakerphone. "Baby girl, you know we would love to. But I don't think it's a good time."

My heart pinches at that. It's never a good time. Ever since I moved here, I've been the one going across the ocean to see them, they never come to see me, even if I'm taking care of them financially.

I know my parents are stubborn and don't want to impose on me. But this Christmas will be the first one I'm spending without them in a few years and I don't like the idea of leaving them alone, nor am I thrilled about being alone myself. It's been so hard without Rubina.

"When will it be a good time?" I ask quietly.

She sighs heavily. "Nova, you chose to move to a rock in

the middle of the Pacific. You know your father hates to fly, especially with his arthritis now. We're quite happy staying here."

"But...it will be just you two."

"I know," she says, and her voices drops softly. "I know. But we have each other and we'll get through it. I know it will be hard on us all without her here, but you know she's in our hearts and that's how we'll see it through."

My mother has always had a voraciously spiritual side and I think it's her faith alone that kept everyone from falling apart after Rubina died. She's had to deal with the threat of Rubina dying for years and I suppose when you're a mother, it's only faith and love that can keep you going through it all.

"Okay. But that won't stop me from worrying about you both."

"I know. And it won't stop us from worrying about you."

"You're the one who tells me worrying doesn't change anything."

"And yet we do it anyway."

"Okay, I'm at work now. I'll call you in a few days to check in."

"You take care baby girl. We love you."

She hangs up and I can feel a thread being cut somewhere in the middle of the ocean.

Feeling despondent and melancholy, I head up to the office, prepared for another day of nonsense with Kessler.

I mean, seriously. The last thing I expected to see on Friday after work was his penis, but there it was. Just waving in front of me at half-mast.

Thank god the whole story about the chicken was ridiculous. I didn't doubt him because he did seem awfully shaken up and I think he would have thought up a better excuse to wave his giant cock around than to be attacked by another cock. But the ridiculousness of the matter kept it from being real.

Because, lord, it could have gotten very real. I shouldn't have even been the slightest bit turned on at the sight of him like that but there was a very raw and powerful part of me that was. It's like my body remembered just what it was like to have that beast pumping inside of me and it was immediately game for more.

My body is a traitor.

Luckily my mind was able to shut it all down before things got weirder and I got out of there fast.

That said, after I was done with my volunteer work and I drove back home, the first thing I did was crawl into my bed and bring out my vibrator. It doesn't have the personal touch of Kessler's cock, but it did the job. Several times over. Until the post-orgasm, late-night shame washed over me.

Maybe shame is too strong of a word. It's not that I'm ashamed that I'm still turned on by that man, it's more that I'm disappointed. For five years I wasn't even allowed to think about him when it came to my erotic fantasies. I stuck to people like David Gandy, or Jeff Goldblum, or my surfing instructor who looked like Jason Momoa. Okay, so my vagina has eclectic tastes.

But Kessler was off-limits. It was the only way to get over him. That and dating a whole bunch of guys who, sadly, never measured up in the end.

Now, he's been back for a week and not only is the sweaty monster setting my loins on fire, but he's doing so in this weird dominant position of power way. He's my boss, and as much as I balk against that term and the sad reality of it with every ticking second of my day, for some reason it just fuels my sexual fantasies.

The forbidden and all that shit.

"Good morning," Kate says to me in her deadpan voice as I walk in. "Hey did you hear about what happened here over the weekend?"

"What?" I ask, pausing by her desk.

"I think some of the custodians had an illegal cock-fighting ring somewhere in the building. Maybe even the office. There were feathers everywhere this morning."

I exhale loudly, feeling exhausted. "I swear, if we could just go a day without saying the word cock."

"You okay?"

"I'm fine."

"You don't seem fine. You seem wound up tighter than a whale's asshole. You should have come out with us on Saturday night."

"Whale's asshole?" I repeat.

"Yeah. Because it has to be water tight. Otherwise the whale would be in a lot of trouble. Think about it."

I wave at her dismissively. "I'm going to go work."

"Okay but we need to have drinks this week because we still have a lot to discuss," she calls out after me as I go down the hall.

I close my office door, sit down at my desk and attempt to get to work.

Normally on Monday mornings I have a meeting with Mike to go over the rest of the week. I don't think Kessler ever got that memo and I'm not about to bring it up. The less I see him the better, and I have great satisfaction making him go through Mahina every time he wants to talk to me.

The only problem with that is that Mahina has been called into his office frequently.

And, well, not only is she a bright go-getter but she's all sorts of gorgeous.

Native Hawaiian. Expert surfer (her ex was that Jason Momoa-looking guy).

And Kessler's type with her being seventy-five-percent legs or whatever his Russian model ex was.

I shouldn't be jealous. I'm fairly secure with myself. I know my good sides (hair, skin, face, waist, arms, booty) and my bad (undereye circles, cellulite, jiggly thunder thighs, boobs that could be bigger). And I really do love sex, which I've been told repeatedly is a great asset.

But even so, I'm thirty, Mahina is young(er) and, well, I guess there's a tiny part of me that wants to keep Kessler's roving eyes to myself.

Because the fact is, his eyes are roving. Every time he lays them on me, they never stay in one place very long, unless they're soaking up my lips and attempting to hold my gaze. Otherwise they're constantly running over me like hot flames licking out from a fire, burning my breasts and my waist and my hips and my thighs.

I close my eyes and breathe in sharply through my nose. I'm the problem now, not him. I need to get this runaway libido under control.

I briefly consider calling up Roger, or maybe another ex that hasn't been tainted via Vegas hooker, when there's a knock at my door.

"Come in," I say.

It opens. It's Mahina, her impossibly long dark hair swinging in her face. Ugh, I would kill to have my hair that shiny. "*Aloha kakahiaka*," she greets me cheerfully. "How was your weekend?"

"Great," I tell her. It wasn't great. It was boring. "How was yours?"

"Same old. I was surfing at Sunset Beach, I should have

stopped by your house and said hello. So, uh, Mr. Rocha would like to schedule a meeting with you."

I give her a tired look. "When?"

"Now, I believe."

"Where?"

"Right here is fine," he says, suddenly appearing behind Mahina. "Thank you Mahina, I'll take it from here."

She gives him a sheepish smile that borders on high school crush and then scampers away to her desk down the hall.

"I guess we both share the same assistant now," Kessler says, leaning against the door. It bothers me that he doesn't look sweaty at all, as if being a sweat monster was his one weakness. Oh who am I kidding, seeing that sweat drip off of him only brought memories of our slick bodies tangled beneath the sheets.

"She's *my* assistant," I manage to say.

"Actually, according to Desiree, she was also Mike's assistant. Oh wait, no." He taps his fingers against his manly chin in false contemplation. "Desiree said that you were essentially Mike's assistant. But I told her you were more qualified than that."

I swallow down my pride in a bitter pill. "Thank you."

"So anyway, I need to talk to you."

"Is this about our weekly meeting?"

"Weekly meeting? No." He steps in and shuts the door behind him and then strolls over to the chair across from my desk and takes a seat. "I need to talk to you about something urgent."

I frown, my heart picking up the beat. "What?"

He gives me a shy grin, the type of grin that makes the dimples pop on his scruffy cheeks. He doesn't have a Hawaiian tan yet, but once he does, he's going to get pretty dark thanks to that Portuguese blood of his and those teal eyes are going to pop even more. Maybe that's half the reason why my body turns to goo around him, his eyes are my favorite color in the whole world.

"I need to ask you a favor."

I stare at him. Worried. I hate favors. "What favor?"

He chews on his lip for a moment. "We have a leprechaun problem."

I blink. "...Leprechaun?"

"Cockroaches," he elaborates.

There's that word cock again.

"Is that what you call cockroaches in the Yukon?" Fucking Canadians.

"No, it's what Hunter calls them," he says. "Point is, we have a cockroach problem. The whole house has been invaded."

I shudder, scrunching up my face. "Ew."

"Yeah, that's putting it mildly. Hunter's been afraid of leprechauns since we got here and I only realized on Friday when he put a fucking dead roach in my hand just what his version of leprechauns were. Let me tell you, it was scarier than the Leprechaun movie."

"That wasn't scary," I tell him.

"That's because you don't find any movies scary," he says.

I shrug. "I don't know, the real-life horror show of a cockroach infestation sounds much worse."

"It is. I thought maybe it was just the bathroom so Loan and I got to setting traps—"

"Who is Loan?" That weird jealousy spear is poking me again.

"The nanny," he says. "She's Vietnamese. Quiet, except at odd times. She's a good egg though, Mike set it up."

"The same Mike that gave you this job and then put you in his cockroach-infested house?"

"That's the same one. I don't know how he's been living there but..." he trails off and now it's time for him to shudder. "Anyway, either Mike is a giant slob or he's been blinded because of that porn star, but either way, the house is infested from top to bottom. The traps don't work and we can't do much more because of Hunter. I think he's picking up some sort of asthmatic response to them too."

"Shit."

"Speaking of shit, have you seen cockroach shit? Looks like coffee grounds. That's what I fucking thought it was, like Loan was just messy with the Starbucks blend in the morning but oh no no no."

"So..."

"So I spent the weekend trying to figure out what to do. When I realized it was a losing battle, I called the exterminators. They came by yesterday and took a look around. The main guy was a real Clint Eastwood when it came to cockroaches. He said it would take three nights, maybe more. Fumigation started today."

Oh god. Please don't let this go where I think it's going.

He continues, his brows raised in a pleading way that makes my heart sink. "I looked at hotels but because it's me, Hunter, and Loan, one room just wouldn't work, and because it's the holiday season now, almost everything is booked up except for places on Waikiki charging three grand a night. Then I asked around the office and the only offer I got was from Teef but I don't feel like living with ten of his cousins. Then everyone mentioned that you had a large house all to yourself..."

Fuck.

I knew this would bite me in the ass one day.

When I first moved to Honolulu, I was in a tiny one-bedroom studio in Pearl City for six months. I was working hard and barely had time for the fact that I was in Hawaii of all places. I finally made my way out to the North Shore, courtesy of Teef who took pity on me and needed to show me what was so great about Oahu.

I fell in love.

It felt so different from Honolulu and the south shore. The north shore was wild and lush and uncontained and free. The beaches were empty, the surf was loud, and the waves were behemoths that made me shake even standing on the shore. It was so green it hurt my eyes and the flowers that sprouted off the power lines were a sign that nature was just a misstep away from taking over civilization.

It spoke to my soul, my spirit. For the first time since coming to Hawaii, I understood what Aloha was.

It was love.

I had to move there immediately.

I found a room in a large plantation house in Hale'iwa that needed fixing up. I started out having three roommates. As time went on, I started working on the house in my spare time. Eventually the owner wanted to sell and I put in the first offer. Because I'd already put so much of my own spirit into the place, he agreed to sell it to me.

It wasn't cheap but I'd just moved up into my current position and the bank approved me and the rest was history. I had a roommate, Cinthia, to help along with the mortgage until last year, and since then I've been alone.

So, Kessler isn't mistaken in that I do have a large house with lots of room. But it's the kind of room I was hoping my parents would take me up on.

Not the man sitting across from me.

But I'm also not a heartless wench, even if I feel like I

am sometimes. He's obviously in a tough spot, plus he has his son and nanny to worry about. To be honest, I'm really curious about Hunter. I wonder how much of him looks like Kessler, how much the Russian model. Does he have Kessler's eyes? His olive skin tone? Has he picked up on the funny way he pronounces things sometimes?

"You want to move in with me?" I ask.

He bites on his lip and I ignore the urge to do the same. "If it's not too much trouble. Just for three nights. That's the estimate the roach guy gave me anyway. We can even carpool in the morning. It will be fun."

I cock my head, brows to the heavens. *Fun? Are you serious?*

Kessler ignores that look. "So you're okay with this?"

I sigh and lean back in my chair. "Of course I'm okay with it. As long as you don't mind living out on the north shore for a few days. Believe me, it's miles from Honolulu."

"I haven't been yet but I've heard it's beautiful."

The way he says beautiful, the way his eyes hold mine, fire intensifying in them, sends shivers down my spine that I try desperately to hide.

"Okay well..." I say.

"After work today we can move everything over," he says. "We don't have much stuff as it is. And don't worry about Hunter. I mean, he's a toddler so he's half-angel, half-fiendish troll, but he's a pretty good kid if I do say so myself. And Loan just keeps to herself, you won't even know she's there."

I nod, swallowing. "Okay then. Then it's settled."

He grins at me. "I won't forget this," he says, as if it's going to buy me some favor in the future.

How about you give me your job in exchange, I think, even though I'm giving him a fake smile.

I keep it plastered on my face until he leaves.

Instead of heading straight home after work like I usually do on a Monday, I drive to Mike's house where Kessler proceeds to get all his shit out of the house. Because of the evening downpour that rolls around like clockwork this time of year, I sit in my car and watch through the rain-soaked windshield. I could have just told them to meet me at the house but figured an escort was a more personal way of moving.

Besides, it looks horrid. The exterminators have already put up tents around half the house, so when Kessler starts bringing out his luggage, it looks like they're fleeing a post-apocalyptic scene.

It isn't until a slender women—who I assume is Loan—holding a child in her arms—who I assume is Hunter—comes out do I see the dilemma. Kessler's fancy sports car isn't enough for everyone.

Eventually the bags get moved into my trunk and then I get Loan as my passenger.

"Hello," I say to her as she shuts the door, shaking the rain out of her hair.

"Hello," she says to me curtly, giving me the once over before putting on her seatbelt.

Okay, so Kessler never quite told me how much English Loan knows. I never had a nanny growing up, but a girl across the street did, a Swedish one that her father eventually ended up banging according to my mother, and she didn't speak a word of English.

I'm pretty awkward with small talk so I don't say anything while I drive out of the hills and to the freeway, turning up the music on the radio. You don't hear Jack Johnson here as much as you think you would but I figure he's pretty good for putting people in a relaxed mood. I mean, who can be angry when you're thinking about banana pancakes?

It isn't until we've crested the mountains and started heading down towards the north shore that Loan turns to me. "Do you have Wi-Fi?"

I stare at her for a moment before looking back to the road.

"Do I have Wi-Fi?"

"At the house."

"Of course. Five G."

She nods. "Okay. Good signal?"

"As good as it gets out there," I tell her. "Why, are you a video gamer?"

I swear I see a touch of a smile on her lips. "No. I like to Facetime my boy."

"You have a son?"

She nods, staring out the rain-streaked window. "Yes. Hai is my son. And my husband is Binh. In English their names are Ocean and Peaceful."

"That's lovely. I had no idea. So where are they, in Vietnam?"

She nods. "In Hanoi. Binh owns a restaurant. My mother looks after Hai. I'm just here for a few years to help bring in some money. It's better this way than for me to stay there. This way I only have to work a little and I'll bring in the same amount as if I worked a lot there."

"How old is Hai?"

"He's thirteen now," she says. "I'll go back for good when he's sixteen. I still visit every year. Once he came here, he loved it."

"That must be hard to leave them for so long."

She shrugs a shoulder. "It is hard but it must be done and so I do it. It's how you get through it."

She doesn't say anything after that, but she doesn't need to. Her words had so much conviction in them it was hard for me not to ruminate on them for the rest of the drive.

Finally, we pull up to the house.

No surprise, the place is painted a dark teal, though you can't tell that from the faint light of the road. It's large, slightly raised above ground with a sprawling lanai and a copious amount of ti bushes and bamboo along the edges of the property that I keep between tamed and unruly. I'm about four blocks from the shore, so if the night is calm and you listen hard, you can hear the famously powerful surf.

Tonight though, it's raining. It's often raining here, hence why it's so lush and green, and in a way it reminds me of home.

With Kessler parking behind me in the driveway, we make quick work of getting everything inside, even though we all get soaked in the end.

It's only then that I finally get my first proper look at Hunter.

The boy is gorgeous. Gorgeous in a way that makes my heart ache.

I briefly have flashes of Kess and I together, the times that he was so tender and attentive with me, the way he made me feel like I was the only person in the world. It was during those times that my mind and heart ran away with me. Where I started to wonder, what would it be like to marry him? To have his children? Where would we live, what would our children be like?

I pictured them with a lot of me, of course, maybe curly black hair and bronzed skin and full lips. I also pictured them with blue eyes, maybe green, and a strong jaw. There were a million variations of all the *could-have-beens* running through my head.

And yet seeing Hunter standing before me, his actual son, I'm totally floored because even though he's not my child and Kessler is totally new at this parenting thing, I see a product of my imagination come to life, just a million times more beautiful.

Hunter must take after his mother when it comes to the color of his sandy blonde hair and pale skin, but his curly waves, his light eyes and dark brow are totally Kessler. Even though he looks a bit shell-shocked to be where we are, in a totally strange and foreign house, adorably clutching a Kahuna Hotels pineapple stress ball to his chest, he looks like he's ready to laugh at any second.

That's pure Kessler. And when I glance up at Kess, who has been watching me carefully as I take in his son, I know my approval means something.

"Hey Hunter," I say to him, crouching down to his level. "We haven't officially met yet. I'm Nova. This is my house that you're going to be staying in for a few days while those nasty cockroaches are cleaned up."

"Leprechauns," he corrects me. "They live at the bottom of the rainbow."

"Or the bottom of the toilet bowl," Kessler says. "Either one. Should we find you your room, buddy?" He glances at me for guidance.

"Of course," I say, walking down the hall. "There's one guest bedroom down there," I say, looking at Loan. "You could use that if you want. It has a nice view of the mountains in the back and there's the bathroom right here. On the other side is this room I use as a study but there's a really comfy pull-out couch in there that might be good for Hunter."

Loan nods and takes Hunter's hand, leading him to the rooms for his approval.

"And where am I staying?" Kessler asks in a low voice. "In your room?"

I give him a withering glance. "Yeah right. Of all things to not forget right now, let's not forget you're my boss."

"I can forget if you can," he says, wagging his brows.

I reach out and slap him across the chest. "Hey. I'm serious. I didn't help you out for any other reason than I'm a good person and I felt sorry for your son and your nanny. Both of whom have to put up with you now on a daily basis. So, if you're going to test your luck in any sort of way with me, I'm going to kick your ass to the curb. The others can stay."

He stares at me in challenge and I know from the way his eyes search mine that he's looking for some sort of weakness in me, some way he can come out on top. But the fact is, he no longer has the upper hand. He's currently homeless and I'm his helping hand. Actually, it probably pisses him off in some way, having to depend on me like this.

I can't help but smile.

"Uh oh," he says, leaning in close as he frowns at me. "I don't like that smile. I know that smile. That smile has rarely led to anything good."

I raise a brow. "Just behave yourself, okay there, sweat monster?"

"Sweat monster?"

I nod at his forehead which is already glistening. "Sorry, I forgot to mention I only have AC in my bedroom."

"And I'm not sleeping there."

"Correct. Let me show you where you are sleeping," I

tell him, heading up the stairs and incredibly aware that my ass is swinging back and forth in his face as I make the climb. My skin practically heats up knowing his eyes are locked to it.

Actually Kessler's bedroom isn't that bad. It's right across from mine, the entire upper floor just our bedrooms and we both have an en suite. It has a large fan, plus the windows face the ocean so you have that sea breeze always coming in. I originally wanted that room to be mine, but mine was the room I'd got when I first arrived and I'm too attached to it to switch.

"This is yours," I tell him, opening the door and flicking on the light. I'd recently gone through and cleaned all the rooms and changed all the bedding in the hopes that my parents might come for Christmas but we all know that's not happening now.

He walks inside, hauling his suitcase to the middle of the room, and looks around.

"Did you decorate?" he asks.

I nod. "I did."

"You know it looks like I walked into a room at a Kahuna Hotel."

I grin sheepishly. Okay, so I may have a problem with pilfering Kahuna Hotel swag whenever I get the chance. It's a pro of working in marketing, I get to test the products out, which means I have golden pineapple-themed everything. Including bedspread, which Kessler is inspecting right now.

"Really?" he asks. "It's going to be like sleeping at the office. Shit, did you steal those paintings too?" He points at the walls.

"I didn't steal anything," I hiss at him. "They were leftovers. Now if you'll excuse me, I'm wet and it's been a long day and I'm ready for bed."

I turn and head out of the room, half-expecting him to say something with regards to the *wet* comment.

Instead I hear a faint shriek.

I turn around and poke my head back in his room.

"Was that you?" I ask. "It sounded like a little girl."

He's standing by the bed but his eyes are glued to the space above the doorway. I step inside and look up.

There's a gecko perched on the wall, minding his own business.

"What?" I ask, looking back at Kessler who seems frozen on the spot.

"What is that?"

"What is that?" I repeat. "That's a gecko."

"He's huge," he hisses, eyes wide. You'd think he was staring at Godzilla.

"That's why his name is Dwayne Johnson," I tell him.

He does a double take. "I'm sorry, he has a name?"

"Yeah."

"Dwayne Johnson?"

"He's a big gecko."

"You're crazy."

"Geckos are good luck. You're crazy to be afraid of them."

"I'm not afraid of them," he says sharply. "I just don't like lizards. It's a natural dislike to have."

"First chickens, now geckos. Are you sure you had a cockroach infestation at your house and they aren't actually fumigating for ladybugs?"

"Oh ha ha," he says dryly. "I'll have you know in the Yukon, I grew up wrestling wolves and bears."

I fold my arms across my chest. "Oh really. Let me guess, it was essential for hockey practice."

"I'm just saying, no sane person lets lizards stay in their house, let alone gives them names."

"Geckos eat mosquitos and cockroaches," I tell him. "We'd be more screwed without them than with. Now, if you're really that afraid, I can remove him for you but if he wants to, he's going to come right back in here."

Kessler closes his eyes and takes in a deep breath. To see him with his massive arms and wide chest and shoulders like boulders, all six foot two of this sweaty burly hunk of man meat, shaken up because of a gecko is probably the most amusing thing I've seen all year.

"Just think of him as the Geico gecko," I tell him, grabbing the door and starting to pull it shut. "Imagine him talking to you in a British accent." I clear my throat and do my best English impression. "Don't mind me, Mr. Rocha. I'm just your friendly neighborhood gecko, stationed here so you don't get eaten alive by mosquitos at night. Nothing to fear here, just a little lizard to watch over you and sell you car insurance."

"You can go now," Kessler says, shooting me a dirty look as he throws back his bed covers.

"Are you sure?" I continue in the accent.

"Good night, Nova."

I grin at him. "Good night, Kessler. Don't let the geckos bite," I tell him right before I shut the door.

I'm practically giggling all the way to bed.

CHAPTER SIX

KESSLER

I BARELY SLEPT LAST NIGHT.

I didn't even know I had any sort of reptile phobia until I saw that miniature dragon hanging above the doorway and suddenly it was like some switch got flipped in me. Perhaps if I hadn't been accosted by chickens and cockroaches over the weekend, I wouldn't be so jumpy about the thing but the fact is, I'm not a fan of geckos.

And for the life of me, I don't get how Nova can stand them either. I mean, she lets it live in her house. She's given the little Godzilla a name.

Dwayne Johnson. I mean what the fuck?

Suffice it to say, when I finally did succumb to sleep it was the middle of the night and my body was too tired to pretend that there weren't lizards running all over me.

Because I'm staying with Nova now, something I'm already regretting thanks to her lizard friend, she's the one who's driving us to work this morning. Thank god, because I am way too rattled by everything to think straight and the whole North Shore of Oahu has me totally turned around.

I mean, it's a gorgeous place but it's completely different than Honolulu. It's the place where you want to sit back in a hammock and have a beer and let your mind run free. Perhaps run naked through the jungle. I can see why Nova wants to live here, but I'm not so sold.

After I've said goodbye to Hunter and Loan, and Nova has given Loan the low-down on the area and where to go and what to see, we get into Nova's Honda Civic and head through a small town full of quaint and colorful buildings before we pull onto a highway.

It's a grey morning and humid as fuck and I've already downed a bucket of water so far, so it's no surprise when I tell Nova to pull over so I can take a leak.

"Can't you hold it?" she says distastefully, as if I have zero control of my bladder.

"I can, I'm not Hunter," I tell her. "I would rather not sit here uncomfortable for the next hour."

It's already bad enough I'm exhausted, I'm stuck in this car with you, who hates me one minute and hates me a little less the next.

"You better not make us late," she says, pulling the car down a narrow dirt road bordered by fenced cow fields where we bounce along pot holes for a few feet until she stops by a bunch of wild bushes with white flowers. It's almost too pretty to piss on. Almost.

"Late?" I say with a snort as I get out. "We're on Hawaii time, we're already late compared to the rest of the world."

That was one of the annoying things about working for the company in California. If you waited for corporate to get anything done, you had to wait a long time. When they started work at nine, it was already eleven or noon on the mainland.

I've just finished pissing when I hear some shaking from

beneath the bushes. Not wanting to stick around and see what it is, I zip up my pants and hurry back to the car. I'm over getting caught with my pants down.

I get in the passenger seat and Nova pulls away, heading down the long road, reddish dust flying up behind us.

"Highway is back there. Where are you going?" I ask as we're heading toward a barn. "Going to take me cow-tipping?"

She gives me a sharp look, as if I've majorly offended her. "Who told you about that?" she hisses.

"About what?"

She frowns at me and then pulls the car around in the turnaround. "It was too narrow to turn around back there," she says, ignoring me.

We're heading off back down the road toward the highway, the car bumping along the potholes at a steady speed. I'm about to tell Nova that maybe she should slow down when we pass by the bushes I pissed on earlier and a chicken comes darting out across the road in front of the car.

"Ahhhh!' Nova screams, immediately swerving as if she's trying not to hit a child and as she whips the wheel around, we go careening off the road right into the fence pole.

The impact is sharp and the seatbelt cuts into my neck just as the airbags inflate and slam me in the face. Everything comes to a stop.

"Are you okay?" I ask Nova, frantically trying to battle the air bag but it's like hitting a dusty balloon.

"I guess so," I hear her mumble through it all.

The impact was pretty gentle as far as car crashes are concerned but even so, I'm worried. "Are you sure? Don't move, I'll help you."

I open my door to get out, the airbag practically punching me in the face, and quickly survey the damage as I make my way behind the Civic. The fence post is at an angle, the front of her hood is pushed in a bit and a headlight is broken. We've also attracted the attention of all the cows.

I open her door, peering at her.

She glances up at me, face against the airbag, covered in fine white dust. To my relief, she doesn't look hurt but her pride sure does.

"You look like you had a massive cocaine party," I tell her, gesturing to the powder from the airbag that's all over her face.

She gives me a wane smile. "So do you."

"Are you sure you're okay?" I ask and as she's nodding, I hear a familiar squawking sound from the front of the car.

Suddenly the same chicken that ran across the road and caused us to swerve is staring right at me with beady yellow eyes, seemingly unharmed.

"Oh sweet Jesus, it's *him*," I say.

"Who?" Nova says, trying to see around the airbag.

I point at the rooster. "It's that motherfucking chicken!"

"Is he okay?"

I glare at her. "Is he *okay*? Why the fuck didn't you hit it? That's the same fucking chicken from the office."

She rolls her eyes. "Oh my god, Kess."

"It is!" I look back at the chicken and he flaps his wings several times, stirring the dust in the road before putting his head back and letting out a familiar battle cry. "It's him! Did you hear what he said? That's his war cry!"

"It's not the same chicken," she says, attempting to get out of the car. Her movement scares the chicken, which then darts back across the road and under the bush. "There is a mountain range between us and Honolulu and there are millions of chickens. They all look the same."

"They do not," I say, helping her undo her seatbelt and carefully pulling her out of the car. "That one has white spots on his chest and I looked into his eyes and those eyes told me everything I needed to know. That motherfucking chicken is out to get me."

She stares up at me and it's only then that I realize we're just inches apart. The proximity to her does something to my brain, unraveling it, and for a moment I've forgotten all about the chicken. I reach out to brush the powder from her hair which she's pulled back into a ponytail and her eyes widen at my contact.

"Are you sure you're okay?" I ask her, wishing I could let my hand drift down her head, down her neck, across her shoulder. Wishing I could just continue touching her for no reason at all other than nothing has ever felt better.

She nods, slowly, as if she doesn't want me to stop touching her either.

I can feel the sweat prickling at the back of my neck.

It's hot out and it's getting hotter.

Then she abruptly moves to the side and my hand falls to nothing. She goes to the front of the car and then puts her hands over her face, taking in a deep breath.

Oh right. The car.

"It's not so bad," I tell her.

"I can't drive this now," she says through her hands. She lets out a muffled shriek. "Ahhh, we're going to be late."

"Late? Who cares. Nova, we were in a car accident, work should be the last thing on your mind."

But as her hands fall away and I see the sharp line between her brows, I know it's everything that's on her mind. "You don't understand, I was supposed to pitch an idea for the holidays with George, some newsletter discount."

"George is a nice guy, I'm sure he'll understand that his employee has been in a car accident. Hell, I was just in this car accident too. What the hell were you doing swerving like that?"

Her eyes fly, sharp as knives. "I'm sorry I don't like running over innocent animals."

"That wasn't an animal, it was a chicken and more than that, it was *that* motherfucking chicken, so he wasn't fucking innocent after all. That chicken deserved to be under the wheels of your car and we deserve to be driving to work right now and arguing over something else that's stupid."

"Stupid?" she says. "If we ever argue about something stupid, it's probably because it came from you."

"Are you calling me stupid?"

I know I shouldn't be bothered by that comment and I normally do let a lot of things roll off my back, but being called stupid or dumb has always aggravated me, probably because it's such a stereotype to put on hockey players, probably because it's a sore spot because I wish I had gone to college. It was always part of my plans.

I'm watching her carefully. I know she wants to say it, I know it bothers her so damn much that she's had to go to school and work her juicy butt off. I know she thinks I got everything handed to me in life when that's never been the case at all.

The sweat is now creeping down my face and getting in my eyes.

Why the fuck is it so hot? It's not even sunny out!

She purses her lips for a moment. "You're the one who said we argue about stupid shit."

"Well, we do. All we do is argue."

She snorts, looking away. "You wish. I know arguing turns you on."

"It turns you on too," I point out, starting to unbutton my shirt. "Remember that time when you accused me of stealing your idea for the hotel lobby?"

That got her attention. Her nostrils flare as she gives me daggers. "You did steal my idea! Like you would have ever come up with having cucumber spa water on your own."

"No, it was my idea," I tell her. "I saw it at another hotel so I *stole* it."

"Well I came up with it organically. And why the hell are you taking off your shirt, are you turned on already?"

"It's fucking hot out!" I yell, wrestling with the already damp shirt as it's sticking to my skin. I practically rip it off, throwing it on the roof of the car.

And now Nova is speechless.

Which is both a nice respite and somewhat rewarding since she's staring at me with her eyes wide and mouth open, something she immediately tries to hide.

"You can ogle me, it's fine," I tell her, raising my arms out.

I know I have a damn good body. When you consistently workout every morning for an hour and watch what you eat, you're very aware of the reward. Plus I'm naturally bulky and muscular, which is why I was such a good defenseman. When I came skating at top speed and threw people into the boards, they were out for the count.

Now of course I wouldn't mind doing the same to Nova, throwing her up against the car and having my way with her, sweat be damned.

"I'm not ogling you," she manages to say, a bit too late.

I grin at her, making sure everything is flexing. And as

her eyes coast over the rigid planes of my abs, they pause at my crotch, where, yeah, I'm pretty fucking hard as well.

"I can't believe you're turned on," she says, shaking her head in disgust. "Put your shirt back on and your boner away, I can't talk to you like this."

"Hey baby, I thought this was the Hawaiian way. If you can't beat 'em, join 'em, right?"

"Please don't start beating anything," she says, eyes at my dick imprint again. "You're so inappropriate."

"Because arguing with you turns me on? Or because I'm thinking about what happened the last time we argued, when you insisted that the cucumber water was your idea. Do you remember?"

"I'm not revisiting memory lane with you," she says, and starts to walk past me to the driver's side. "I need to get my phone to call roadside assistance."

I reach out and grab her, my hands wrapped around her forearms, pulling her in until she's almost pressed up against my chest.

I grin down at her, at her eyes that hover between being anxious and wide and devilishly curious. "Of course you remember," I murmur, leaning in closer. She smells like honey today. "The way we argued in your office afterward. You got so hot for me, so wet, you were begging for it. I fucked you right there on your desk, right up your tight little ass."

She swallows loudly, her eyes turning into mahogany saucers. "That didn't happen," she manages to say, her voice low and throaty.

"Oh right," I say, biting my lip for a moment. "We had angry sex up against the wall. The whole doing you on your desk was what I was imagining last Friday when I was jerking off to you in the washroom."

She blinks at me but somehow doesn't seem all that surprised. "Was that before or after the chicken attacked you?"

"Before," I murmur. "I was interrupted. But you can bet I finished that fantasy back at home."

Nova doesn't blush often but she's blushing now, her cheeks darkening as she averts her eyes. "You're sweating on me," she says after a beat.

"I know. I'm starting to think that you're the reason it's so fucking hot here."

"That's cute." She cocks her head. "Need I remind you that you're my boss? I don't like it any more than you do."

"But I do like it," I tell her with a grin. "I love the fact that I'm your boss and I get to order you around and tell you what to do."

She laughs. It's a genuine laugh too, a beautiful sound. Because she knows I haven't been able to order her around or tell her what to do, but lord knows I won't stop trying. "You're impossible," she says. "Now can you let me get my phone or do I have to knee you in the balls?"

Her smile is sweet but her eyes tell me she means business.

"Still feisty," I tell her, letting go of her arms and watching her bring her purse and phone out from airbag hell. "Tell me again why we didn't work out?"

She's about to dial when she stops, cold.

Uh oh.

That was maybe the wrong thing to say.

She raises her chin to look at me.

I swear I see a glimmer of something witchy and green in her eyes, like somewhere inside her I just threw a bunch of gasoline on an industrial fire.

"You want to know why we didn't work out?" she

repeats. Slowly. Her words like miniature bombs. "Really? You want to know?"

I try to shrug. "I was just joking..."

"No, really," she says, taking a careful step toward me. "You seem like you want to know."

I should probably protect my balls at this point.

"Look, let's just forget I said anything," I tell her quickly. "Call Triple A and we can get going. I'll call Loan to pick us up."

"We didn't work out because you never wanted us to work out," she says, eyes sparking as she pokes her finger into my bare chest.

I wrap my hand around her finger and pull it off. "That's not true at all."

"You told me, and I remember this so, so clearly, that one morning after you slept over at my apartment for the first time, months after we started fucking. You said, *I think we should call this off. I don't want things to get complicated at work.* To which I said, *things won't get complicated. We're allowed to date people in the office.* To which you said, *but we aren't dating, we're just fucking.* To which I said, *oh. I thought this was turning into more.* To which you said, *you know I'm not that kind of guy.* To which I said, *you're right, I did know that.*" She pokes her other finger in my chest, harder now. She's grinding her teeth as she talks. "So we stopped sleeping together, just like that, because you didn't want to complicate things and ruin our friendship and you didn't want commitment and *what* did you do two days later?"

Oh god. She knows.

"You fucked Stacy, the god damn front desk clerk, the same clerk you knew had a crush on you, the same clerk whom you once said wasn't your type. You were screwing her just two days later, you fucking asshole."

Okay. She's got me there. But even though I don't really have anything to defend, I still feel like I've got to try.

I raise my palms, staring at her finger instead of the hatred billowing in her eyes. "It didn't mean anything."

"What didn't? Stacy, or us?"

"*Stacy*."

"How is that supposed to make me feel better? That's even more insulting."

"Look, the two of us were just having fun and you knew I didn't want a relationship, so you went along with it anyway. What, did you think you were going to change me?"

Her nostrils flare again. Okay, wrong thing to say, part two.

I stumble on. "I mean, you seemed to take it well. You never showed much interest in me if my cock wasn't buried deep inside you, so how was I supposed to know you'd care?"

She shakes her head, taking her finger away and turning from me. "Why am I even talking to you about this? Why do I even bother?"

"I don't know but you brought it up."

"You brought it up!" she yells, whirling around. "You *just* brought it up. And now that it is up, are you fucking dense? You really thought it was just about sex for me and that was it?"

"Of course I did!" I throw my arms out. "Why would I think any different! You never told me anything, you never opened up. The only time I saw you vulnerable was when I was making you come. And maybe that's one reason why I liked to make you come so fucking much, it was the only time you let your guard down, where you'd let me in, let me see who you were underneath."

Shit. I had no idea where any of that came from but apparently I haven't been the only one harboring some resentment over the last five years.

It's caught her off guard too. She's breathing hard, her forehead creased. I both want to pull her into me and hold her and tell her I'm sorry for even yelling at her like this, and at the same time I want to kiss her, strip her bare, see if maybe she can belong to me this time around.

"I keep things close to my chest," she says carefully, taking in a deep breath. "That's just how I am, and I have my reasons. And one of those reasons is so that men like you don't walk all over me. I knew you didn't want to commit, so yeah it was my own fault for thinking you could maybe commit to me. I'll own that mistake. But to see you so callously move on like that..."

I sigh heavily, my heart a sinking rock. "I know. I felt bad about it and I feel even worse now. I made a mistake and I did some stupid shit. I was a different person back then. We both were."

"I know." She says, her attention going back to her phone. "So let's just let bygones be bygones and pretend you and I never ever happened."

"That's not going to be easy," I tell her.

Because I don't want to pretend we never happened.

I want to do the opposite.

I want...I think I just want a second chance to see if things can work this time around.

But from the way she's glaring at me as she dials the phone, I know that's never going to happen.

She hates me, and if she doesn't hate me, then she's going to be indifferent and I'm not sure which one is worse.

"Easy or not, I wiped you from my memory once, I can do it again," she says, putting the phone to her ear.

I flinch. Ouch. Okay, whatever *this* is, is worse.

"I'm still your boss," I remind her gently. "You'll still see me every day and I'm still living in your house until those cockroaches are gone."

But if she's heard me at all, she doesn't show it. She just nods and says, "Hello, hi, my name is Nova Lane and I'm a Triple A member and I've just been in a minor car accident."

I exhale loudly and grab my shirt as I lean back against the car. She tells the guy on the phone that no one is hurt and there are no injuries.

But that's just not true at all.

CHAPTER SEVEN

NOVA

IT'S BEEN A *DAY*.

And that's putting it mildly.

After the disaster of a morning, Triple A towed my car away and then Loan was able to pick us up and take us back to my house where we went into Kessler's Audi.

If I thought the commute was awkward before, now it was unbearable.

We weren't talking to each other.

Kessler made a few attempts but, in the end, I turned up the radio and he got the hint.

I was mad.

Fuming.

And, well, a little embarrassed if I'm being honest.

The whole blow-up we had at each other was a long time coming, and it wasn't until we were yelling at each other like a bunch of children that I realized all of this could have been dealt with years ago. Back then it was just easier to cut and run.

And I still don't regret it. After all, he's the one who

slept with Stacy right after I was sleeping with him for months. That shit hurt, more than I thought possible.

But what was even worse than the whole Stacy thing was the fact that I was in love with Kessler and he broke my heart when he broke things off. Regardless of what happened afterward, who he slept with or whatever, I was a wounded animal, crawling off to heal somewhere.

It ended up being Hawaii.

I just never realized that not everything was so one-sided. I know I wasn't open with Kessler because I knew what kind of a man he was and I knew I had extra reason to protect myself. What I didn't realize was that Kessler noticed. More than that, it seemed to have bothered him. When he was yelling at me, I heard the emotion in his voice, I saw the sincerity in his eyes. Maybe if I had let him in more, maybe then things would have ended differently.

Or not, I think with a sigh, leaning back in my office chair and closing my eyes. *Whether you protect yourself or not, when you fall in love, it's going to hurt.*

A knock at my door snaps me out of it. It opens and Teef pokes his head in. He's never been very good at waiting for a response.

"Hey lady," Teef says, with his big, white, toothy smile as he bites the end of a banana. "I heard about your accident earlier. So sorry there. The *malihini* said it was a chicken?"

I can't even smile at that. "Yeah," I say tiredly. "It was a chicken. I was better off running it over."

"I can relate," he says. "Listen, if you need a ride home, I can give you one."

"Thanks. But Kessler's my ride. You know the whole cockroach thing." It's the only reason it's convenient that he's been working late too.

At that, Teef stops chewing, looking shocked. "Oh. No. See we're the last ones in the office. Kessler is gone, sis."

"He's what!" I cry out, pressing my hands into the desk.

Teef backs up, thinking I'm about to launch over the desk and tackle him. "I'm just saying, he's not in his office. I'm about to leave."

I grumble. "Whatever. It's fine. I'm fine. Maybe he forgot."

Maybe he's mad at you, too.

"You sure?"

"I'm sure Teef, I'll figure it out. I'll see you tomorrow."

"*A hui hou*," he says quickly, closing the door.

Well fuckity fuck.

How could Kessler forget about me?

I suppose it doesn't help that I didn't talk to him for the rest of the day. Maybe he wiped me out of his brain as easily as I once did. Who knows, he could have driven all the way back to Mike's before he remembered the whole cockroach thing.

If I wasn't in a foul mood before, I am now. I'm tempted to pick up my phone and call him and yell or text a flurry of expletives, but decide against it. I have every right to be mad that I'm stranded at the office but I still don't want to give him the satisfaction of my reaction, just in case he did it on purpose.

Instead I pick up the pineapple stress ball and I launch it across the office so it hits the wall with a somewhat satisfying *whack*.

Then I pack up my stuff, bring out my phone and try to find an Uber as I head to the elevators.

The door dings open even before I get a chance to push the button and out steps Kessler.

"Where are you going?" he asks.

"Where have you been?"

"I stepped out. I thought you'd be working a little later," he says. "Were you planning on walking?"

I put my phone away in my purse. "I was calling an Uber."

He folds his massive arms and I don't know if that's his distraction technique, like him taking his shirt off earlier. Whatever it is, it works, because now I'm picturing him without his shirt on, the way his sweaty, naked torso looked against the backdrop of the mountains this morning, the only good thing about the car accident.

"Did you really think I would have left without you?"

I shrug. "I don't know. Maybe you forgot. Maybe you didn't care."

He shakes his head, frowning. "You're unbelievable. I'd like to think you'd give me a little more credit than that. Just because you said you wanted to let bygones be bygones, doesn't mean I'm not driving you home...to your own house. What kind of man do you think I am?"

A frustrating one, I think. *With one hell of a body.*

"I'm sorry," I mutter, staring down at his fancy shoes that are now appropriately scuffed. "I guess I wouldn't have blamed you."

"Why, because we had a fight? You know I love fighting with you, Supernova."

I glance up at him and it's like all the air is squeezed from my lungs. The way his hair has curled just so around his ears and the nape of his neck, the shining depths of his jewel-toned eyes, permanently bordering on something wicked and lewd, the hint of a smile on his full lips.

And just like that, I'm staring at him like a dumb idiot, pretty much the same way I did when I first laid eyes on him all those years ago and my heart skipped ten beats at once.

But I'm not that person anymore and because I have a shred of dignity, I clear my throat and say. "Okay, well we better get going so we can stop by Panda Express."

He laughs as he pushes the elevator button. "We aren't going to Panda Express."

"Uh, it's Tuesday," I tell him. "Chinese Food Tuesday. It's a thing. It's my thing. And I told Loan she could have the night off from cooking."

He narrows his eyes at me. "I know. I recall you telling *my* nanny that she could have a night off," he says as the doors open and we step in. "But Panda Express isn't even real food."

"Have you had their Beijing Beef?" I ask incredulously.

He gives me the *Oh Nova* look. "Trust me, I've taken care of dinner."

"So we're going to McDonalds then?"

"I'm starting to think you don't know me at all," Kessler says. "And that's fine. You can get to know me all over again." I'm still staring at him, so he says, "I'm taking care of dinner. I'm cooking. I went out and got groceries, that's where I was just now."

"I didn't know you could cook," I tell him. "I mean, you never cooked for me before."

"Palm Desert Kessler is not the same as Honolulu Kessler. Hope you'll start figuring that out soon."

I know what he means by that, for me to start forgetting all that shit between us, Stacy and otherwise, and start fresh. But damn if it isn't hard to let go.

By the time we get back to my house, the sun is just setting behind us, shooting rays of pink and gold over the jagged mountain range and I've tried to look at Kessler with new eyes.

It helps once we get inside and he immediately starts making himself at home in the kitchen. With my only apron tied around his white dress shirt, he tells us to relax with some drinks while he cooks up macadamia-nut crusted mahi mahi.

I sit in the living room with Hunter and Loan. Even though he's playing with some GI Joes and a pineapple pillow and Loan keeps getting up to spy on Kessler in the kitchen, telling him he's doing something wrong every now and then, it's nice to have some company over. I'm not anti-social. I've had Kate over a few times, sometimes Mahina or Teef come over if they're surfing on the North Shore, and once I had Desiree over for tea.

But it's nice to be with people who aren't my colleagues.

Except for Kessler of course. Though it's still so new working with him again, that it's not the same. It makes me realize that outside of work, I actually don't have a lot of friends. It's like I've made my job and my colleagues my substitute family. *Ohana.*

Which I don't think is a bad thing but it does make me wonder if I need some sort of separation between my work life and my personal life.

Who am I kidding...I don't have a personal life.

But tonight isn't the night to dwell on it. I'm tired, from the morning and from the glass of wine, and by the time Kessler is done cooking, I'm ready to eat and go to bed.

I have to admit, the food is amazing. Kessler really does know how to cook, which makes him even sexier than he was before. There's nothing I find hotter than a man who knows his way around the kitchen, knows exactly what food needs what spices, has the creativity and a delicate touch. Actually, all of those skills translate well to the bedroom too.

Which I know too well when it comes to him.

Seeing him sitting across from me, watching him laugh with his son next to him, I'm hit with a million competing feelings all at once. Everything maternal inside me is coming alive, like my frigging ovaries are in bloom for the first time.

It's not crazy to want this, I tell myself. To want a man and a child, to have a family in your home, a family of your own.

And yet I'm not sure if it's just the whole scenario that I want or if it's him. If it's Hunter. Loan even. The whole shebang.

It is crazy to want that, I go on. *And I think you've had too much wine.*

I haven't and to prove a point to myself, as soon as dinner is over I pour myself another glass and head out onto the lanai.

"Ahhhh," I say in a long, low exhale as I close the screen door behind me and welcome the cool ocean breeze. I light the array of citronella candles around me, sit back in my favorite teak chair, and take a good long sip of my wine.

It's not long before the screen door slides open and Kessler steps out. "I'm not interrupting quiet time, am I?"

I glance up at him, his face shadowy from the dim light of the porch overhang. "Not at all. Are you sure I can't help clean up?"

"Loan's already taken care of it. She's fast."

"Where's Hunter?"

"Down for the count. I read him his favorite bedtime story and he was asleep a few pages in. I think all the fresh air is doing something good to him."

"Sedating your child," I laugh.

"In a way," he says, sitting down on the chair next to me. He takes a long swig of the Kona beer in his hand. "I don't know. Back in San Francisco, I felt like we were under this perpetual cloud, aside from the actual fog. It made it hard to see my future. It made it hard to see Hunter. It's hard to explain. He was so unhappy, you have no idea." He exhales, and I can see all the worry and pain on his face. "I didn't know what to do until Mike called and that's when I knew I had to take it. I had to come here."

"Did you know you'd see me?"

His head lolls to the side and he gives me a small smile. "Of course. It was one of the first things Mike said. He said, you used to work with Nova Lane, you'll be working with her again. Honestly, it was a selling point."

"Right."

"I'm serious. I wanted to know what happened to you. You know, I never stopped thinking about you. I never stopped wondering what you were doing, how you were. When I moved onto Rockstar, I wasn't in touch with the people at Kahuna anymore, so I had no one to ask. Is it too much to ask you now...how have you been these last five years?"

I stare at him blankly. "Are you serious?"

"I am," he says, features grave. "What happened? What happened that made you like this?"

My hackles automatically raise at that. "Made me like what?"

"You know what," he says, refusing to be intimidated by my death glare. "You're like a tap that's been shut off."

"All dried up, is that it?"

"You used to have such a shine to you, Nova. Just like your name. You could obliterate every other star in the sky.

Now it's dimmed and I don't know why. Was it...was it me?"

If he had asked me that a few weeks ago, I probably would have said yes. I would have blamed him. I would have said that he's the one that dimmed the lights inside me. But now I know that's not true. He didn't help, but I can't blame him for everything. Not when I can blame myself.

I bite my lip and stare up at the stars, looking at their light, feeling their indifference, how the lives of us down here take nothing away from them. "My sister died."

Silence falls between us. In the distance, the shore breaks.

"I'm so sorry," he says softly. "What happened?"

I look at him, the honesty and concern on his face, and only then do I realize he has no idea. If he did, he wouldn't ask.

I swallow hard and run my fingers along the rim of the wine glass. "She had problems. A lot of problems. Mental health problems, then drugs. It was just such a constant in our lives, the worry, and then one day we didn't worry anymore. Police found her OD'd on the streets of down-town Seattle. Two years ago, around Christmas."

Kessler adjusts himself so he's facing me squarely, fingers clasped. "I had no idea. I know you mentioned you had a sister a few times but..."

"I never talked about her with you. Not the way she really was. It hurt to talk about it. It was...embarrassing to talk about it. We used to be so close growing up, she was my idol and I was her shadow, but she was always suffering. My parents saw it, I saw it, we did what we could to help but fuck if it wasn't impossible because her own demons had her and she couldn't rid herself of them. She fell into the darkness only because she couldn't help herself and our help wasn't enough." I take in a deep, shaking breath. "Her name was Rubina and she was so beautiful and so fucking tortured and I distanced myself because it was better for me. In the end, it wasn't better for her."

The tears want to fall but I don't let them. I keep them back, even though it's like keeping a herd of wild horses behind a fence, begging to be let free. To hold them in place is against their nature but I know if I let them go, they'll keep running and running.

"I'm so so sorry," he says, his voice rough. "I wish you had told me."

"To tell you would be to admit what a shitty sister I was, and I wasn't ready to face that yet. But believe me, I'm facing it now."

Kessler nods, slowly, his eyes searching my face, and I expect him to say something to try and make it better, but he doesn't. "I get it," he says. "I get it."

I don't know if he does get it. It's hard to imagine a guy like him having to go through such a thing. But we all have our devils inside us, some of us just know how to dress them up better.

"So what about you?" I ask him. "You have any regrets?"

He raises his brows. "Me? No."

"No? I thought we were about to have a little pity party here, man," I tell him. "I open up to you, you open up to me."

"I'll be as open as you want me to be," he says. "Believe me, just ask and I'll tell you. But I don't have any regrets."

"Not even the Russian con?"

He shakes his head adamantly. "Nope. Not her. If it wasn't for her, I wouldn't have Hunter. If I didn't have Hunter, I wouldn't be here right now, talking to you. Every single thing I've done, every single choice I've made, good or bad, has led me to right here and right now. Even if I was absolutely miserable at the moment, I couldn't regret a thing because we never know where tomorrow leads. We never know the choices we'll make and the path we'll go down."

"Whatever is meant to be is meant to be?"

"Shit yeah," he says, nodding enthusiastically. "Don't you feel that?"

I shake my head. "That would mean my sister is meant to be dead. And I would do anything to turn back time and change things."

"But what would you have done?"

I shrug, feeling defensive. "I don't know. Anything. Something. Got her into rehab."

"Surely you already tried that."

"Well my parents did. All the time. It's partly why my father sold the motel, so they could afford to put her in a treatment center. But it never worked out. She never stayed. She was so broken and in the end so were we." I close my eyes and lean back in the chair, listening to the chorus of crickets and cicadas. I really don't want to talk about this anymore.

We don't say anything for several minutes, both of us wrestling with what I said, or maybe Kessler is wrestling with something else. Finally, he says, "Oh great, Dwayne Johnson's here."

I open my eyes to see him staring up at a gecko by the porch ceiling light. "That's not Dwayne. That's Jeff GeckoBlum."

"Of course it is. Let me guess, you've named them all."

I nod, happy to be onto another subject. "If you've noticed a lack of mosquitos out here, it's because of them. There's Dwayne Johnson, Jeff Geckoblum, Bruce Lee, and

Sylvester Stallone. Sometimes I'll see some other ones but they're the regulars."

He stares up at the gecko with comedic disgust, much the same way I imagine the actual Jeff Goldblum would. "How are you sure they're all the same geckos?"

"How are you sure it's always the same chicken?"

"Hey," he says, pointing at me. "If you saw the chicken in the washroom, you would know the one we saw today was the same fucking one."

I laugh. "You're insane."

"You're the insane one, Gecko Lady."

"Whatever. I'm going to get more wine," I say, easing myself out of the chair. "Then I'm going to bed."

"Oh, by the way," he calls out after me as I'm about to open the screen door. "I talked to the exterminator guy today. They're going to need at least another day before we can return home."

I sigh. Of course they are.

I WAKE up to a pinch on my arm.

My eyes fly open and I don't have to hear the high-pitched whine in my ear to know what's happening.

There's a fucking mosquito in my room.

Okay, here's the thing about me.

I *hate* mosquitos.

I mean, I loathe them.

Public enemy number one.

I don't know when this vendetta against them started. I'm going to blame camping trips growing up in the Pacific Northwest, where my father would drive us out to the

Olympic National Park every spring and we would get eaten alive.

Since then, they're the bane of my existence and it's only gotten worse. The mosquitos in Hawaii are different, too. They're top-notch predators. They're smaller, quicker, relentless. They don't land on the wall and bumble around like they do on the mainland. No, here they go straight for you at the speed of light, darting at you, anticipating your every move. You don't even hear them half the time.

As it is, I can't fall asleep until the mosquito is dead, and that means I'll wake up in the dead of night and go absolutely ballistic, even if it takes several hours to hunt that one mosquito down.

Like I'm about to do.

I roll over and quickly flick on my nightstand light. My mouth is dry from the wine earlier but I ignore it. I only have one thing on my mind right now.

It won't be attracted to the light—it's too smart for that—so I have a little contraption.

I get up and reach into the side table drawer, pulling out my head lamp and place it on my head like a crown, switching the light on the end on. Then I grab my fly swatter and my insect repellant spray, climb on top of my bed, and wait.

There's a reason why I let Dwayne Johnson and the other geckos in the house—they're the number one mosquito killers. Unfortunately, Dwayne's probably too scared of Kessler to come back in the house.

I stand on top of the bed for a good five minutes before I'm dive-bombed.

I yelp, start swatting the air violently, then jump off the bed, following the blood-sucking bug as it zooms across the room. If it could just skirt along the wall for a minute, I could get a good shot. Once it's in my sights, I rarely miss.

Except this time, it refuses to do anything but come back right at me, straight into my headlamp.

I shriek again, thumping into my dresser before flailing around in a frantic circle, spraying the repellant like a fire-hose with one hand while I swat the air with the other.

"Jesus Christ!" Kessler calls out.

I stop spinning to see Kessler in my doorway, his eyes pinched shut, wiping them with the heel of his palm.

"Oh my god," I cry out, coming over to him. "Did I spray you?"

"Right in the fucking eyes," he cries, trying to look up at me, eyes red and wet. "Why are you trying to mace me!?"

"It's mosquito repellant!"

"Same difference," he says, eyes blinking rapidly. Then he frowns at me. "Why are you wearing a headlamp?" Then his eyes trail down my body and only then do I realize that I'm wearing a tiny cropped camisole and booty shorts. Now he's laughing, still rubbing his eyes. "What is going on?"

"There's a mosquito in my room," I tell him stiffly, looking around for it. I'm not going to let him distract me, even though he is standing there in just his grey boxer briefs and I can clearly see the outline of his half-hard dick. I swear the man always has a boner ready to go. It's my fucking kryptonite.

"So?" he says. "You're wearing a headlamp to fight a mosquito? You look like you're going to work at a fucking coal mine."

"I can't sleep until I kill it," I tell him. "So, if you're not going to help me hunt it down, I suggest you leave."

Then I see it zip over my bed, heading to the opposite wall.

I run over and jump on the bed, watching as it tries to land above the headboard. I take a leap, striking it like a praying mantis. "Got you, bitch!" I yell but when I remove the swatter, the mosquito flies away, unscathed. "Shit!"

Meanwhile Kessler is laughing his ass off behind me and I can't tell if those tears are from laughter or from DEET in his eye. I whip around to give him the stink eye, realizing he had a very good view of my butt as I did all that. "What?" I hiss.

"This has to be the most ridiculous, most adorable thing I have ever seen," he chuckles, gesturing to me. "Maybe even the sexiest."

I give him a withering stare. "Are you going to help me or no?"

"Well I'm up now," he says. "And I doubt I'll be able to go back to sleep with you yelling and thumping about in here. Show me where the sucker is."

"That's the thing. You don't know where he is. They're sneaky."

"It's just a mosquito."

I gesture to the wall behind his shoulder. "There's a gecko behind you."

He jumps, shrieking "Ahhhh!" like a little girl as he spins around.

There is no gecko behind him, I'm just trying to prove a point.

"You were saying?" I say.

"That's not funny."

"Neither is this."

"It's kind of funny," he muses and suddenly his attention is captured, his eyes darting to the side. "I've spotted it," he says.

"Where?" I jump off the bed, trying to point my head-lamp in the right direction.

He points to the wall. "There."

I see a dark smudge and slowly approach it, fly swatter raised in the air. I peer at it as I get closer and it's only when I'm up close that I realize it's actually a dead mosquito that I must have killed some other time and—

Suddenly a million creepy crawlies are running up and down my sides, tickling me and I'm yelping, spinning around, realizing it's actually Kessler who's doing it to me, his fingers making quick work of the bare skin of my waist.

"You dick!" I yell at him, punching him on the chest and shoulder but the tickling only intensifies and now I'm doubling over in the worst kind of laughter, trying to escape, my headlamp slipping off and crashing to the floor.

Kessler wraps his arms around me, picks me up and spins me around and the next thing I know, his hand is disappearing into my hair and he's leaning in and...

Dear lord.

He's kissing me.

I'm momentarily stunned as his lips press against mine, full and soft and sweet.

But just for a moment.

A moment before I realize how wonderfully familiar this kiss is, how well his lips meld to mine, how easy it is to fall into this rhythm of our mouths. Wet, warm, silk, his tongue slips against mine and I'm taken, I'm falling, I'm hungry. My hands go to his hair, so wonderfully thick and I wrap my fingers around the strands, tugging until it elicits a moan from him, the kind of moan that makes me wet between my thighs.

It's been so long since I felt like this over a kiss, over

anyone, that my body is practically weeping for more of him, for this to never end, for this—

"Daddy!"

Hunter's cry breaks us apart and Kess and I stare at each other wide-eyed and I can feel his heart pumping as fast as mine, our lungs heaving, almost breathless.

Then the biggest, most incredulous smile spreads across Kessler's face.

"*Daddy*," Kessler whispers to me in awe. "He's never called me Daddy before."

Suddenly the kiss is forgotten as Kessler basks in his fatherly milestone. He turns around to face Hunter who is standing in the doorway in just his pajama top, totally naked from the waist down. Such a mini-Kessler already.

"What is it Hunter?" Kessler asks him, pride choking his voice.

Hunter smiles. "Daddy. I pooped on the floor."

I snort.

Kessler's mouth drops, the wind taken out of his sails. He glances back at me with a sheepish shrug. "Okay. Well. That happened. I guess I'll go deal with that."

I bite my lip to keep from laughing and watch as Kessler walks over to Hunter, taking his hand. "Okay buddy, show me where you pooped."

"Good night Kessler, good night Hunter," I call out after them.

"Bye!" Hunter cries out as he disappears down the hall, Kessler giving me an apologetic look over his shoulder.

I go over and close the door, leaning back against it, trying to calm my racing heart. Even though I needed that kiss like nothing else, I'm grateful for Hunter's interruption, though I'm sure Kess doesn't quite feel the same way.

It's just that I was seconds away from giving in, giving

him everything, in a way I could never get back, in a way that would complicate our car wreck of a relationship even further.

I need to keep my head on straight.

I need to keep my heart in the clear.

I need to remember what happened the last time Kessler and I got together this way. No matter how good it feels, no matter how badly my body needs it, it's my heart that will pay the price.

Somehow I fall asleep without having killed the mosquito.

CHAPTER EIGHT

NOVA

"YOU PUT the lime in the coconut and you drank 'em bot' up," Bradah Ed sings, as the waitress passes us our drinks, that happen to be in coconuts.

"Oh yum," Kate exclaims, sipping from her straw. "Remind me why we don't do these touristy things more often? I mean, what is the point of living in fucking Hawaii if you can't sit on Waikiki Beach at sunset and drink out of fucking coconuts?"

"You swear a lot, Kate," Bradah Ed says, sipping on his drink while eying her with disapproval. "Show some respect."

"Respect to who? Her?" Kate gestures to me. "She's got an even worse potty mouth than I do."

"Please don't mention potty," I mumble under my breath, thinking about Hunter last night and his incredible timing.

"Why, do you have to go?" she asks, looking concerned as she puts her hand on my arm. "I can take you to the restroom if you don't think you can make it."

I swat her hand away. "I'm fine, I've just had two drinks."

"This is your third," Bradah Ed says.

"What are you, the drink police?" Kate asks.

"I am a security guard," he says, raising his chin. "It's my job to be concerned about the tenants of my building. That's why when I heard you were going out for drinks, I figured the right thing to do would be to escort you here and make sure you're safe."

I roll my eyes. Bradah Ed seems like the worst security guard on the surface. He's awkwardly tall and stick-thin and constantly smells like pot. But he's a pretty loyal guy, even though I think the reason he's having drinks with us—on our girl's night, mind you—is because he's trying to score with Kate.

Which I don't think would ever happen. Kate tends to go for white boys with man buns, at least that's her pick of the moment, and Bradah Ed is Hawaiian Filipino with a shiny shaved head. She does seem to enjoy rubbing it when she gets drunk though.

At the moment, she's behaving herself.

I sit back and stare at the people on the beach. We're outside of the bar at the Outrigger Hotel, the perfect place to watch the tourist world go by and do some research. Even though we have a large Kahuna Hotel on the beach down near the Honolulu Zoo, I try to spend most of my nights out in the arms of the competition. That's always been my strategy and it's paid off. In fact, it was my idea and plan to revamp our hotel's bars into something hipper and sleeker and more in tune to today's traveler that won me my last promotion.

Who the hell knows what it's going to take to win my next one.

I'll have to outdo Kessler, and even though I know I have the chops to do so, it's kind of hard when he's my boss. I wish I could call up Mike and yell at him. I don't care that he's fallen in love with a porn star, I really don't (though I do wish I knew her name so I could look her up), I just want to know why I wasn't chosen as his replacement. Didn't he like me? Or if he didn't like me, couldn't he at least see what I've done for the company?

But tomorrow Kessler and I have a meeting with George and Andy, the VP who spends half his time in the Arizona office. I don't even think Kessler has met him yet. We're both supposed to come up with new marketing ideas, probably for Valentines Day, and I've been trying to figure which one to swing past them. We've been taking Kahuna Hotels in a younger direction, hence why my revamp of the hotel bars has been so popular. But I know where Kessler used to work, our competitor, have really pushed that hip, sexy edge. I'm sure whatever Kessler pushes on them will speak to that, so I have to take a classier approach.

"Earth to Nova," Kate says, waving her hand in front of my face.

"What?" I tell her, fiddling with my cocktail umbrella and bringing my attention back to the present.

"I was talking about Kessler's Big Dick Energy."

I nearly spit out my drink. "What are you talking about?" I glance at Bradah Ed.

He shrugs. "Don't look at me. I didn't come here to talk about other guy's dicks."

She lets out a disgruntled moan. "Auuuurgh. Don't you guys know what's going on in the world at all? Don't you know memes?"

"All I know is there is a hottie over there giving me the eye," he says, leaning back to scope out a chick in a bikini sitting at the bar, glancing coquettishly over her shoulder at us.

"How do you know she's not checking out me?" Kate asks, insulted, apparently.

"You wish," Bradah Ed says, getting out of his chair while sipping on his coconut and smoothly moving over to the girl. "I'll see you guys later."

"Forget about him," Kate says with a dismissive wave.

"I already have," I tell her. "So, uh, why were you talking about Kessler's dick?"

She grins at me, wagging her brows. "Wouldn't you like to know? No wait. You do know. Let me guess, you've already seen it since he's been here."

She's not wrong but I'm not about to bring up the chicken incident or the amount of times he's had a boner around me.

And I'm definitely not going to bring up the fact that we kissed last night.

No, I'm taking that one to my grave.

I swear it.

"Kessler's my boss, need I remind you," I tell her.

"So? You think I haven't seen inter-office relationships? The hotel I worked at before I came here, Moonwater Inn, I was shacking up with one of the cooks at the restaurant, meanwhile my friend ended up sleeping with the boss. It was all sorts of complicated like *whoa* but they're married now with a kid, if that gives you hope. But believe me when I say I can see these things coming from a mile away."

"And so what do you see with me?" I ask her, point blank.

She gives me a small, knowing smile. "I see you falling for his Big Dick Energy."

"Okay, so run that Big Dick Energy past me again. What is that?"

"Well," she says, leaning forward so her hair falls in front of her face. "BDE doesn't just describe a man, nor does it describe sexuality or the size of your member. It's about the powerful aura you give off. Me, for example, I give off BDE."

I can't argue with her. I don't really know the definition of the term yet, but it already makes sense.

"Cate Blanchett also gives off Big Dick Energy, as does Sam Rockwell. You get my drift?"

"You're just listing off people you want to bone. Including yourself."

"Well it's impossible not to want to bone people with BDE. You have BDE and you know I think you're hot stuff, hot stuff."

"And I guess Kessler has it too?"

"Oh yeah," she says with a wide grin. "He's just brimming with BDE. It helps that I know he has a real big dick to begin with. He walks into a room and everyone turns around to stare. It's not just that he's a massive burly handsome fuck, but that he knows what he wants in life and is going for it and it's exuding from every pore in his body."

I'm not going to argue with her over that either. Kessler does have BDE, whether it comes from his sense of self or his actual big dick. But with that explanation, I'm starting to think I don't have it.

I thought I knew what I wanted in life.

I'm not sure what I want anymore.

You know, a voice whispers in my head. *You know what you want, what you need.*

"Shut up," I mutter.

"Are you talking to me or yourself?" Kate asks.

"Myself," I say, before busying myself with the drink. Damn these coconuts go down fast.

"Did something happen with you and Kessler?" she asks after a moment.

I should just ignore it and laugh and say "no way" but something inside me, probably the lime or the rum in the coconut, has the truth spilling from my lips.

"Not really," I tell her. "Okay, I have a bit of a problem."

"I knew it," she says with conviction, practically pounding her fist on the table. "Tell Kate everything."

I'm not going to tell her everything, but I do say, "There's something you didn't know about us. And by us, I mean back in the day. We, uh, well we slept together for a few months, like I'd said, and then he broke it off because he couldn't commit." I pause and she gestures for me to go on, looking bored because she already knows all of this. "And the truth was, I was in love with him."

She stares at me for a moment before slowly stirring her drink. "And?"

"And...he broke my heart. My boss is the man who broke my heart. He's my level-ten heartbreaker."

"So?"

"So?! You ever had your heart broken?"

"Yeah."

"On a level-ten scale?"

"Yeah and it sucked. But I mean this is pretty obvious, Nova. You moved all the way here after you guys broke up, and ever since I've known you, you've dated a lot of guys but never committed to one. I've been in your shoes, I know what it's like. You're trying to forget and he did a number on you and sometimes there are people in your life that affect you more than you think they should. They take up more space in your heart than you originally made room for them, like when a goldfish outgrows its tank."

I stab my pineapple with the straw. "You come up with surprising analogies sometimes."

"It's true," she says. "So you were in love with him and you had your heart broken. So what? We all get our hearts broken if we're lucky enough."

I shake my head vehemently. "I wouldn't wish it on my worst enemy."

"But what's the alternative?"

"The alternative is that you end up loving someone who loves you and you live happily ever after."

"That will happen, just chill about it. The alternative you should fear is the one where you never get your heart broken because you never fall in love. That's sad."

"That's smart."

"No, it's sad. How can you say you've had the human experience unless you've fallen in love? And part of falling in love means that you're likely to get hurt. To suffer over a broken heart is...well, that's what helps to build Big Dick Energy. You think Cate Blanchett hasn't cried over someone before? She has. She's taken that and let it fuel her."

I don't even know what this Kate is talking about now. "All I know is that I fell in love against my will."

"Right, and you fought against it and it still happened and you still got hurt. So fuck all that. It's not smart to avoid the inevitable. Just open your arms and let it in. Believe me, it's much better when you're not fighting it. It makes the highs that much sweeter."

"I'm not in love with Kessler," I tell her.

"I never said you are. But you were, and it's not a big deal and nothing to be ashamed about. Just accept it happened and move on."

"It's kind of hard to move on when I work with him."

"Right, but moving on doesn't mean you're closed off to him. Moving on just means you're both moving on from the people you were. It doesn't mean you're moving on from him."

She's making sense. I don't need to move on from Kessler necessarily, but I do need to move on from the people we once were and the relationship we once had with each other. That needs to be put to bed, or it's going to haunt me and mess up any good thing that might come from this.

But I'm getting ahead of myself. He kissed me and it's like the stitches unraveled and my heart cracked back open. Just an inch but an inch is enough. I'm vulnerable again in more ways than one. I need to move on from the people we were but that doesn't mean I need to move on with him in the picture.

Dear lord, how am I going to survive these three months?

Drinking. I'll do it by drinking.

"I need another coconut," I tell Kate.

She purses her lips together as she observes me. Then she nods in approval and orders us another round. "This means I'm not driving you home anymore."

"I'll get an Uber."

"Kessler could pick you up."

"I'll get an Uber," I repeat.

"Fine, but if you get an Uber driver named Harold with a 4.8 rating and a white Prius, you should totally unload on him. He gives great advice."

I'm momentarily offended that Kate unloads her problems on an Uber driver instead of me, but it only makes me realize that maybe Kessler isn't the only person I'm not open enough with.

Things need to change.

But as the evening goes on and the drinks keep coming and the sun goes down, Kate and I decide to bar hop. We walk down Waikiki, flirting with surfer boys and chugging back piña coladas and mai tais, but the only thing that changes is that I get increasingly drunker—to the point where my memories all start to blur even as I'm living them.

"Where are we now?" I ask Kate. It's dark. I'm sitting on the beach, sand up my ass, leaning back against a coconut palm.

"We're getting you a ride home," she says from above me.

I glance up but only see her silhouette beneath the palm tree, so I go back to closing my eyes. "Do you think it's dangerous to sit underneath a coconut tree? Do you think maybe our hotels should give guests helmets to wear?"

"What are you talking about?" she says. "Nova, these better be drunk ideas and not actual ideas."

"Coconut helmets," I go on. She doesn't get it. I am a genius ahead of my time. "Because it's dangerous. They could crack your head open. I could die, just sitting here." I mimic a coconut coming off the tree and hitting me on the head. "Just like that. *Splat*. We need to take care of our guests, Kate. We could make the helmet in the shape of a pineapple."

"Actually I think a coconut would be more appropriate."

"Oh my god, you're right," I slur.

"Okay," she says cheerfully, and I hear her clap her hands. "Your ride is here."

"My ride? We were talking about coconut helmets. Oh,

oh, how about coconut bike helmets so you can ride a bike and also protect your noggin from coconuts. They're not only a problem for pedestrians."

"Nova?"

I freeze. Kessler's familiar sexy voice has infiltrated my thoughts.

I open one eye to see him standing beside Kate and peering down at me. "How are ya?" he asks.

I frown. "Why are you here? You're going to steal my coconut idea like you did with the cucumber water!"

"You got her pretty drunk, Kate," Kessler says to her.

"I did no such thing," scoffs Kate.

"Where is my Uber?" I cry out. "Why did you call Kessler? He's a jerk. A Big Dick Energy jerk."

"What about my big dick?"

"She wants to take a ride, me thinks," Kate says.

"Kate you whore, you're a liar!" I yell up at her.

"Hey, I meant a ride in his car. By the way, I just saved your ass by getting your boss man here to pick you up. I wouldn't send you in any Uber in this state, other than Harold, whom I do think you need to talk to."

"Who is Harold?" Kessler asks, and is it my imagination or is there an edge to his voice?

Jealous?

"Harold is my favorite Uber driver," Kate explains. "I told Nova she could unload all her problems on him."

"What problems?" Kessler asks, and I can tell he's asking me.

I clamp my lips together. No problems. Not anymore, now that I have my brilliant coconut helmet idea.

"I think she's all torn up and twisted because of you," Kate says.

"Kate shut your face!" I yell, attempting to get to my

feet. The sand is a liar, it's not a stable surface at all and I start pitching to the left.

Kessler reaches out with his Big Dick Energy arms and catches me. "I have you all torn up and twisted, Supernova?" he asks, and I can tell from the tone of his voice that he is just loving this. God, his ego is insatiable.

"Let me go," I sneer at him.

"As much as I would love to see you faceplant in the sand, I'd hate to make your problems any worse than I already have."

"You can handle her?" Kate asks.

"Oh," he says, pulling me close to him and all I smell is his sweat and his pine-scented deodorant and my eyes are closing. The last thing I hear before I pass out is, "I can handle her."

KILL ME.

Kill me now.

There is sunlight streaming through my window, making my face hot. I'm dripping in a big bowl of sweat. I can hear roosters crowing incessantly in the distance. My stomach contents are fighting their way up my throat. My head is pulsing so fast and hard it's like road construction inside my skull.

I am hungover as fuck.

And right now, it's all that I am, all that matters, all that exists.

There is no escape, there is only pain, there is...

Wait a minute.

I am in my bed, right?

I slowly, painfully, pry open one eye and glance around.

It's my room all right, but something is different.

For one, the AC isn't running and I normally turn it on at night, but then again I can't remember much of last night other than Kessler picking me up from Waikiki Beach and then I was stumbling through the house, stepping on Hunter's toys, and then I was on my knees in the bathroom, hurling my guts out while Kessler held back my hair and Loan made some kind of ancient tea she said was good for detoxing.

Then that was it.

Now I'm here, in bed.

But Kessler never turned on the AC.

Which also explains why the window is open.

Which also explains why I can hear the neighborhood feral chickens.

Which...doesn't explain why the sun is on my face.

It's a Thursday.

I get up at seven a.m. to get ready for work.

The sun doesn't get over those mountains and into my window at that time.

Which means...

I quickly sit up, my head backhanded with a headache, and wince as I pick up my phone.

It's eleven a.m.!

Oh my god, I slept in.

I slept *way* in.

Why the fuck didn't Kessler wake me up?

"Aaaaaurgh," I cry out and then notice that there's a giant bottle of water on my bedside table, plus Advil, plus a note that says:

Didn't want to wake you. Take two of these and call me in the morning,

Your sweat monster, Kess.

For a second I'm touched by the gesture and butterflies start to fly in my stomach over the fact that he took care of me and called himself my sweat monster. But then those butterflies wither and die when I realize he's at work right now, at the meeting with George and Andy, and I'm not.

That asshole did this on purpose!

He wanted me to sleep in so I could miss work so he could go in and tell them that Nova was too hungover to make it but don't worry, he's the boss and he can handle it and gee she's not all that dependable anyway. This is sabotage! This isn't him pretending to be caring and kind, this is *personal*.

I immediately dial his number. I don't have time to angry text him, I'll probably fill it all up with dumb typos and I can't have him own me in grammar either.

But there's no answer. Of course there's no answer, he's probably in that meeting right now.

I get up. I am a ball of rage. I am a ball of rage who barely makes it across her room without doubling over because oh my god, I'm going to be sick. This is why I need to stay away from Waikiki Beach. I'm not twenty-one and on vacation. I'm thirty, and for every step forward I seem to take toward my career, it feels like I'm taking two steps back.

And all of those steps have me always crashing into Kessler.

I manage to make my way to the washroom without throwing up and, after I've washed my face a million times, my skin ashen, my dark circles looking like I've smeared coal under my eyes, I make my way downstairs. Thank god I'm in a baggy t-shirt and shorts. I have a feeling Kessler must have helped me undress last night and at least he didn't stick me in my tiny camisole and a thong.

"There you are," Loan says from the kitchen where she's slicing up a sandwich. She nods to a pot on the stove. "I was going to bring you soup."

I lean against the doorway and breathe in deep. It smells like ginger and chicken and lemongrass and it immediately calms me.

"You don't look so good," Loan says to me. "Here, sit down. Hunter!" she calls out. "Lunch is ready."

Hunter appears from the living room where I realize he's been watching Moana. It's pretty much been on repeat since he's got here.

"I want a Hei Hei," he says, gesturing to the chicken on the screen as Loan helps him up into his chair.

"I wouldn't ask your father for one," I say under my breath.

"You already have a Hei Hei," Loan says.

"I want that one," he says. "And I want to go see Maui at the beach. I want to put on baby soup."

I glance at Loan, brows raised. *Baby soup?*

"What are you talking about, Hunter?" Loan asks. "Do you want some soup?"

"Baby soup," he says. "I want to put it on and go swimming."

"You mean...bathing suit?" I guess and Hunter nods.

"Yeah I want to swim and you swim in a baby soup."

"Do you know how to swim?"

He shakes his head. "No. Will you teach me?"

"I could but I think that's your daddy's job."

"We could go to the beach though," Loan says, looking at me for approval, as if I'm Kessler's partner now.

I shrug. "Sure. I'm sure that would be great. I guess I'm stranded here today."

"You need to rest," Loan says. "You are very loud when you throw up."

I wince. "Sorry." I sigh. "Maybe I should call an Uber and go to work." Even though now the mention of Uber has my mind going back to Harold and oh god, what had I said in front of Kessler? I didn't say anything embarrassing last night, did I?

"You stay here," she says. "Mr. Rocha said for me to take care of you."

"Of course he did." So he could look like Mr. Big Shot at work.

I have half a mind to call him up again and yell at him, but then my head starts to pound, and the soup is wonderfully distracting and before I know it, Loan and I have packed up a beach bag and we've walked the four blocks to Kaiaka Bay Beach Park.

I have to say, even though I feel rotten and I'm still seething over Kessler and having to miss work like this, I've had worse days. It's nice to talk to Loan, and the longer I'm around her, the more she opens up, particularly about her life in Hanoi with her family.

"You don't have a man in your life?" she asks me, rather bluntly I might add, as she slathers more baby sunblock on Hunter's arm and ties his little straw hat on tighter.

"You know, I'm glad you're talking more but jeez..." I say with a chuckle, brushing stray sand off my towel.

"No man because of Mr. Rocha," she says, letting Hunter go so he can continue to make lumpy sandcastles beside us, the sand going everywhere, including back on my towel.

"Mr. Rocha has nothing to do with it," I tell her, giving her a steady look over my sunglasses.

"Mmmhmm," she says stone-faced. "I would say otherwise. There was something going on between you once."

"Why do you say that? Let me guess, he looks at me a certain way," I say wryly.

"No."

"Oh." I'm strangely deflated.

"You look at *him* a certain way."

I sit up straighter, propped on my elbows. "How so?"

"Like you hate him."

I shrug. "Well, you're not too far off with that one."

"Because you love him."

"Whoa, whoa, whoa." Now I'm fully sitting up, my bikini top nearly coming off and I have to quickly retie the string around my neck. "That's just not true."

She nods. "It is. I see things. I know things."

"You know nothing, Miss Loan."

There's a small quirk to her lips. "I know things," she says again, "because that's my job. I've worked for many families and I know the signs when one of them is cheating on the other and I know the signs when someone is falling out of love and I also know the signs when someone is still in love, and you are still in love. It's the truth, Miss Nova."

I shake my head, glad that Hunter has taken no interest in what we're talking about. I can't imagine how confusing it must be so far for him, having his mother for the first three years of his life, then having her go away, replaced with a father he never knew, then moving over here to Hawaii where he's now with us. Kessler was right when he said he was adaptable.

"Okay," I admit. "So maybe I was in love with Kessler once. But that went away when we broke up."

"What ends can start again."

"He annoys the," I glance at Hunter, "*heck* out of me."

"As I said, you only hate him because you still love him."

"I don't want to talk about this anymore," I say quickly, my headache coming back. "I'm going for a dip."

"Suit yourself," Loan says, as I get up and walk toward the surf, hoping a quick swim in the ocean will set me right.

"Baby soup!" Hunter cries out.

CHAPTER NINE

KESSLER

I KNOW Nova is mad at me even before I set foot in her house.

I know because I saw a bunch of missed calls from her all day but no messages.

No texts either.

I know when she gets really mad, she saves herself for a big argument, like she's conserving her anger in a giant reservoir, waiting for the right time to open the dam. Errant messages and texts don't cut it with her, they merely take away from the big explosion

I have a feeling I'm going to be a victim of that big explosion the moment I go inside.

Which is why I'm sitting in my car in her driveway and staring at the house.

Even though she was right in that arguing with her does turn me on, sometimes she can be downright frightening. She used to love my dick but you often hurt the things you love and I have no doubt she thinks a lot of problems can be solved with a kick to the groin.

Eventually Hunter spots me as he appears at the screen door and yells, "Daddy!"

I have to say, it gives me strength.

The other night when he first called me Daddy, I felt like a motherfucking king on top of the world, higher than cloud nine. That was hot on the heels of the fact that I just kissed Nova and her lips felt even more amazing than I had remembered. I didn't even care that I had to clean up Hunter's shit on the floor because two of the most important things in my life were both happening at once.

"Hey, Hunter," I call out to him as I get out of the car, remembering to grab the stuffed sea turtle I picked up for him at the gas station along the way.

I go up the steps, slowly, smiling for Hunter but I feel like my back is being used for target practice, like Nova might appear at any moment.

I open the door and step inside, scooping my son up into my arms and giving him a squeeze. "How was your day, buddy? I brought you a friend." I show him the turtle which he eagerly grabs.

"Crush," he says. "He was in Finding Nemo."

"That's right, it's totally Crush," I tell him, even though it's a rather cheap knockoff, but that's what you get when you go shopping for gifts at Exxon.

I walk down the hall and look in the kitchen where Loan is at the stove cooking something in a giant pot, gently placing Hunter back on his feet.

"Hi, Mr. Rocha," she says without glancing at me. "You're home early. Dinner won't be ready for another hour."

"That's fine with me," I tell her, as Hunter runs off with Crush. "Where's, uh, Nova?" I ask, warily looking around, as if I'm about to ambushed.

"She went for a walk."

"Did she look mad?"

"She always looks mad."

"Yeah, I suppose you're right."

"Moving day tomorrow, right?" Loan asks.

"Unless the exterminator calls before then, yes."

"I like this house. Maybe we can stay here with Miss Nova. Tell that Mr. Mike we don't want to stay in his house. Cockroaches can live a month without their head."

I both sigh and shudder at once. I've been thinking about it because, even though I'm sure the cockroaches will be gone, I've gotten used to this blue house on the North Shore, with the town of colorful houses around the corner. But I would never impose on Nova that way. She has her life here and after her drunken confessions the other night, it's apparent that she really doesn't want me messing it up.

"I don't think Miss Nova would approve," I tell her.

"Hmmm maybe," she says. "I'll miss her though. You should bring her around to the house then."

"We'll see," I tell her even though I highly doubt Nova will ever come over.

"You'll miss her too," she says.

"I'll still see her at work every weekday," I remind her, even though, yes, I actually will miss her in this context, away from the office walls. Surrounded by geckos.

And even though I know she's mad at me because I let her sleep in and she missed work, I decide that it's my last night here and perhaps I should welcome the fight.

"I'm going to go for a walk, see if I bump into her," I tell Loan.

"I thought you would," Loan says under her breath.

"What was that?"

"Be back in one hour," she commands.

I have no idea where Nova might go but even so I walk around the block, taking in the evening. The sun is starting to set and a lot of people are either just getting home from work or hanging out in their yard, drinking beer and BBQing. Nearly every person I see raises their hand in greeting and says "Good evening" or "Hey" or "Aloha." They're all in good spirits, happy to be outside in the fresh warm air, enjoying life.

I'm starting to get it now, this Aloha spirit. It's still far too hot and humid for me and I flinch at every chicken I see thinking it's *that* motherfucking chicken. I only recently discovered there's a place called Ice Palace Hawaii with an adult hockey league starting up in January, but I'm not sure if that will be enough for me. My idea killed it at today's meeting with the big bosses but I can't guarantee this job will turn out to be more than temporary.

Yet Hunter seems to be thriving here and it's already brought us closer together, plus Loan seems like a great fit for our mini family. And even with the heat and humidity, there's something both primal and purifying about the sweat, about living in a land this lush and wild that makes you want to strip all your inhibitions away and run around naked in the jungle.

Of course there's only one person I want to do that with.

And there she is, wading into the surf, the faded remains of a golden-red sunset coloring the water.

Right now, she's a Supernova.

"Hey," I call out to her.

I'm at the beach closest to the house. I should have figured to check here first.

She's in the water up to her waist, her back to me, her shapely curves setting fire to the waves around her.

She glances at me over her shoulder but her face is in shadows. I'm going to assume she's not happy to see me.

"How are you feeling?" I ask, kicking off my shoes and socks on the grass before stepping into the soft sand.

"Seems the salt water is the only thing healing me today," she says in a low voice, the sound nearly swallowed by the lapping waves. I can tell she doesn't want to talk and I should probably turn around and go back to the house, spend time with Hunter, help Loan with dinner, do something.

But like a Supernova, she's caught me in her pull and I'm too stupid to leave.

"The last time I saw you that drunk I think it was New Year's Eve, back in the day."

I can tell she's glaring at me. "Why are you here, to tell me what an idiot I was last night, or to tell me everything I missed at work?"

"I just wanted to see you," I admit, stepping back as the waves chase my toes.

"And why the hell do you think I want to see you?"

Feisty, feisty. Just a few more pokes and she'll unleash that reservoir.

"Maybe you needed some eye candy."

"Oh, fuck you."

"Wow, I thought the water would be cooling you off."

"I was fine until *you* got here."

"Do you always go swimming at night? Don't you worry about sharks?"

"The only shark I see is standing on the shore."

"*Zing.* You know, I thought maybe you'd be, I don't know, grateful."

I can see her eyes flash in the shadows. "Grateful?"

I shove my hands into my pockets. "Not many people

would let their employee have the day off because they have a hangover."

"That wasn't your choice to make!" she hisses at me, coming forward a few steps until her body is positively glistening in the last light. She looks amazing in her tiny bikini, the strings look so fragile I imagine it wouldn't take much to undo them.

And there I go, getting hard again.

I clear my throat. "I'm an executive and I made an executive decision to let you sleep it off. I pride myself on being a kind and just boss."

"You're a conniving asshole, that's what you are. You didn't do that because you felt sorry for me, you did that so you could sabotage me!"

"Sabotage you?" I frown. "What the hell are you talking about?"

"You knew I had an important meeting today," she says. "It was a meeting we both should have been there for, not just you."

"How is that sabotage?"

"Because you know that your job is temporary and that if anyone is going to take it from you, it's me. So why not make me look bad?"

"Why would I make you look bad?" She's really lost it now.

She grumbles something and starts heading deeper into the water, trying to escape me.

Without thinking, I quickly take off my shirt and undo my pants until I'm in my boxer briefs. It's dark enough now that it looks like I could be in swim trunks, and there's only a few people on the beach anyway, hanging out at the other end and drinking.

I hate being in water for many reasons, so I'm not taking

this lightly that I'm going in after her, in the motherfucking ocean of all places. But by the time I'm splashing in up to my chest and my feet are still firmly on the bottom, I've grabbed her arm and I'm pulling her back to shore with me.

"What the hell are you doing?" she says, and tries to swim away but even in water, I'm stronger and my legs are firmly rooted.

"I need to get one thing straight with you," I tell her, pulling her toward me, her breasts pressed up against my chest, her lips mesmerizingly close to mine. "I am not your enemy. Okay? You can go on thinking that all you want but it's not true. I am not your enemy. I'm barely even your boss. I am your equal and you are mine."

"I am not yours," she says but her words falter.

"You very much are," I murmur, my voice growing rough as the rest of me burns with impatience.

The other night was only a taste.

I'm starving for the rest of her.

Before she can protest, before she can duck out of the way and swim from me, I grab her face in my hands and kiss her, hard. There is no softness here, the only silk comes from the bracing ocean waves as they roll through us. This kiss is fast and powerful and bruising, my mouth pressed against hers until she's kissing me back, our lips, teeth, tongue tangling.

If this is the explosion I was looking for, I've got it.

She's moaning into my mouth, her hands around my neck, legs wrapping around my waist as her tongue continues to dance with mine. She's gone wild and I'm fueling her flames, one hand pushing her bikini top aside until her gorgeously perky breasts are free. My mouth dips into the water, tasting the salt, sucking her nipple into my mouth until she lets out a sharp cry, her head going back into the waves, her neck exposed as the water runs down it.

Nova has never looked sexier. No woman ever has. I have a combustible star in my grasp and I know I'm playing with fire and I don't care if she takes both of us out. I want her, I need her, just like this, unleashed like the waves.

"Kessler," she whispers, and her hand is sliding down the lines of my abs all the way to my dick. She pulls it out of the band of the boxer briefs, gives me a hard stroke from root to tip and now I'm groaning with a mad sort of lust, like if I don't come inside her right now I'm going to die.

"Fuck me," she whispers, her mouth at my neck, tasting and sucking and biting as she strokes me harder and tighter with her fist, the water all friction.

I manage to pull myself together and not blow my load right there. It would be so easy, everything about this is so perfect, especially as the moon is rising and the twilight is fading to a narrow, electric blue strip at the horizon. I'm not even thinking about the fact that I'm in the ocean at night, all I'm thinking about is getting her off.

"I'd fuck you all night long," I tell her, sucking her lower lip into my mouth with a grunt. "But I don't have a condom here and it's not up on the shore either. That won't stop you from coming though."

I shove my hand down the front of her bikini bottoms and her legs spread wider around me, hanging on for balance and to give me easier access. We're still about chest high in the water and if the people at the end of the beach looked over here, there's no question it looks like we're getting it on.

I don't care. Nova doesn't care either. In fact, whenever she looks over my shoulder at them, she gets this wicked, almost decadent look in her eyes, like it would bring this to another level if they were watching us.

Yes. This is the Nova I remember.

And yet this Nova now is so much more, on so many levels.

She's my equal and she's mine, that's all there is to it.

With a heated grin I slip my finger along the lushness of her clit and then thrust it inside her.

She gasps, her nostrils flaring as her grip at the back of my neck stiffens. She's tight, so fucking tight and the lack of lube from the water doesn't help. Luckily I know how to get her wet in a second.

I take her earlobe between my teeth and tug at it, sucking hot and wet in my mouth, while stroking my thumb around her clit in a quick circle. The combination has her moaning my name, her legs falling even more open to let me in.

Yes, let me in.

Let me in deeper.

Let me see all of you.

My gorgeous fucking universe.

I slide my finger out, slowly, teasingly, then plunge two back inside her. Then three.

"Kess," she murmurs, eyes pinched shut as she tightens around me. "Don't stop, don't stop."

"I wouldn't fucking dream of it," I tell her. I grunt as I start working her harder, tapping her swollen G-spot, knowing if I keep at it she'll be coming on my hand in no time.

"God I want you inside me," she manages to say before she kisses me with everything she's got. "I need you."

Fuck, I've been dreaming about hearing those words.

Those words have been fueling so many fucking fantasies.

Not just in the last week or so.

But the last years.

"I am inside you," I murmur into her mouth. "And I'm about to make you come so fucking hard, you'll think you're drowning."

I kiss her, violent and rough.

My fingers work her into a frenzy.

Before long she's opening wider around me, her head going back until her hair dips in the water and her bare breasts and arched neck sparkle in the moonshine.

"Don't stop, don't stop," she cries out, breathless, and I'm sure her voice is carrying over the water, or maybe it's swallowed by the waves.

She comes hard, pulsing around my fingers, milking them like a vice and even though I wish it was my dick inside her, my dick that's so fucking hard it might shatter if provoked, I'm glad I had her come this way. To see her in the wild like this, free and bare and open. See her vulnerable and real and raw, just for me.

No matter what happens between us after this, I know this is a memory that will sustain me for a lifetime.

But even as Nova comes and starts to right herself, shaking off the satiation and stupor of the post-orgasm bliss, she's already slipping through my fingers.

It was the one thing that used to bother me after I slept with her. How much of a man she acted, for lack of a better word. How after she'd come, she'd wipe away all sense of vulnerability and go back to business like nothing happened.

It's happening now, right before my eyes.

"We better go back," she says, pulling away from me

and haphazardly tying her bikini behind her neck. She gives me a small smile. "Loan will kill us if we're late for dinner."

I smile right back, grateful that at least I'm not getting the deep freeze. "You got that right."

And so we don't talk about it while we step out of the surf and onto the shore. My legs are almost shaking for some reason, like it took more out of me to keep from drowning out there.

And we don't talk about it while we walk down the street back to her house, either.

And we don't talk about it when we go our separate ways to get ready for dinner.

And we don't talk about it during dinner.

Or after.

The only thing I say is, "Are you okay?" while she's heading to her bedroom to sleep.

For a moment there's a look in her eyes that says she's not okay.

It's not in a bad way.

It's not that I've ruined her.

Or that she feels ashamed.

It's that she needs me.

Wants me.

In her bed tonight.

She doesn't have to say it but I can read it off her, just like I saw a raw glimpse of her in that water, when I was thinking about how I dreamt about this, how she was thinking the same thing.

But it wouldn't be Nova if she didn't nip that in the bud.

"I'm fine," she says, giving me a quick smile that signi-fies whatever happened out there in the waves was meant to stay there. "I'll see you in the morning. Don't forget me this time."

I nod and hope my smile looks more carefree than it feels. "I won't. Good night Nova."

"Good night Kess."

And to think I could ever forget about her.

Not when she's across the hall.

Not when she's across the office.

Not even if she's across an ocean.

CHAPTER TEN

"KESSLER SAID you were upset about missing yester-day's meeting, so we figured we could hold another one."

I blink up at George who is standing in my office doorway alongside Andy Walters, the VP. Both of them are staring at me expectantly and I'm not sure if it's planned or not but they're both wearing the exact same Hawaiian shirt. "I'm sorry, Kessler said what?"

"Yesterday, he said you were upset you weren't here," George said with a knowing smile. "I told you to stay away from those drinks in the City of Sin, they aren't much better here on Waikiki." I stare at him. "Anyway, meeting in the office in five minutes."

And then they're gone.

What the actual fuck?

Kessler said I was upset?

I pick up my phone and dial Kessler's extension, but of course he's not picking up. He never seems to pick up when I'm calling.

How convenient.

So I sit back in my chair and stew for a moment.

Everything is *way* out of control right now.

It was bad enough when Kessler kissed me the other day in my bedroom, bad enough when I got drunk and he had to drive me home.

Bad enough when he finger-banged me in the ocean last night.

Now he's told the upper-ups I was *upset* that I missed the meeting?

Calm down, I tell myself. *Kessler might have been trying to do good. He was probably trying to make you look proactive, that you care. He was probably trying to help.*

Yeah, but by telling them I was *upset* that I missed it? That makes me sound like some crazy emotional female!

You are a fucking crazy emotional female.

Oh god, now my thoughts are turning against me. I don't need this right now.

There's a rap at my door and I look up to see it open with Kessler grinning at me. "Are you ready?"

My eyes blaze at him. "Did you tell George that was upset that I missed the meeting?"

"Uh yeah. You're welcome."

My lower jaw wiggles as I try vainly to dissipate the anger. "Do you know you made me sound like some crazy woman?"

"Isn't it good to be upset about that kind of thing?"

"Okay, how would you like it if I said the same about you? That you, Kessler Rocha, were upset because you missed a meeting because you were hungover."

He thinks about it for a moment, then says, "Doesn't matter. Come on."

He walks off down the hall to the boardroom.

Fuckity fuck it doesn't matter.

I grumble to myself and follow him.

My main problem is I was totally ready for this meeting the other day. But now, my brain has been so obliterated by Kessler and his magic fingers, that I don't even remember what my game plan was.

It doesn't help that when I enter the boardroom, Kessler is already sitting down with George and Andy and they're all laughing, obviously some joke that I'll never know.

"Hi," I say to them, pausing by the door before I close it, making sure they know I'm here. "Hope I'm not interrupting anything."

"Not at all," George says, as the three of them exchange a knowing look and it's then that I realize it's me versus three rich white men, and there's no way I'm going to come out on top.

But I still flash them that genial smile and take a seat beside Andy, across from Kessler and George. Jesus, it's like Kessler's already become his right-hand man.

"Nova, we were just discussing Kessler's winning idea from yesterday. Kessler, did you get a chance to run it by her yet?"

Kessler shakes his head but when he makes eye contact with me, I swear I see a triumphant smirk.

Please let me be looking too hard into things. That smirk doesn't belong in this meeting.

"No, I don't think he did."

The only thing Kessler has run past me in the last twenty-four hours were his fingers.

But god, even though I regret it this morning, at the time it was worth it.

That fucking man is way too talented for his own good.

Something glimmers in his eyes and his smirk widens and I realize I might be an open book right now.

Before I can look away, George says, "Well, Kessler, do you want to fill her in? Heck, let me do it. As you know Nova, the meeting yesterday, and by default today, was to try and come up with some new ideas for the new year, once this holiday Christmas crap blows over. Originally we wanted to focus on Valentine's Day, but Kessler had the brilliant idea of making every day Valentine's Day when it comes to the Kahuna Hotel. Inject a little sex appeal, if you will."

Oh god no. *We don't need Kessler's kind of sex appeal. He hits you over the head with it. Kahuna Hotels is all about subtle sensuality. If that!*

These are all the things on the tip of my tongue along with my ever familiar warning, courtesy of the singer Banks: *Try to look smart but not too smart to threaten everything they say.*

"Sex appeal?" I manage to repeat.

"Condoms," Andy says, slapping his palm on the table. "Pineapple-flavored condoms on a stick."

"Like a lollipop," George offers with a grin.

My jaw had become unhinged and I'm having a hard time closing it. "Condoms?" I eventually say, looking at Kessler.

He grins at me. No, it's that *smirk* again.

"I thought it would be a good idea," he says. "You never know when you might need one."

He holds my gaze even though I know what he's referencing.

Last night.

As if that's not completely inappropriate right now.

George goes on, "We figured putting the pineapple-flavored condom-pops in every hotel room would be an easy way to say, hey, come spend your sexy times with us."

"But at the same time," Andy continues, "protect your-self from STDs."

"Safe sex is cool now," George adds.

Oh my god. Get me out of this fucking room.

I look at Kessler and he's grinning at them and I am watching carefully to see if I see a hint of embarrassment, like he gave this idea as a joke and now they're running with it and he's Canadian so he's too polite to tell them otherwise.

But no. He's just grinning.

Like a rat bastard.

"So what do you think, Nova?" George asks, and it's then that I notice how pink his cheeks are and oh god, this is hell because he's actually embarrassed to be talking about condoms with me.

I swallow all the bile and resentment and try to put my most fake smile on.

"I'm not so sure that's the right approach," I say.

Immediately George and Andy glance at each other and then look at Kessler and it's never been so apparent that this is one big boys' club. I mean it was always a given, but this is the first time I feel like they're not bothering to hide it.

This is the first time I feel like I can't compete.

It's these men against me.

"So, Nova has had some excellent ideas too," Kessler offers as he clears his throat. "That's why she couldn't wait to hold this meeting again."

Now, I'm not sure if Kessler is honestly trying to help or trying to throw me under the bus. As much as I hate our relationship at the moment, I have been trying to give him the benefit of the doubt. I don't want to think the worst of him, it just naturally happens. And so when last night he said we were equals, I felt his sincerity.

I just don't know if he knows what being equals means.

I mean, he's a man. How can he? The idea he throws out there gets all lapped up, but could you imagine me doing the same? Coming into a meeting with the CEOs and pitching fucking pineapple-flavored condoms on a stick? They'd all think I'm a whore and then they'd laugh me out of the room. To get the respect that he gets, I have to work three times as hard.

Thank fuck I'm a hard worker.

I sit up straighter and give Kessler my most pleasant smile, which he immediately balks from because that motherfucker knows what it means.

"Coconuts," I say and when everyone stares at me with blank expressions, I go on. "Coconut helmets."

"Coconut helmets?" George repeats.

"Coconut bike helmets," I elaborate. "Because I think that Kahuna Hotels should start implementing a bike program. We've all seen it take off in major cities, including Honolulu. People want to be responsible citizens. They don't want to call a cab or an Uber and use harmful emissions if they don't have to. In cities around the world, bikes and scooters are taking over, providing a cheap, fun and environmentally-friendly way to travel. I think if Kahuna Hotels started providing free cruiser bikes to their guests—with coconut bike helmets with our logo—we'll appeal to the hip and environmentally friendly traveler. It's sexy these days to do what you can to stop climate change."

I sit back in my chair, trying not to feel proud of myself for completely pulling that out of my ass.

I glance briefly at Kessler and see that even he looks impressed.

"Hmmm," George says. "That's not a bad idea. Hey, it might work well with the free condoms, Kessler. Think about it. During the day you go for a ride and at night you go for another ride."

Oh. God.

Stop.

"Makes perfect sense to me," Kessler says with one of those jovial *I'm one of the boys* laughs and I don't think I've ever hated him more.

Kessler goes on, that smirk returning. "It works perfectly, Nova. Travelers these days want their finger to be on the pulse of everything new. They want to feel things from the inside out. They want to be knuckle-deep in tomorrow's promises."

This motherfucker is feeding me straight-up innuendo during a meeting.

That's no accident.

I lash out and kick him under the table.

George leaps up in pained surprise.

"Ow!" he cries loudly. "What the—?"

Oh *shit*.

Wrong shin.

"I am so sorry," I exclaim, "I was just crossing my legs."

"Holy moly, Nova," George says, practically weeping at this point. "Do you wear the pointiest shoes in the world?"

"I am so sorry," I say again, getting to my feet, because if I stay in this god damn meeting one minute longer, I'm going to burn the whole room down with me in it. "I think I need more potassium or something. Leg spasms. I'm going to go talk to Teef about it, he always seems to be eating bananas."

"Nova," Kessler says but I don't even look at him. I'm out.

I walk out of the boardroom and down the hall, right to my office.

I probably should have gone to the elevator and headed out for lunch, or gone to the washroom where I could dab myself with a cold towel and calm down these rage flashes, but instead I go in my office and slam the door.

I'm pretty sure the whole office shook.

I'm about to go Supernova.

My door flies open and Kessler barges in, doesn't even knock.

"What is going on with you?" he asks. "Are you okay?"

I'm speechless for a moment and can only gesture wildly with my hands. "Am I okay? No!"

"What happened? Why did you kick George?"

The idiot actually looks confused.

"You happened. Finger on the pulse? Knuckle-deep?"

"I thought it was funny."

"It wasn't funny!" I yell. "Those are my bosses."

"They didn't know what I was talking about."

"It doesn't matter. You're my boss too."

"So I'm being inappropriate?"

"Hell yes you are. This is exactly why yesterday was a mistake."

He flinches like I've backhanded him. "Look, I know you're mad and I'm sorry I made a joke. We always joke about sex."

"Not this time! This time it's personal!"

"Why?"

"Because of what you just said. You're my boss now. Letting that happen yesterday was…"

"A mistake. I know. But we can act like adults here."

"Okay let me know when you plan on starting."

He raises his palms in surrender and I notice the sweat

starting to bead on his forehead. "I'm sorry, okay? I was inappropriate and I especially shouldn't have hinted at anything between us or said any innuendo because I'm your boss. But just so we're clear here, you're not innocent in this at all, Demi Moore."

"Demi Moore?" I say incredulously.

"Yeah. Disclosure. I know you've seen that movie."

"Oh my god," I say, stomping over to him, waving my arms. "Just get out. Go."

"Fine, fine," he says and I'm pretty much shutting the door in his face.

I lean back against the shut door, running my hands through my hair, trying to regain my temper. He's not being professional at all but maybe he's right with his Demi Moore comment. I'm not exactly professional either, trying to kick him under the table and all that.

He at least deserved it for the condom idea, the voice in my head says.

God, that's right!

I whip open the door and storm down the hall to his office and I can feel heads poking up over the cubicles watching me as I go but I don't care.

I barge right into his office, slamming the door behind me. "I'm not done with you yet!"

He's sitting down at his chair, aiming the AC remote at the unit and stares at me in a mix of surprise and fear as I storm over to his desk.

"Condoms!" I yell at him. "Your idea was condoms?"

He blinks at me. "Uh, yeah."

"What is wrong with you!?"

"What? Don't pretend that you're some prude suddenly. Believe me, I know you're not a prude."

"I'm not being a prude, you're just turning this company into a joke. We can't give condoms to our guests!"

"Why not, at Rockstar we had condoms available, along with a little sex kit they could buy from the mini bar."

"This isn't Rockstar. We don't stoop to that level."

"Hey I'll have you know the sex kits were my idea."

"Of course they were *your* idea," I tell him. "Who else would think of such a thing?"

He gets out of his chair and takes off his blazer, hanging it on the back of his chair. "You're just upset that the bosses liked my idea best."

"Best?"

"Better than yours. Coconut bike helmets? Like that's sexy?"

"It's a good idea and you know it!"

"No, a good idea is keeping with the times. You yourself said you wanted to turn Kahuna Hotels into something that's tailored to young couples and professionals. None of this family shit, just young, sexy and hip, a place where you'd even Instagram the toilet. That was your objective and you did it with the revamp of the hotel bars. You made a place where people could go to work and not be disturbed as well as try and pick up the hottie next to them. Why are condoms any further off? I mean, those bar hookups are going to go back to the hotel rooms and guess what, they'll need condoms."

"Pineapple ones? On a stick? Kessler, it's going to look like a lollipop. What if someone does bring their kids here? Next thing we know children are going to start eating condoms by accident."

"You're the one who said to stop catering to families. Besides, parents have to get laid and have fun too."

"I know you fucking do," I say under my breath.

"Excuse me?" Kessler says, coming around the desk to me. "I need to get laid? You're the one who came all over my fingers last night."

"You're the one who keeps bringing that up. I'd like to pretend it never happened."

"Yeah fucking right," he says, getting right in my face. His nostrils are flaring, his eyes burning into mine. "You go on pretending, but I know that last night you closed that door to your room and you got off thinking about me, thinking about my big fat cock squeezing inside your tight little cunt. Those fingers weren't enough for you, nothing is enough for you when I'm in the picture."

"You're so full of it," I sneer at him, staring at his lips, hating the words that are coming out of his mouth, hating how much they're turning me on, hating how that mouth makes me feel when it's flush against mine.

"You wish you were full of my cock," he says, grabbing my hand and placing it right on the stiff length of him straining against his fly.

I want to laugh but it dissolves in my throat as my fingers curl around his dick, feeling the heat pulse through the fabric into my palm.

I'm fucking *aching* for him. I hate what he does to me, I hate that I should push him away and call him out for being inappropriate when all I want to do is sink to my knees and do inappropriate things to him.

"I hate you," I hiss at him.

He smirks. "You only hate that you want me."

"Same difference."

"I don't think so," he says, his hand going to my hair and making a fist in my strands. I grip his dick harder in response. "I can practically smell how wet you are. You want me to shove up that little skirt and make your eyes cross when I slam inside you. You want me to fuck the hate out of you."

"I'd like to see you try," I say.

Then before I can stop myself, I'm kissing him.

It's angry.

There's power behind it, all mashed lips and teeth and tongue, a fight for dominance, a lust fueled by raw frustration and need and everything else that's been swimming inside me for days, weeks, years, ever since we broke up.

I'm undoing his pants, taking his cock out, feeling his heat in my hand, the veins and the blood pulsing and the familiarity of it all. Big Dick Energy, indeed. I'm aching to be a part of it.

"Fuck yes," he whispers into my mouth, yanking back on my hair until my throat is exposed. "Go wild with me."

"I'm not doing anything with you except getting off," I snap at him, as he licks along my neck. "So hurry up and fuck me."

"You know I love it when you talk like that," he says, grabbing me by the waist and spinning me around so my stomach and breasts are pressed down on his desk, my back to him. "You know what it does to me."

He shoves up my skirt and moans at the sight. "White lace," he says thickly. "Pretty flimsy looking. Did you wear these on purpose so I could tear them off of you?"

"Shut up," I tell him, because the thought did go through my head when I was getting dressed this morning and I don't want him to know how much I think about him.

But who am I kidding? He knows.

Why else am I bent over his desk right now, my ass wriggling in his hands, begging for him?

He runs his thumbs underneath the bands of my thong

and with one quick snapping motion, rips the underwear in half. "Oh, you definitely wore these on purpose."

Then he's running his hands down my inner thighs, spreading me wider, and he's dropping to his knees behind me. I instinctively grip the edge of his desk, my breasts pushed up against a stack of books on Hawaii, and I brace as I wait for his tongue.

It starts off slow, licking me right behind the knee, causing shivers to cascade down my spine in electrifying rivers.

Fucking hell.

He's barely done anything to me and I'm already losing all sense of self control.

With his hands gripping my thighs, fingers pressing in so hard they're almost bruising, he works his way up, his beard scratching my sensitive flesh as he continues to lick and nibble.

I can't control the moans slipping out of my mouth, even when I feel him smiling against my skin, loving every second of the pleasure he's bringing me.

I decide to let it go. If this means he thinks he wins, if this feeds his ego even more, fine.

"Just fuck me," I blurt out.

He chuckles, the vibrations running over my thighs and up inside me where I'm so damn desperate for him, it's pathetic.

"Someone's impatient," he murmurs, his thumbs now in the crease between my pussy and my inner thighs. He gives me a squeeze, pressing his thumbs in and then he's licking me out from behind. His flat, strong tongue dips inside me, tasting me, and he's moaning loudly now, enough that my eyes roll back in my head.

I whimper a bunch of nonsense, not sure what I'm

saying, just knowing that I'm begging for more, begging for him, and I hate that I have to beg for it but this is what Kessler does to me. He strips me of everything that holds me together and fills in the missing pieces.

"I've missed this," he says hoarsely, and I can hear the lust dripping from him. "Your taste, your skin, every secret, hidden spot." He grabs my ass cheeks and spreads them, then pauses. "Tell me that I'm the only man you let do this to you."

Before I can answer he licks up my ass, eating me out in a wet, arcing curve and I'm moaning loud. "Jesus."

"I take that as a yes," he says, sounding so fucking satisfied but I don't care because so am I. He continues to probe me with his tongue and eager lips. It's so wrong, so bad, so dirty to have my boss tongue-fucking my pussy and ass like this, bent over his desk like I'm being punished in the best way. Fuck if I care, though.

But when I'm close to coming, he pulls back and then spanks me hard across my ass. "Fuck, Nova," he groans, smacking me again, the sounds filling the air. "So fucking good. I'm going to give it to you so fucking good."

Even in my horny stupor I remember he needs a condom but I don't have to tell him, he's opening a drawer and I hear the tear of the wrapper.

I brace myself, my hands already cramping as I grip the edge of the desk and he positions his cock at my entrance, slowly pulling it back up and down in a long, sensuous tease, mimicking what his mouth was just doing.

"This has been in my dreams," he says, his voice so rich and husky it makes me even wetter. "You, just like this."

"Over your desk, ass in the air?" I ask.

He laughs. "I'll take you anywhere, Nova," he says, and with one swift thrust he pushes deep inside my pussy, so deep it feels like the air is being expelled from my lungs. I gasp, a cry dying in my throat, the pain mingling with the sweet until he pulls out fully.

Suddenly I'm hollow without him there.

"Please," I tell him. "More."

He smacks my ass again with the flat of his palm and then he's pushing in again, his long thick dick stretching me to the point of pain. "Nova, Nova," he murmurs, breathless as he pulls out and thrusts in again. "Jesus, I don't think I can last long."

"As long as you make me come," I warn him, because if he doesn't there will be hell to pay. I'm not getting done like this just for his enjoyment.

"Still a greedy girl, huh?" he moans and then his grip on my hips tighten and he starts to pick up the pace, thrusting in deeper, longer, harder until the desk starts to shake. His hips piston into my ass, creating a wet slapping sound and I know that despite the AC blowing, he's sweating on me. Nothing has felt hotter, the slick sounds, the way he's exerting himself, grunting with each powerful thrust.

"Come for me," he bites out. "Fucking come for me."

"Fucking make me," I tell him through a moan, and he adjusts himself so the curve of his dick is hitting my G-spot. He is the only man to ever make me come like this and my body is tensing up already, anticipating how earth-shattering these kinds of orgasms are.

And then it's rising up inside me and I'm letting go. Kessler works me harder and harder and I'm swept away by the tide, pounded by waves as the orgasm takes over. I'm crying out loud, so loud that I have to shove the pineapple stress ball on his desk in my mouth to keep from alerting the whole office what's going on in here.

I bite down, *hard*.

"Fuck," he swears. "I'm coming, I'm coming."

He grunts loudly, his pumps slowing, but I feel like I'm somewhere on the ceiling, completely obliterated. If I were to look down, I'd see him hunched over me, his toned bare ass flexing as he milks every last drop out of himself.

"Nova," he says, and I open my eyes, staring at the painting across the room of a Waikiki sunset. Suddenly I'm half on this earth, in this office, in this reality, half in the stars where my body is still floating, my mind stunned by the galaxies whizzing past, at what Kessler was able to bring out of me.

But then the other half takes over. The dominant half. The one that sits up straighter, pushing aside all the hazy strands of the orgasm and realizes what happened.

I just had sex with Kessler on his desk.

Motherfucker.

"Are you okay?" Kessler asks, stepping back.

I pull down my skirt and quickly flip over. His brow is cocked as he eyes me and slowly slips off the condom. "I'm fine," I say, licking my lips, trying to appear cool, calm, collected.

Then I notice the open drawer beside me.

It's absolutely stocked full of condoms.

And not just any condoms.

Novelty condoms.

"What the fuck?" I ask. "Why do you have so many condoms?"

"Market research," he says.

My eyes snap to him. "*What*?"

He gives me a wary smile. "I was doing some research for my condom idea. I went to the ABC store and stocked up on the novelty condoms. Where do you think I got the pineapple lollipop idea?"

"Please don't tell me you used one of those condoms to fuck me."

He grins and picks up the wrapper and tosses it at me.

"It's piña colada flavoured," he says proudly.

I stare at the plastic wrapping that has a picture of a piña colada and says *Hawaiian Flavored Condom Pop*.

Oh my god.

"These are novelty condoms!" I yell at him.

"So?"

"So? You can't rely on these!" I grab my hair. "Oh my god, I can't believe I just let you fuck me with a piña colada dick!"

"Hey, you love that piña colada dick," he says, obviously insulted.

I shake my head, edging away from the condoms. "Now I have to go out and get Plan B."

"What?" he says, picking up a cheap paper-wrapped one that says *I got lei'd in Hawaii*. "They don't say you can't use them for real."

"You're unbelievable. No wonder you got someone pregnant."

"Hey," he snaps at me, frowning before he tosses the condom in the wastebasket. "That's not fair."

"And market research," I cry out, gesturing to his giant stash. "Please don't tell me I'm a test subject."

"Oh come on, that's the conclusion you're jumping to?" he says. "Can't you just stop being so bitter and distrustful for one second?"

I gasp. Oh no he didn't.

I'm done here.

"I'm going," I tell him. "And because it's Friday night, I'm going straight to my volunteer work after I pick up my car. I trust by the time I get home tonight, you'll be moved out of my house, because I really don't want to see you."

"All because I fucked you with a piña colada dick?"

I shake my head. "Just...it's fine. It's fine, forget it. I need to think."

He rolls his eyes. "Oh brother, here we go with the thinking. Let's see what crazy conclusions you're going to jump to, what strange reasons to hate me you're going to conjure up."

I should have something to say back to that but, actually, he's kind of right.

Of course I don't want to admit that.

I open his door. "Have a good weekend, Kessler. Stay away from the piña coladas."

And then I leave, walking through the office with my head held high, ignoring any looks that I might be getting because of what just went on in there. Nothing to see here folks, just horny Nova making very bad decisions.

As usual.

CHAPTER ELEVEN

KESSLER

"HO, HO, HO," I say in an extra deep, jolly voice.

"Hmmmm," Teef says, leaning back and striking a pondering pose as he looks me over. He leans in and tugs my beard to the right. Then to the left. "Maybe no ho, ho, ho. You have this Gandalf vibe going on. Just say *Mele Kalikimaka*."

"Mele what?"

"*Mele Kalikimaka*. It means Merry Christmas."

"Can't I just say Merry Christmas?"

"I believe that's politically incorrect."

"And Melekalamalaka isn't?"

"No. And it's *Mele Kalikimaka*. Cookie?"

He's brought a tin of what appears to be homemade sugar cookies in the shape of a Christmas light and holds one up to me. "On second thought, you're just going to get crumbs in your beard."

"No cookies, no ho, ho, ho. Remind me why I volunteered to be the Kahuna Hotels Santa?"

"Because you're the new guy, you're the only one who

hasn't done it yet, and I don't believe you volunteered, you were offered up like a sacrificial holiday lamb."

It's the Kahuna Hotels corporate Christmas party, and Teef and I are backstage at the festivities. Every year they hold it at the Kahuna Hotel on Waikiki Beach, where the pool area spills out onto the beach. There's a luau and a stage for a hula show, which I think is rather redundant since no one here is a tourist, but everyone's families are here and the kids seem to love it.

Which is why they also need a Santa Claus.

Thankfully I'm playing a Hawaiian Santa, which means though I have a very fake white beard attached to my face and a giant velvet Santa cap, I also get to wear board shorts, flip flops and a Hawaiian shirt, which is stuffed with many Kahuna Hotels pillows to get that Santa paunch. Or perhaps they made the exception for me since I'm already sweating in this and they probably knew I'd go up in flames in a full-on Santa suit.

"So what do I have to do again?" I ask Teef, as he peers out around the wall to look at the crowd.

"Just sit on the surfboard throne and then kids will sit on your lap and then you give them a present from the bag beside you."

"That's it? No chit chat? No, were you a good boy or girl?"

"I don't know man, do whatever."

"You were Santa last year, what did you do?"

"I protected my nuts, that's what," he says through a mouth full of cookie. "Some of them *keiki* have poor motor skills. But there's only like ten kids so it'll be over fast and then you can go on stage for the hula."

"For the what?"

Just then "Jingle Bell Rock" starts up from the loudspeakers by the pool. Teef pounds me on the shoulder. "Good luck, brah."

Teef walks off just as Bradah Ed strides over, slurping from a coconut. He's got a red hat on with fake elf ears.

"I'm Bradah Elf, here to escort Santa Claus," he says.

I eye his drink and swipe it from him. "Give me that," I say, taking in a deep sip through the straw.

It fucking burns like I've swallowed napalm.

"What is this, pure rum?" I start coughing, giving it back to him.

"You obviously haven't had to get through many Christmas parties," Bradah Ed says, casually taking a sip. "You need more, you know where to find me."

He takes me over to this giant chair made out of surfboards, beneath tinsel and twinkly lights, and I sit down, finally taking a moment to eye the crowd.

Thankfully Teef was right and there aren't that many kids but that doesn't mean every single person I work with and their significant others aren't all staring at me, like I'm part of the entertainment. The only person I don't see is Nova, which bothers me more than it should. Ever since we had sex in my office, she's been avoiding me like the plague. Not in the way she would sometimes before, now it's like she's ashamed of what happened, which hurts because that actually meant something to me.

Yeah, it was dirty hot angry sex, sex that we so desperately needed to get out of our system, sex that was fueled by the past, sex that was inevitable. But it was still sex with Nova and seeing her come with me inside her brought my feelings for her to another level, like I'd walked through another door, into another universe.

Unfortunately, it seemed to do the same with her, in the opposite direction. For the last week, all I've gotten are curt responses and quick, stone-faced glances. She's not even mad at me anymore, which is no fun. I'd rather have that raging Supernova on my hands than this cold indifference. She gives me a bigger chill than my AC unit, and I have that thing on full blast.

I just hope she's not avoiding the holiday party because of me.

"And who do we have first up?" Bradah Ed says, gesturing to the front of the line.

Oh shit.

It's Hunter and Loan.

I mean, I knew they were here, obviously. I just didn't realize until this second that Hunter might recognize me in my Santa get-up and, well, that could ruin the idea of Santa Claus for every kid here, including him. The last thing I want to do is prove that I'm not really St. Nick.

"Ho, ho, ho," I say to Hunter in my deepest voice, holding out my arms for him while glancing quickly at Loan. "Merry Kalamata olives."

Loan winks at me as Hunter gets in my lap. "We're so honored to meet Mr. Santa," Loan says. "Hunter has been a very good boy this year."

"Oh, ho, ho," I bellow. "Is that so Hunter? Have you been a good boy?"

He nods shyly, apparently star-struck. Thankfully he's not inspecting me too closely or else he'd totally see his hapless father beneath the fake beard.

"Well, Hunter, since you've been *such* a good boy this year, what would you like for Christmas?"

Please say it's something money can buy, please say it's something money can buy.

"Um," he says. "I would like...a submarine."

Whew. "A submarine? For your bathtub? I'm sure that can be arranged."

"And a mom."

Oh fuck.

"Your mom?" I repeat. This is the worst-case scenario, this is what I've been fearing all this time. That he'd miss his mom so much, that I could never measure up as a father, that I'll never be enough for him.

"No, Santa, *a* mom," he corrects me. "I would like a mom for Christmas."

I look at Loan with wide-eyes and she gives me a sympathetic smile. I'm sure she sees this a lot but even so. I almost make a remark about Miss Loan being his substitute mom and the fact that his real mom is out there somewhere, but all of that is too much for a three-year old and, hell, Santa wouldn't know that anyway, as all powerful as he is.

"That's a difficult request, Hunter," I tell him, feeling all sorts of choked up and winded, like he'd just punched me in the gut. "I can definitely get you a submarine but I'll have to do some research about the mom thing."

"What about Nova?" he asks.

Oh shit, no.

"Who is Nova?" I feebly play along.

"Nova is my father's friend and I really like her and I think she'd be a good mom."

"You know I'd have to ask this Nova," I tell him.

"She wouldn't mind. I can tell."

I look at Loan again and sigh, picking Hunter up and handing him to her. "Okay, I'll see what I can do."

"Sorry," Loan mouths to me and I'm so exhausted suddenly that Bradah Ed has to reach into the present bag and hand a gift to Hunter.

"Man, that was rough, brah," Bradah Ed says as he leans into me. "Though if you ask me, Nova might be up for it."

I shake my head and wave up the next kid. Now isn't the time to get into that with him, though I could definitely use more of his rum.

Thankfully the rest of the Santa shit goes smoothly and only one kid tries to go for my nuts, which I managed to block with a present, and then the hula show starts up.

I manage to get a few hearty gulps of Bradah Ed's rum before I'm hauled up on a stage lit by tiki torches, young athletic girls dressed in coconut bras and grass skirts surrounding me.

Now what?

Bradah Ed climbs on up and stands beside me.

"Who wants to see Santa do the hula?" he says to the crowd.

"Heck yes!" a thoroughly drunk George yells, his mai tai splashing all over the place.

Fucking hell.

"Just follow my lead, Santa," Bradah Ed says to me, seconds before he rips off his shirt and throws it across the stage.

Turns out skinny Bradah Ed is fucking ripped. A hula girl comes over to him, ties a grass skirt around his waist, and then he's off and doing the hula moves with his hypnotizing rippling abs, while a small ukulele and slack-key guitar band start playing.

I don't know what I'm doing. The moves seem slow and easy enough but all the kids in the crowd are laughing their little asses off. I guess that's the whole point, that Santa comes up here and makes a big fool of himself. The only thing I hope is that the pillows don't start slipping out. That would be a hard one to explain.

But after the first song, I'm starting to get the hang of it and now all the kids, Hunter included, are at the front of the stage, copying the hula dancers. It's pretty fucking cute.

And then I see her.

My Supernova.

At the back of the crowd, beer in her hand, talking to Kate, staring at me.

Laughing.

Of course she's laughing. This is probably making her year to see me up here like this. With the beard and the faux belly, she's probably imagining what I'm going to look like in a few decades.

Well, there's no point hiding it. I commit myself to the moment, to the character, to the hula, to...

No.

God no.

There.

To the far left, on the other side of the pool, is *the* chicken.

Not just any chicken.

The motherfucking one.

And he's looking right at me.

Bright beady yellow eyes.

Spots on his chest feathers.

It's *him*.

"You okay?" Bradah Ed whispers in my ear. "We're almost done here."

I realize I've completely stopped moving.

I can't help it.

I can only see the chicken.

It's coming toward me now, at a fast pace, like it's in a hurry.

Going around the pool...

I feebly try to move my arms in whatever pattern the hula dancers are doing around me but I can't look away, not now.

He's out to finish what he started.

"Oh no you don't," I say to myself, shaking my head, a grin spreading across my face. I've got him right where I want him.

"Kessler?" Bradah Ed says, hula-ing into my side. "I mean, Santa?"

"Shhh," I hush at him, watching as the chicken starts running parallel to the stage. No one is paying it much attention, but only because they don't have the relationship with the cocky bastard that I do.

Then, as if he knows what I intend to do to it, it starts running away.

I don't even think.

I *go*.

I start running down the stage at full speed and leap off, launching myself through the air, arms open wide, the chicken right below me like a landing pad.

I land with a painful thump in a flowering bush, colliding with the chicken in a flurry of squawks and flying feathers and flowers.

Everyone gasps.

The music stops.

I can't see anything except for the plant and feathers, my hands are around the chicken's throat for a moment but then it starts pecking at my forehead and pulling at my beard.

I'm rolling out of the bush now, onto the ground in front of the stage.

The children are crying.

And the chicken is getting the upper hand.

The pecking intensifies and then the claws are scratching down my hands and now they're tangled with my beard and somewhere in the background I hear someone yelling "Stop it Santa, stop it! Let the chicken live!" but I have no choice now.

I'm no longer trying to kill the damn thing, I'm trying to defend myself.

And I'm not even doing a good job at that.

Finally, the chicken starts to ease up and then it's gone.

I'm being beaten with something and I realize that Bradah Ed is standing above me, whacking me repeatedly with a palm frond.

"Now that," he says to me, "was a cock-a-doodle *don't*."

"Oh god," I cry out, covering my face with my hands. "Did everyone see?"

"Uh yeah, they're all staring at you like Santa has gone crazy, so why don't you straighten your beard, get up, give a smile and a wave, and I'll help you out of here, okay?"

I nod.

Bradah Ed helps me up and pain shoots through me.

I manage to wave at the shocked crowd and then Bradah Ed announces, "That chicken was trying to steal presents so Santa was making sure he didn't get yours. I'm going to take him to see his reindeer for a minute."

He leads me off of the patio area and onto the beach, pulling me along the sand until we're far enough away from the hotel and I collapse beneath a palm tree.

"Now here, take this," Bradah Ed says as he crouches down beside me, handing me his flask from his pocket. "I have more where that came from but you seem like you need it now."

I take a long swig from the flask and wince, the alcohol running onto my hands and burning the cuts and scratches.

He takes it from me, has a small sip before giving it back. "Now, you want to tell your bradah here why you fucking crazy?"

"That chicken," I start to say, not realizing how crazy I really do sound. "We've met before."

"Uh huh. But this obviously ain't about a chicken, eh? Why don't you tell me about Nova?"

I take another gulp of rum. "Nova? What does she have to do with any of it?"

"I ain't no doctor, Kess, but there's something going on with you two. I don't really care, I believe in sex for everyone, inter-office, inter-spacial romances or whatever you want to call it. But I noticed you saw her while you were on stage and it was only then that you saw the chicken. Are you even sure it was the same chicken you have a vendetta against?"

"Hey, the chicken started it. He has the vendetta against *me*."

"So what happened with you guys? Not the chicken. Nova. You broke up? I know Nova, she's just as shook up by you as you are with her."

"I don't want to talk about it," I mutter, bringing my attention to the waves and faded silhouette of Diamond Head in the distance. Sometimes I have to pinch myself that I'm in Hawaii, especially the more I fall in love with the place. Then sometimes I have to wonder how fickle paradise can be. Your problems don't take a vacation.

"Well maybe you oughta talk about it with someone, or else every chicken on this island is going to be in trouble. Hell, maybe you should start by talking it over with her."

"We're not so good with talking," I admit, then finish the rest of his bottle.

"Then communicate in other ways, brah," he says,

taking the empty bottle from me. He looks down the beach and then starts to sing, "Woah oh here she comes, watch out boy, she'll chew you up."

"Why are you singing Maneater?" I ask, and look to see Nova approaching us.

I see.

"I was just leaving," Bradah Ed says to Nova as he passes her. "Take it easy on him. It ain't easy being Santa."

Nova laughs softly and stares down at me. "Why do I feel like this is a reverse of a few weeks ago. You, drunk and sitting on Waikiki Beach. Me, hovering above you obnoxiously."

"Except you weren't Santa Claus."

"No, I definitely wasn't."

I glance up at her but can only see shadows on her face. "Do you think Hunter was traumatized?"

She laughs and sits down on the sand next to me. "Hunter was laughing. He thought you were trying to get him a Hei Hei for Christmas."

I breathe out in relief and lean back against the tree. "Why did you come over here?" She adjusts herself so she's sitting cross-legged, and up close I see her long black dress is dotted with shimmering sequins. "You look beautiful, by the way," I add.

She gives me a quick smile, her face now lit up by the faint glow of nearby tiki torches. "Thank you. I came here because I'm worried about you."

"Could have fooled me. You've been avoiding me."

She sighs and rests her elbows on her thighs. "I know. I'm sorry."

"You regret the hot sex, don't you?"

She laughs. "It's hard not to when you put it that way."

"I'm serious."

She glances at me and shakes her head, positioning herself so that she's facing me head on. Her hands go to my face and she pulls off my beard until it's under my chin. "I'm sorry. I can't take you seriously with that thing on. You look like you had your face dipped in glue and then shoved in a vat of cotton balls."

"Are you saying I wasn't a very convincing Santa?"

"Well the *keiki* seemed to believe you and that's the most important part."

"I think I fooled Hunter," I muse. "I asked him what he wanted for Christmas and he told me he wanted a submarine and a mom."

"A *mom*?"

I nod. "Yeah. So that was rough."

She scrunches up her nose. "I bet. I'm sorry."

I stare at her, how beautiful she looks under this light, under these stars, wishing that our gentle little moments like this could last forever. They're just as impactful as all of our explosions.

"He said you could be his mother," I say softly.

Her eyes widen. "Oh shit."

I reach out and touch her hair, pushing it behind her ear. "He said you'd be into it."

"Oh he did, did he?"

"The little guy likes you."

"Yeah, well, he's easy to please."

"So am I."

She gives me a wry twist of her mouth. "In a very different way."

"I like you."

"Kessler," she says, but before she can say anymore I lean in and kiss her, soft and sweet and warm.

But the kiss just lasts a second before she's placing her

hand on my chest and gently pushing me back. "It's not a good idea, Kess."

"Is it the beard? Do you want me to put the beard back on?"

She gives me a small smile, her eyes brimming with sadness as she looks up at me. "No. It's not the beard. You and I together...what happened the other week at the office just has to stay that way. In the past."

"We're good together," I tell her, trying not to plead but Bradah Ed's rum is coursing through me. "You know we are."

"We're good at fighting," she says. "And we're really good at makeup sex. But Kess, you know where this is headed. It'll end the same as it did last time, in heartbreak."

"Heartbreak?" I repeat.

She bites her lip and nods. "You broke my heart."

The admission hits me deep in my chest, shattering all my ideas about her, about us.

"I didn't...I didn't know."

"I wasn't just hurt and humiliated when you broke it off and moved on to Stacy. I was heartbroken. Kessler, I was so in love with you. Maybe it was the young stupid obsessive kind of love that only comes on hard the first time you fall but...I fell for you. I loved you."

She's talking in past tense, but it feels real all the same.

I can barely talk, barely think. I just know I need her. I want nothing more than to hold her and kiss her and see if she can love me again.

No one has ever loved me like that.

Or at all.

"You were in love with me?" I manage to say. "Why didn't you tell me?"

She shrugs, looking off down the beach, the moonlight

reflected in her glossy eyes. "Because I was protecting myself. Because I didn't want to be vulnerable. Because I thought it would protect me from being hurt. Because I knew in the end you would hurt me."

Fuck. "You should have told me."

"Why?" She glances at me curiously. "Would it have made any difference at all? Would you have stayed with me?"

I want to say of course it would have made all the difference in the world but the truth is, it wouldn't have. I was a different person then. Younger. The things I wanted then weren't love and security, they were cheap thrills and hot sex with different women. I loved being with Nova but I didn't love her back then, and that was the truth.

I didn't love anyone back then, including myself.

"See," she says gently. "I knew that it wouldn't make a difference. And it's fine."

"It still would have been nice to know."

She runs her fingertips over my brow and I close my eyes at her touch. Every cell in my body is begging for her, wanting to know what it's like to have her heart. I want her heart, to possess it, to protect it and never let it go.

"Well, you know now," she says.

"I wouldn't break your heart again," I tell her, grabbing her hand, holding it tight in mine. "I swear I wouldn't."

Her smile wanes. "You're a good man, Kess. A good man with good intentions. But you're my boss now, and if you're not my boss, that means you're leaving in two months. I can't go through all of that again. I don't know how I'd survive losing you twice."

She sighs and pulls away, getting to her feet. "I'm going back to the party and then I'm going home. Want me to say anything to Loan and Hunter? You can't hide out here forever."

I reach up for her hand and she grabs it, trying to haul me up but I just hold her still. "Stay with me. Tonight. Come back with us. Please."

Her lips press together in thought and she swallows and for a moment I think maybe I've convinced her. Maybe she could take pity on me above all else.

"You'll be all right, Kess," she says, pulling her hand away. "Just sleep it off. I'll see you on Monday."

Then she's walking off down the beach.

I don't think she knows she's taken a piece of my heart with her.

CHAPTER TWELVE

NOVA

"AND HAVE yourself a merry little Christmas now."

"Augh," I cry out, picking up a pineapple pillow and tossing it over to my iPod dock where it's currently playing a range of holiday songs, including this one, the world's most depressing. Lord knows why I'm doing this to myself on Christmas morning, alone in my house, drinking spiked eggnog in my coffee and shedding a pathetic tear every now and then.

But the pineapple pillow misses and hits a painting on the wall, which proceeds to fall down and smash on the bamboo floors, glass going everywhere.

I moan. It was my favorite painting from the Kahuna Hotels collection. Just the profile of a Hawaiian girl at sunset, her long wavy hair turning into a lei of plumeria flowers which then turn into waves. I always stare at her and think she's got it going on. She's free. She's at peace.

Now she's shattered on Christmas Day, lying on the floor in pieces.

So fitting.

To make matters worse, Judy Garland's mournful singing about the most depressing Christmas ever goes away and the playlist replaces her with Paul McCartney and what I do believe is the worst Christmas song in the history of Christmas songs.

"Simply having a wonderful Christmas time," he sings and my whole body literally shudders.

Or maybe that's the pounding at my door.

I get up and make my way down the hall, opening the front door to see Kessler with Hunter in his arms and Loan behind him holding a giant turkey in a pan.

"Merry Christmas!" Kessler booms, practically shoving me aside as they all barge into my house, Loan giving me a giddy smile as she hurries on past, heading straight to the oven.

"I'm sorry, I thought you guys moved out weeks ago," I say, following them down the hall.

"As if we would let you spend Christmas all alone," Kessler says, just as Hunter goes, "Santa came last night!"

Such an innocent expression and yet I'm conjuring up the image of Kessler dressed as Santa and things are already so inappropriate in this brain of mine.

"Did he now?" I ask Hunter, while Kessler smirks.

"Yes!" Hunter yells. "I got Hei Hei and I got a whale and I got a submarine for the bath tub and I got some more army men and I got other stuff."

Thank god there is no mention of a mom.

"Wow, Hunter, sounds like you got some pretty awesome presents," I say to him, reaching over and messing up his hair. I glance at Kessler. "Not a pineapple in sight."

"Hey," Kessler says to me, putting Hunter down. "I'll have you know the pineapples are very popular. Besides, your house still looks like you ransacked the merchandise department."

"I told you I did," I remind him. "Did you know we even made pineapple shaped back massagers at one point? They vibrate."

This gets his attention, his brows arch devilishly. I don't know why I'm even flirting with him like this, two seconds ago I was crying over a broken painting.

"Oh shit," I say, quickly reaching down and grabbing Hunter before he has a chance to run off to the living room. "Sorry little dude, I forgot I have broken glass over there. Just hang out with your daddy for a bit while I clean it up."

"You said shit," Hunter says, laughing. "The word is poop. Remember I pooped on your floor, right over there." He points to the kitchen where Loan is standing.

"I recall," I tell him.

"I cleaned up the poop, I might as well clean up the glass," Kessler says, grabbing a dustpan from the hall closet like it's second nature and heading over to the painting. He nods at the iPod. "Nice tunes."

"Please don't tell me you like this song."

"I love this song."

I groan, my head in my hands. "This is why we could never work, Kessler."

When he doesn't say anything to that, I look up to see him staring at me oddly, like he's almost hurt by what I said.

But he recovers quickly with a shrug. "It's Sir Paul. And Wings. Band on the Run."

"But it's not Band on the Run or Live and Let Die or Let 'Em In, or any of the songs that make Wings awesome. It's this vile piece of saccharine Christmas bullshit. How could you love this song?"

He grins at me and starts sweeping up the glass. "I don't

know. I just do. In fact, now that I know it bothers you so much, I might just love the song even more. Hey Hunter, do you know this song? We should sing along. It goes like this: Simply, having, a wonderful Christmas time."

And then Hunter starts singing along on cue.

The irony is the kid could be signing it instead of Paul McCartney and no one would know the difference.

"Sim-ply! Hav-ing! A wonderful Christmas time!" Hunter starts yelling.

Oh my god. "Look, did you come here to annoy me on Christmas?" I say to Kessler as I pick up the painting from the floor. "Is that your present instead of a lump of coal? Because you are doing a good job."

"I came here to keep you company," he says. "And you're welcome."

"What if I didn't want company?"

"You'd rather be alone drinking eggnog at ten a.m., trashing your house and listening to songs you hate?"

He's got me there. "Besides," he goes on. "Maybe I wanted the company. Maybe Hunter wanted to see you."

"I'm pretty sure Loan wanted a day off."

"She wants to cook the turkey, it was her idea. Look, we're all kind of marooned on this same island away from family, so why not just have a castaway Christmas together."

I hate how clever that sounds, a castaway Christmas. It reminds me that when it comes to marketing and ideas, Kessler is rather good at his job, even though I wish he wasn't sometimes. But that's my own insecurities talking, something I should probably get a handle on.

"What are you thinking?" he asks, peering closely at me. At this distance I can see the flecks of green and blue that come together in his eyes to make them seem teal at times.

"I'm thinking you might have the most beautiful eyes I've ever seen," I say, and the words surprise me as much as they surprise him.

"Nova Lane, paying me compliments?" he says in a low voice. "It's a Christmas miracle."

I look away, feeling strangely embarrassed. We've gotten closer—or at least friendlier—in the week since the Christmas party, when I found him on the beach and admitted I used to be in love with him. I wasn't planning on telling him that, it just happened, but the moment the truth came out was the moment I felt a weight lift off my shoulders, a weight that had held me down for years.

He had wanted me to tell him back then, even though we both knew it wouldn't have changed anything, that he didn't love me and probably wouldn't have. But me telling him now, I feel like it already has changed something. Maybe it's just me finally letting bygones be bygones. Maybe it's my heart's way of preparing for something, clearing the way for the future.

I don't know and I don't want to think about it too much. I've been so guarded for so long, the death of my sister throwing me into a deeper chasm, that even thinking about being open again is scary.

Especially when it comes to my level-ten heartbreaker.

And yet Kessler is in front of me and in those eyes of his that I just admitted were the most beautiful I'd ever seen, I see a different version of him. The one who doesn't want to be a heartbreaker, not on any level. Not with me.

"Nova!" Hunter yells out. "Simply, having, a wonderful Christmas time!"

Kessler gives me a sheepish smile that makes his dimples pop. "Sorry."

I shake my head and laugh and then remember something.

"Hey Hunter, I got you a Christmas gift!" I tell him.

"You didn't have to do that," Kessler says.

I shrug. "I was going to bring it to work and give it to you. It's not a big deal."

I go over to the tiny stack of presents I have by my tree. I originally was going to ignore the whole Christmas thing once I learned my parents weren't coming. It was just too hard without them, without Rubina. But then I thought ignoring Christmas wasn't going to make it go away. So I embraced it. I went to a tree farm and got a small pine that smells oh so heavenly and decorated with millions of teeny tiny sparkling lights. It's very girly and very pretty and I love it.

I pull out a box and hand it to Hunter. "Here you go."

Hunter takes it and sits on the floor, eagerly tearing into it.

"Whoa!" he cries out, lifting it up for his dad to see. "Maui!"

Specifically, they're *Moana*-themed inflatable water wings.

I glance at Kessler who looks thoroughly surprised. "Hunter told me he wanted to swim, like Maui from the movie," I explain. "So I thought you could teach him. I got him these water wings to help."

"Oh," Kessler says quickly. He's acting rather odd. "Huh. Well, yeah. That's good."

"Daddy," Hunter says, putting on his most adorable voice. "Can we go to the beach? Today?"

"Now?" Kessler bites his lip, slowly nodding. "Yup. Sure. Okay."

"You good?" I ask him quietly. "Are you upset I didn't get you a present?"

"What? No." He smiles. "I'm fine. But I did get you one."

"Well I got you one too."

A box of macadamia nut chocolates. Not the most original Christmas gift, but that's what happens when you do yours last minute at the ABC store. I just hope he didn't buy me a bunch of flavored condoms.

"You just said you didn't."

"I was playing my cards right and seeing how the day went. If you were naughty or nice."

"You know I'm nothing but naughty."

"Oh I know. Which makes you oh so nice."

There I am with the flirting again. I should knock it off but it's just so damn easy with him. It's making me smile from the inside out.

We promise to give each other our gifts later, and Kessler seems to get over his hesitation about the beach. Perhaps it reminded him of what happened the last time we were there. We tell Loan we'll be back and she seems more than happy to be at peace in the kitchen, cooking up a feast and watching Vietnamese dramas on my Netflix.

Going to the beach on Christmas Day is pretty much tradition in Hawaii, and it's absolutely packed with families. I'm glad we only had to walk a short bit because parking would have been a nightmare, but we manage to find a spot in the sand near where a jetty of rocks stick out in the water, creating a pool of sorts that's safe for kids.

I can tell Hunter wants to go right into the water and try out his Maui wings but we decide to eat lunch first. I packed a cooler with some ahi poke I got at the Suprette in Kahuku and kalua pig burritos. Normally I'd grab some kombucha from the Sunrise Shack but being Christmas and all, I've brought a bottle of Veuve Cliquot and some POG juice. I like to call it "POG Cliquot."

"Okay, you're going to have to explain all this food to me again," Kessler says, looking over the spread as he takes a nibble of the poke. "I mean this is good, whatever this is, but I don't know what it means."

"You mean you've been here a month and you haven't had poke yet?"

"Oh that's how you pronounce it. Po-kay. I thought it was poke, like this." He pokes me in the side, making me giggle.

"Stop it. And yes, po-kay. In Hawaiian you pronounce every single letter. Makes it a lot easier when you think of it that way. Like Merry Christmas is..."

"Merry Kalamata olives."

I roll my eyes. "Mele Kalikimaka. If you saw it spelled out, it would read the same way. And this burrito is filled with Kalua pork, which is like the pork you eat at a luau, all shredded."

"And Pog? Weren't there trading cards called Pog?"

"They were milk caps and they came from this POG, which stands for passionfruit, orange and guava. To have champagne and POG is basically a Hawaiian mimosa." I stare at him for a moment. "I really need to get you acclimatized to this place."

"Hey, I've acclimatized. If you haven't noticed, I've stopped sweating."

I peer at his brow. "You're sweating a little."

"I'm glistening," he corrects me. "It's like a glow. Everyone here has that glow. Now I glisten like the locals do."

I look him up and down, focusing on his large forearms

and biceps sticking out from beneath his soft t-shirt. "Well I definitely thought you would be a lot more tanned by now."

He gives me a look. "In case you don't remember, I work long hours five days a week. All these people who walk around Hawaii all tanned are either natives or they work in Sunrise shacks and surf schools. Or are tourists who have time to work on their tans all day. We work inside and I'm always wearing suits."

"Then explain why I'm tanned?"

"Your mother is from the Bahamas," he says.

"It's because I make time to play. So should you."

"You know I'll play with you any day, Supernova. And you're a liar. You don't make time to play. Tell me how often you come to the beach?"

I clamp my lips shut because he's got me there. "I'm here now."

"So am I. I work a lot and so do you. Maybe we both work too much."

"Maybe we're both afraid of what happens if we step back," I say.

He raises a discerning brow, studying me. "Well, well, well. Another Christmas miracle."

"What?"

"I've never heard you associate the word fear with work before."

I shrug, taking in a deep breath. I used to be scared to talk about this with anyone, let alone Kessler, but since I discovered how good it felt to be honest the other day with him, I'm letting my guard down. "It's true. For me, anyway. I'm afraid that if I stop working so hard, if I stop trying so hard, that everything I've worked for is going to slip away from me."

"That's not going to happen, Nova," he says. "And I'm

not saying that as your boss because we both know that title is bullshit. Everyone sees the work you put in."

I shake my head. "They don't. George doesn't."

"You know it wasn't George who recommended me to take Mike's place. That was Mike himself. I know George didn't agree and Desiree wasn't sold. That's why I'm temporary, on probation. I guarantee it would have gone to you. You deserve it. You're the best at it and they know it."

"Then why did Mike recommend you?"

He shrugs. "Big hockey fan."

"You're serious?"

"Have you seen inside his house? It's like a fucking shrine to the NHL. I have a theory that he's set up cameras all over just to watch me shower and shit, probably has Loan cut locks of my hair at night." He shudders.

"I can't believe you never told me that," I tell him. "You knew that's what I thought."

"I know. I didn't want you to be right and I especially didn't want you to know that you're right. There's nothing more dangerous."

I punch his arm. "Well, if it makes you feel any better, I do think you're great at the job. Aside from a few blunders. Like the condoms."

"Just you wait and see, it will be a huge success. As will the bike program."

"Now you're just being nice on purpose."

"Does this mean we can't argue with each other anymore?"

I laugh. "Don't worry, we have plenty to butt heads over."

"But seriously," he says, twisting to face me. "I think it would be good for you to just take a step back and relax about everything. You live in this beautiful place that's filled with Aloha and you're like the sarcastic *ha* part of the word."

"That's a new one," I mutter. "I'll relax more when you relax more."

"Well I can't. Not yet. I want to stay here. I want to keep my position. I need to keep working hard. I need to prove myself. It's what's driving me at the moment."

I give him a small smile. "But those are all my reasons too. And I'm after your job."

He holds my gaze and it's then that we realize the kicker of this situation. Even if we get along, even if we start opening up with each other, even if whatever kind of relationship we have, whether it's a friendship like this or friends with benefits or something more, it will always come down to the fact that he has the job I've been working toward.

And even though I would have done anything for Kessler in the past, throwing my career goals aside for him doesn't seem right. Not now, when there are no guarantees of our feelings for each other and a future together.

He gives me a steady look. "Do you want me to step aside?"

Yes.

No.

I shake my head. "I don't want it to be that way."

"And I don't want to either, because I want to be here and I will fight to be here. Maybe I got the job because I was playing for the Kings for a year, but that doesn't mean I don't think I deserve it, and it doesn't mean I don't think I'm good at it." He pauses. "But Nova, I want to stay here. For you."

I swallow. "For me?"

"Yes. But I don't even have you. And I'm not sure if I'll

ever get you, I mean really get you, unless you take my job and let all of this go. Do you know what I mean? Do you see the problem?"

I see the problem. I've always seen the problem. "Catch-22," I say.

He exhales and runs his hand down his face before looking back at me. "So what do we do?"

"Nothing, I guess," I say with a tired sigh, already distancing myself from it. "Just keep doing this. Go for a swim."

"Yeah, swim!" Hunter says, stomping excitedly on his sandcastle.

"What about the food?" Kessler says.

"We'll come back to it later," I tell him. "Come on."

It takes a lot of extra sunscreen on Hunter and some struggling with the inflatable wings before we're ready to go. I'm grateful for the change in subject, but Kessler is back to being cagey about the water. Maybe our talk hit him deeper than I thought. As much as it would be touching for him to step aside for me, it's not what I want from him either.

I think...I think I just want him.

The thought alone already has me feeling like I'm drowning.

I go into the water, holding Hunter's hand, Kessler holding his other.

Of course, I'm not a mom, I don't have a ton of experience with kids, I have no idea how to teach a kid to swim. I kind of thought Kessler would for some reason.

But he looks just as confused.

"I think you should lift him up and walk in the water with him," I tell Kessler, as the waves lap at Hunter's feet. "Just get him used to being in it. But don't let go yet, even though he has the wings."

He frowns, then looks out at the waves, which are especially calm for a December day. "I think *you* should."

"Why me?"

"You're a woman."

"So?" I lower my voice. "I'm not his mom."

"I know that but I just think it's a woman thing to do."

I peer at him. "You're not glistening anymore. You're sweating. What's going on?"

"I'll tell you later."

"Tell me now."

"I can't."

"Kessler," I warn him. I glance down at Hunter who is looking up at us impatiently, wondering what the hell is going on.

He sighs. "Fine." He scoops Hunter up in his arms and then gingerly walks into the waves. I'm right beside him. As we go, Kessler keeps staring down at his feet in the water.

"Are you afraid of sharks?" I ask him.

He shakes his head. "No. Well, I mean, who isn't?"

"I don't get it, you're acting afraid of the water. You've been in this water before. With me. *Remember?*"

He looks at me quickly. "I remember. That was different. I always kept my feet on the bottom. And you were very distracting."

"What was I distracting you of? Oh my god. Kessler." I whisper, "Do you know how to swim?"

His pained expression says it all.

"Oh my god," I cry out softly. "How is this possible? Everyone knows how to swim."

"Not everyone," he snaps. "Hunter doesn't."

"I'm going to learn," Hunter says knowingly. "I'm only three."

"Kessler..."

"What?"

"Why didn't you tell me?"

"And have you revoke my man card?"

"Oh come on, no one can revoke *your* man card. I just don't get how that's possible. You're a hockey player. You grew up skating on frozen lakes and rivers in the Yukon. What happened if you fell in?"

"Uh, then you die."

"I don't want to die," Hunter says.

"You're not going to die, buddy," Kessler says.

I hold out my arms for Hunter. "Here, come here Hunter. Let's practice this."

Kessler hesitantly hands him over to me and I hold Hunter in the water, raising him up when the waves roll through. "You know you're going to have to learn too, Kess. You can't live here and not know how. It's not just dangerous for you, you need to know for Hunter's sake, just in case."

Kessler sighs and starts walking backward toward shore a few steps, until the water is at his waist. "Fine. But you're teaching me."

"Me? Why me?"

"Why do you think? If I go to anyone else, I will have my man card revoked."

"Stop talking about your man card like it's a thing. It's nothing to be embarrassed about."

"Well I couldn't tell that from your reaction. Anyway, sometimes people recognize me. I don't think an article in the NHL Daily News about has-been defenseman Kessler Rocha taking swimming lessons in a kiddie pool with toddlers would do me any favors."

"There's not really a NHL Daily News, is there?"

"There is and I'm pretty sure Mike Epson is their main

contributor."

"Okay fine. I'll teach you. I'll teach both of you. Would you like that Hunter?"

"Yeah! Can daddy have water wings too?"

I laugh. "I would love to make that happen."

Of course when it comes to Kessler, I think the only thing that would fit around his arms would be two inner tubes. The idea of getting two matching flamingo floaties crosses my mind.

"Stop laughing," he says. "I can tell you're picturing things in your head. Silly things."

I stick my tongue out at him.

Hunter starts singing, "Simply, having, a wonderful Christmas time."

But you know what? For once the song makes sense.

CHAPTER THIRTEEN

NOVA

YOU WANT to know the most annoying sound in the world?

It's the sound of a New Year's Eve party favor horn.

There's currently one sticking in through the crack in my office door and going off.

LOUD.

I stare at the door, waiting for it to open wider.

Kessler pokes his head in, smiling with that horn dangling from his mouth like it's a cigar.

"Happy New Year's," he says.

"It's not New Year's yet," I tell him.

"I know," he says, coming inside. "But it will be soon and I'm not about to let you work late on New Year's Eve. Boss's orders. That's me."

I narrow my eyes at him. Got to say, still hate that term, boss. "I have to work on this research."

"No, you don't," he says, leaning over the desk. God, even though the suit can be so stifling here, he looks damn good in one, especially like this when he's not wearing a tie and the first few buttons of his dress shirt are undone and you can see a hint of chest hair and skin.

He gives me a crooked, cocky grin.

He knows I like what I see.

"The office is closed tomorrow," he goes on. "Everyone needs a break. Research about bikes, or what Pantone colors are in for next year or how to beat Instagram's algorithms or whatever it is you're trying to busy yourself with, can wait."

"I'm not busying myself."

"You are. I know you."

"Didn't we just have a discussion about how the both of us work too hard?"

"Yeah, we did, and it hasn't changed a thing. You're not doing this because you have no New Year's plans, are you?"

I shrug. Kate invited me to some massive party on a hotel rooftop, but I know she's only going because some of her other friends are going and some guy she wants to bone will be there. It's the kind of place that will be too loud and chaotic and I'll be alone and while normally I might try to go and score with someone, things are different now.

Things are different now because of the man leaning on my desk, his gorgeous eyes raking over my features, taking me in like a sunset and he doesn't have a camera.

"Well, you do have plans," he says, straightening up. For a moment there I thought he was going to kiss me and damn if I'm not disappointed.

I clear my throat and tidy the stack of papers on my desk. "What plans are those?"

"Plans with me," he says. "Come on, let's go get you all dressed up." He motions for me to get up.

I don't move. "Dressed up? I don't think so."

His lips twist into a smirk and then he's leaving my office.

"Where are you going?" I ask. Funny how I wanted to be left alone, but now that he was here for a minute, I'm bereft without him. Why is it so hard for me to admit that I want to be with him, be around him? Why can't I just be real?

Add that to your new year's resolution, I tell myself, just as Kessler comes back in my office with two garment bags.

"What are those?" I ask, slowly getting to my feet.

He holds up one and shakes it. "This one is a tuxedo for yours truly because I feel like being a Hawaiian James Bond tonight." He shakes the other one. "This is for you. From me. I never did give you your Christmas present."

That's true. On Christmas, after the delicious turkey that Loan cooked, I gave him the box of macadamia nut chocolates and he gave me a piece of paper that said I.O.U. I thought it was funny and forgot about it, but apparently he didn't.

"You know it was just a box of chocolates, you didn't have to get me anything," I tell him.

"I had planned this even before I got those chocolates," he says. "Come on, take it."

I go around the desk and gingerly take the bag from him, unzipping it.

Inside is a long beaded silver dress that looks like it was made from the moon and stars with sequins and sparkles and tassels.

"What is this for?" I gasp, putting my hand in the bag and running it over the dress.

"For tonight," he says. "I need a James Bond gal on my arm for tonight's party."

"What party?"

"The one Kate invited you too. She invited me too. Lots of people from the office are going."

"Aren't we going to be a bit overdressed?"

He laughs, and the sound combined with the crinkles near his eyes makes my stomach do a million flips "When am I not overdressed? As long as you don't mind a sweat monster as your date."

"I don't," I say, smiling at him. "Is it my size?"

He nods. "I know your size, very, very well."

I glance at the label. It says it's a twelve and I'm normally a ten. I raise my brow at him.

"Hey," he says quickly. "The woman who helped me with it says it runs a size small. All I know is that you're going to look like a galaxy was poured all over you. Put it on."

I hesitate.

"Do you want me to give you privacy?" he asks.

Normally I would say yes, but I'm not ashamed of my body, at least I never am in front of him. The way he's always looking at me makes me feel like I'm a damn supermodel. Or at least Rhianna.

And actually the dress looks too tight and delicate to do it by myself.

"No, I think I might need help with it," I tell him.

"Great," he says. "Strip."

I roll my eyes. "Yes, boss."

"Oh god that's fucking hot."

"Shut up," I tell him, pulling off my sandals, which luckily will go with the dress, then step out of my dress pants while unbuttoning my sleeveless hibiscus-print blouse.

Kessler is watching my every move, lust burning in his eyes, as I take off my bra and toss it on my desk, my breasts bouncing free.

"Fuck me," he murmurs.

"You stay back," I warn him.

We still haven't had sex since that time in his office, and the last time he kissed me was just for a second at the Christmas party. We've been flirty with each other since then, lots of touching in rather innocent ways, but we haven't crossed that line again.

And I still don't plan on it, even though I am standing before him in my office in just a black thong. Like usual, he has a raging hard-on that looks like it wants to burst through his pants and come get me.

"I guess I should be stripping too," he says, starting to undo his pants and unleash that beast.

"No." I raise my finger at him. "You help me into the dress first and keep that thing away. If both of us are naked, it's recipe for disaster."

"It's recipe for screwing you senseless is what it is. But okay."

He manages to keep it in his pants and comes over to me, taking the dress out of the garment bag. I turn around with my back to him and raise my arms and he slowly lowers the dress over me.

I can feel his breath at the nape of my neck, hot and ragged, like he's trying to control himself. All I know is if he doesn't heed my warning and tries something with me, if he places those plush lips of his on my shoulder, I'm going to cave in immediately.

It's never been so erotic, so sensual, to be dressed like this. Normally the reverse is true but here in my office, I feel like I'm being uncovered instead of being covered up, like he's stripping me bare.

Kessler pulls the dress down, tugging just below my breasts, at the sides of my waist, below my ass, his fingers grazing my skin as he does so. I shiver, goosebumps running all over my limbs, and his breath hitches behind me. I know he can see what he's doing to me.

God, I want him so fucking bad, I can barely breathe, barely swallow.

Somehow, Kessler manages to hold himself together and tugs the dress down to my ankles before his fingers find their place at my back, slowly doing up the zipper.

"There," he murmurs at my neck and I can hear him swallow thickly. "All done."

I exhale through my nose, trying to regain a sense of who I am.

"Your turn," I tell him, turning around and I gasp.

He's already fucking naked somehow.

"How did you get your clothes off so fast?" I exclaim, my eyes drawn to his big dick that's bobbing in front of me, looking both delicious and deadly.

"Hidden talent," he says, grinning, and I realize this is the first time I've seen him completely naked in five years. Good lord, he needs to come with a warning label, like *do not stare directly at Kessler's dick without an extra change of panties.*

And of course it's not just that damn cock of his, but his muscular legs, his rigid six-pack, rock-hard chest, and arms and shoulders like bricks and boulders.

I'm practically drooling. I have to clamp my mouth shut.

"Hey, no shame in liking what you see," Kessler says with a grin that's growing cockier by the second, just as his cock is growing harder.

I wave him away, averting my eyes before I lose it. "Okay, you don't need my help, just put your damn tux on. I'm going to the washroom to touch up my makeup."

I grab my purse and head to the washroom, leaving the office as he says, "Aww, you're no fun."

But when I look in the mirror, I see the face of someone who *wants* to have fun. The dress is gorgeous beyond belief and it really does look like liquid starshine was poured on me from shoulders to toes. But more than that, it's my eyes that are doing most of the shining. There's something ignited in them that wasn't there before.

There's lust, for sure. Good old fashioned desire. I'm definitely turned on and I probably should just take my panties off and go commando—Lord knows Kess is doing the same—since they're already soaked through.

There's also hope. Hope on the last day of the year. I don't know exactly what I'm hoping for but I know it has everything to do with the naked man in my office.

Hold onto your hope, I tell myself, as I apply extra coats of mascara. *Let everything go for one evening.*

I keep that in my heart as I walk back to the office and see Kessler dressed in his tuxedo.

Of course, the damn man happens to look just as sexy in the tuxedo as he does naked, and that's no small feat.

"Too much?" he asks me, adjusting his bow tie.

I walk over to him and finish fixing it, staring up at him. "Just enough," I tell him, our faces inches apart.

Then before I get the urge to lean in and kiss him, I back off. "Okay piña colada dick, where are you taking me?"

Because downtown Honolulu is removed from the Waikiki area, he calls us a limousine to take us to the hotel where the party is being held. We head up to the roof in an elevator crammed full of people who are also dressed to the nines, thank god, and spill out onto the roof with stunning views of the city.

"Oh my god!" Kate's voice soars above the crowd of partygoers. "Big Dick Energy is here!"

She fights her way over to us, giant umbrella-crested tiki drink in her hand.

"Which one of us is Big Dick Energy?" I ask, happy to see her.

"You both are," she says as she looks me up and down. "Look at you, hot stuff." She looks at Kessler in his tux. "Same to you, big dick."

Kessler smirks. "That's a dangerous nickname to have."

She shrugs and takes a sip of her drink before reaching out and slapping me across the shoulder. "Hey, bitch, you said you didn't want to come to this party."

"I'm very convincing," Kessler says.

"That's the Big Dick Energy," Kate says with a solemn nod.

"Hey it's you guys!" Bradah Ed yells out, appearing beside Kate wearing a black suit and looking pretty spiffy. He puts his arm around her waist and to my shock, she does not shrug him off.

"I didn't know you were coming," he says.

"Last minute surprise," I tell him.

"Well you look amazing. Come on over, we have a table by the fire pit over there. Teef is here too, so is Mahina and her boyfriend."

I look up at Kessler.

"Mele Kalikimaka," he says, and when I look impressed he adds, "I've been practicing."

"You know Christmas is over."

"But it's always the holiday season in my heart," he says, full of cheese, as he takes my hand in his and presses it against his heart.

But when we start walking off after the others, he doesn't let go.

He holds it.

And I hold his hand right back.

Maybe it's not appropriate to do this in front of the people we work with, especially when Kessler and I are so undefined and the only thing people know us as is boss and employee.

But maybe tonight you let that shit go, I tell myself. Maybe tonight you hold him just as hard as he holds onto you.

So I do.

We sit down on the couch by the fire pit and I don't let go. I'm squished against him and his arm goes up around the back of the couch and I settle in next to him.

No one seems to pay any attention. Everyone is worrying about their own problems, focused on their own things. The champagne starts flowing and the DJ gets louder and yet I'm more and more focused on the man next to me.

The things he's slowly doing.

The way his fingers are absently playing with my hair.

The way he leans in to talk to me, murmurs and whispers in my ear.

The way his thigh presses against mine, so that every inch of us is in contact with the other.

We're in our own little world, our own little universe, surrounded by other stars that are getting dimmer and dimmer, leaving only us to shine.

Before I know what's happening, I'm leaning in so close that my lips are brushing against his and my eyes close and I fall into his kiss, sinking deeper and deeper.

It takes the clearing of someone's throat to break our lips apart and I blink at Kessler for a moment, wondering what we've done, before I look over.

Kate is staring at us with a smug look on her face, brows raised expectantly.

But then again, her hand is in Bradah Ed's lap so I don't know what the hell is going on there.

"Maybe you guys oughta get a room," Kate says.

I look over at Teef who is passing around a tin of cookies and paying us no attention, then at Mahina who is making out with her boyfriend. Bradah Ed is sipping on a coconut, clearly enjoying Kate's company.

Kessler grins at me. "Sounds like a good idea," he says, getting to his feet and pulling me up with him.

"What are you talking about?"

"Well this *is* a hotel. It might not be a Kahuna Hotel, but it's still pretty sweet and a room was included in the package."

My jaw drops. "You planned to have sex with me on New Year's?"

He cocks his head. "I always hope for the best," he says. "Besides, I didn't want to drive home. Come on."

"It's not even midnight yet," I tell him as he takes my hand and leads me through the crowd and back to the elevator.

"Are you afraid of missing the fireworks or the count-down?" he asks. "Because I guarantee you won't miss either. In fact, I might be able to get you off before the year is over."

My eyes widen. We're not exactly alone right now and a few partygoers look our way in amusement as we get in the elevator. "Ready to go down?" he asks me.

"Oh stop it." I hit him across the chest.

We don't have far to go. Our room is on the fifteenth floor and from the floor to ceiling windows, the views over Waikiki Beach and the fireworks barge are just as good as the ones on the roof.

"Our hotels need to step it up a notch," I tell him.

But my voice is wavering.

I'm nervous.

I'm really nervous.

Suddenly it's like I wasn't naked with him earlier in the office.

Suddenly it's like I'm standing in front of him for the first time, wondering what his touch is going to feel like when I know it feels like second nature.

I don't know what to do.

I'm frozen in the spot between the windows and the door.

Kessler gives me a soft smile, his eyes burning with warmth. "I forgot to tell you that you look far more beautiful than I could have ever imagined. I'm the luckiest guy in the world." I lick my lips. "I know I only have you like this, in this moment right now, but even just a moment with you is enough. Anything more than that is too good for the likes of me."

Good lord.

This man.

He knows all the right things to say.

He knows all the ways to say them.

Suddenly I'm not nervous anymore because all I feel is want and lust and gratitude. For him, for this moment, for the way his words make me feel. For the way he always makes me feel.

Like I'm all that matters.

That he sees me.

I've just wanted to be seen.

I walk over to him and run my hands through his wavy hair, kissing him passionately until I'm breathless.

Then I drop right to my knees.

Undo his tuxedo pants and let them fall to the floor.

His cock juts out, twitching with his rising heartbeat and I take it in my hands. He's so hard and smooth, like velvet-encased steel and he's growing stiffer with each pass of my fist.

"Oh fuck," he whispers, his hands going into my hair and holding on tight.

I bring my tongue to his glistening tip, tasting salt, letting it run in a wet trail down the underside of his shaft, all the way to his balls and back up around. It brings out a flurry of deep moans from his mouth, the kind you feel vibrating deep inside you.

I love his cock. I love giving him head. He's always so vocal, so appreciative, and while everything about him is so manly, I love seeing him succumb to me like this, knowing that though I'm the one on my knees, that I'm bringing him to his.

I work at him for a while, sucking on his balls the way he likes it, really giving him everything I have. Then I feel him tense up, his grip tightens. I want him to let loose in my mouth, I want to swallow every single drop of him and feel it slide down my throat.

"Stop, please," he cries out, choking on his words.

I pull my mouth away from his tip. "You don't sound like you want me to stop," I say, even though my jaw is feeling stiff as I say that.

Breathing hard, he steps back, taking off his jacket and throwing it across the room until he's falling back onto the plush armchair against the window. "Come here," he says, a total command.

I bite my lip, loving the sight of him sitting back like that, his wet cock sticking straight up like a mast, his pants by his ankles, his dress shirt half-unbuttoned. He brings out a condom from the shirt pocket and tears it open, smoothly sliding it over his stiff length, mouth open as he stares at me.

I go over to him, kicking off my sandals before I pull up the hem of my dress and hold it around my waist while I climb on the chair, straddling him, sliding my underwear to the side.

Both of his hands slide up to my face, holding me, staring up at me with such intensity that it's unnerving. It's like I'm looking into a side of Kessler that I didn't know was there, that he hadn't shown me before. Not just the one who is throbbing with raw, primal lust, but the one that aches for me with tenderness.

It's disarming.

Whatever walls I had left around me are falling into pieces.

I'm like the painting on my wall, shattered around him, not knowing if he's going to come on by and sweep me up and make me whole again.

But I'm no longer afraid.

Not tonight.

I give him a small smile and, without breaking eye contact, I reach under, holding his cock in place while I slowly lower myself down on him. We both suck in our breath in unison as I stretch around him and he fills me, wider and tighter.

"Fuck," I swear, my mouth dropping open. I pinch my eyes shut for a moment but when I open them he's still staring at me, a gaze deeper and more intimate than any I've known. I feel his gaze inside me the same way I feel his cock, like I'm being penetrated in two places and my mind is starting to tumble.

All I feel is him, everywhere.

All I want is him, always.

"Kessler," I whisper, but my words stop there, fading to nothing, because I don't know what to say or how to go on. I don't know how to tell him because I don't quite know how I feel. Words aren't enough.

But maybe that's why our gazes are locked like this. Maybe he can see it for himself.

"Nova," he says thickly, running his thumb over my lips. "I can't believe this is you."

"It's me," I tell him softly.

And I realize that if I'm seeing the Kessler I haven't seen before, maybe he can see me.

Maybe he knows. Maybe words aren't needed anymore.

I bite my lip as I jerk my hips back up and down, his cock sliding in deeper and deeper with each thrust. It feels so good, the slow tight slide, the way he fills me to the brim. Finally, I break his stare and I throw my head back, my breasts spilling out of my dress where he eagerly laps at them with his tongue.

His hands drift down to my waist and he wraps his fingers around me, tight, and begins to thrust up, faster, harder. I knew he wouldn't let me be in control for too long but I don't care, I'll gladly hand him the keys to this ride.

He starts to pump, sliding past all my sensitive places, making my eyes fly open with each hit. One hand slips down below, between his stomach and mine and slips further until he finds my clit. He rubs his rough thumb around it in flat circles, getting wetter and wetter and I'm starting to moan, louder and louder.

"Don't stop," I whisper. I want him to keep going and yet I never want this to end.

"I won't stop," he grunts, his thumb rubbing harder in time with each quick pump of his hips.

Oh god, oh god, oh god.

I don't have much longer.

I open my eyes to look at him and he's staring me like he's been waiting for me, his eyes heavy-lidded and lost to desire. "Nova," he whispers hoarsely, voice drunk with sex. "I...I..."

Then he breaks off, face contorted as he tries to hold back and I decide to push him over the edge. I ride down on him hard, squeezing as I go, until I'm starting to come.

"Oh god," I cry out. "Fuck." My head goes back and I'm riding him slower and slower as the waves rip through me and I can barely hold on.

I let go, collapsing against him as he's thrusting up into me, biting my neck and grunting with each sharp stab of his hips, saying my name over and over again, like he's having a fevered dream.

Seconds later, fireworks explode over Waikiki Beach, the boom ripping through us, our faces aglow with the lights of yellow, red, and gold as they spray over the ocean.

Kessler pulls his head back and looks at me, a lazy grin on his face. "Happy New Year, Nova.

My heart is pounding in my head louder than the pyrotechnics but still I manage to say, "Happy New Year, Kessler."

CHAPTER FOURTEEN

KESSLER

LAST NIGHT FEELS LIKE A DREAM. I know this even before I wake up, that the reality was greater than the fantasy. That what I had in my hands was everything I ever wanted.

Nova.

I roll over and glance at her. She's sleeping soundly, looking completely at peace, her skin dark and glowing against the white sheets, her hair in a wild mess around her head. She looks like she got thoroughly fucked last night.

I can't help but smile, knowing I was the one who put her through her paces. It didn't just stop on the chair, the fireworks going off after our own fireworks did. We continued on the floor, on the bed, up against the glass. I'm fairly sure we fucked until five in the morning, our own party going on longer than anyone else's.

Which is why I'm glad I actually have this room for another night. I'm not sure if Nova will end up staying with me or not, but it doesn't mean I won't try and convince her.

Until then, I just watch her sleep, loving how vulnerable she looks.

I know she has a big soft heart inside her, it just takes a bit of work to get to it.

But that's what makes it worth it.

Maybe most guys would shy away from a complicated woman but I thrive on it. I like the challenge. I like that Nova isn't a doormat and she isn't a pushover. I like that she has ambitions and goals and doesn't balk from hard work. Women like that should be praised. I hate to use the term strong, because strength comes in all shapes and forms, but she is strong, even if she thinks she's not strong enough.

She just needs to open enough. I get how scary it is. I know I broke her heart before and it's hard enough to open up to anyone, let alone someone like me. I know what happened with her sister is lodged somewhere deep inside her and she's doing all she can to bury it or make peace with it or just try and live with it.

I don't want to change a single part of her. I just want to be there with her, by her side, even if she tries to push me away. I just have to earn her trust again, if I even had it in the first place, and that's going to take time.

Do I even have time?

That's the question.

It's January first.

I have less than two months to either win her over or keep my job, and then I might be sent packing with Hunter back to San Francisco. I'll have my son but it's starting to feel more like a family when I have Nova around.

Why are you worrying? Pay attention to what's right in front of you. Pay attention to your life right now.

No regrets.

Nova slowly blinks her eyes open as if she heard my

thoughts. It takes her a few moments to figure out where she is. We didn't get that drunk last night, but it was a whirlwind of sex, and perhaps she thought it was all a dream.

"Hey," I whisper to her.

She clears her throat. "Hey." A slow smile appears on her lips, making her eyes dance. "Fancy seeing you here."

"How did you sleep?"

"Good. With what little sleep I got." She groans and rolls over, the blanket moving away from her chest and exposing her breasts, her nipples tightening in the air.

Dear lord, I thought maybe this morning we could order room service and talk, that I'd be way too worn out to do anything, but seeing her like this has me raring to go again.

"Kess," she says dreamily. "I can feel your eyes on me."

"Don't you dare cover up those tits of yours," I warn her, inching over. "They are exquisite."

She looks up at me and laughs and it hits me deep in the gut.

Her laughter sounds so pure, her smile wide and open and I can't help but think:

I have her.

I don't dare ruin it.

"Come here," I murmur to her, sliding over her body, the cool sheets slipping down my back as I envelop her. With my elbows planted on either side of her head, I peer down at her face, taking in every gorgeous feature as I gently brush her hair off her forehead.

"How are you so unbelievable?" I whisper, running the tip of my nose against hers.

"How so?" she says.

"First thing in the morning and you're a glowing goddess. Tell me your secret."

She giggles. "Well it might have something to do with what we were doing all night long."

"Oh. So you're saying I have something to do with it."

She bites her lip and smiles. "You might have something to do with it."

And you're still here. You haven't closed up. You haven't run away.

I don't dwell on those thoughts for long.

I kiss her, just the soft, teasing brush of my lips against hers, as sensual as a caress.

She opens her mouth to mine, almost timid, and I respond in kind. Our kiss turns wet and warm, like slowly entering a bath of silk, and the lazy, relaxed morning starts to fade away. It becomes ignited as our tongues stroke each other, the heat building inside us until it envelopes us both, fireworks after fireworks.

Her hands disappear into my hair and she tugs at my strands and I'm so damn hard, my cock a stiff rod between me and her soft belly. I know I have to go slow and take my time. I need to stretch this morning out into the next morning, and the next, until all of time just becomes her naked, writhing body in my bed.

I place small kisses on the corner of her lips, down her delicate jaw, down her neck to her collarbone where I gently nip. I shuffle backward on the bed to continue kissing down to her breasts, taking her nipples into my mouth and sucking hard before lapping up in round circles, pinching and squeezing and watching them harden before me.

It spurs me on like nothing else, especially when she starts shifting beneath me, her legs spreading, her moans as light as air, and I'm practically salivating for her.

While my fingers continue to work her breasts, I move further back still, my tongue snaking down her stomach in a long hot wet line until I'm at her hips. I smile to myself as I place my wide hands on either thigh and spread her legs wider, her gorgeous pussy opening up for me.

"Like I said, unbelievable," I tell her. My words come out hoarse and rough and her body tenses with anticipation. I let my eyes do the work of my mouth at first, knowing she can feel them on her skin as I take in every delicate inch of her, from her sensitive inner thighs to her sweet glistening folds.

I can't hold myself back any longer.

With an iron grip on her thighs, I shove my face between her legs and ravage her with my tongue, eating like I'm a starving man. I lick and suck and probe, voracious and uncivilized, drinking her in until we're both moaning for more.

Her hips buck up into my face, her legs squeezing me on either side, her fingers making fists in my hair and holding on for dear life. I can feel how hungry she is for me, the same hunger I feel for her, and I swear if my dick even gets touched at this point, I'll come all over her. That's how fucking turned on I am.

Screw it, I think. There's no way I'll be able to fuck her and not come in a second.

So I keep eating her, licking her up from the inside out until she's calling out my name like a prayer and her thighs are squeezing the life out of me and she's pulsing around my tongue. I swear the whole bed shakes with how hard she comes.

Before she has a chance to come down, I stand up and start jacking off over her writhing body. "Sorry, I have to come," I tell her through a moan and then I'm grunting loudly as I start to orgasm, the feeling ripping through me from my heavy balls to my cock and cum is streaming out in a hot arc, landing on her tits and stomach.

She doesn't look surprised, she's watching the mess, smiling with a lopsided grin as I continue to fuck my fist, milking out every last drop. Then I nearly collapse on her, my legs feeling boneless.

"Fuck," I swear, wiping the sweat from my eyes, tasting her sweet cum on my lips. I quickly grab a towel from the bathroom and gently wipe the mess off her body. Then I climb beside her and collapse. We lie there beside each other on our backs, our chests heaving, trying to catch our breath.

"That was so Canadian of you," she says after a moment.

"What? Cleaning you off?"

She laughs and rolls over, running her fingers down my pecs and tugging at my chest hair. "No, apologizing for coming all over me."

I chuckle. "Can't say we're nothing if not polite."

"Just so we get something straight here, you never have to apologize for coming on me." A pause. "As long as I get to come first."

My head lolls to the side and I give her a smirk. "Won't be a problem there. I'm pretty sure I can make you come without even laying a finger on you."

"Well, you do have very penetrating eyes."

I wag my brows. "One of my many useful qualities. Another useful quality is the ability to order room service. What do you want for breakfast? One of everything?"

She's shaking her head and smiling but I already see something changing in her eyes, like the realization of where she is and who she's with. "I wish. I should get going."

She moves to sit up and get out of bed but I'm on her in a second, pouncing like a jaguar in waiting.

"No you don't," I tell her, pinning her down with my body. "You are not leaving me, not now."

"I should go back to the house, I didn't know I'd be out all night."

I'm not sure if it helps or not that her argument is totally feeble.

"Why do you need to go to your house? To check on your geckos?"

"No, I..."

"You're reaching for an excuse. You just want to leave."

"That's not true. I don't have my toothbrush or toothpaste."

"Look, this may not be a Kahuna Hotel but I'm pretty sure they'll bring that up to the room along with some lomi lomi eggs benedict and a mimosa. You have nowhere you need to be today. It's January first and you don't have to work."

"But you want me to spend it with my boss?"

"Fuck yes I want you to spend it with your boss," I tell her, kissing her. "I'm a damn good boss, at least in the bedroom. And I have this bedroom all day so just forget about going home, forget about all the things you should be doing and just fucking do *me*."

She blinks up at me, thinking it over. "You do make very convincing arguments. No wonder you're in marketing."

"Stop acting like I'm good at what I do. I'm good at everything I do," I tell her, rolling off her to pick up the phone.

"Including modesty."

I give her the stink-eye and call room service, ordering up the aforementioned eggs benedict while Nova requests fried eggs, rice, soy sauce and Portuguese sausage, along with a vat of coffee and a bottle of Baileys.

"Really? Rice for breakfast?" I ask, slipping back into bed.

"Don't knock it unless you've tried it," she says. "You know, you never did tell me how you got into marketing."

Question time? That's a first.

"Maybe because you never asked," I tell her.

"Okay," she says, positioning herself so she's on her side, head propped up on her hand. "I'm asking now."

I reach over and pull up the sheets so they cover her breasts. "I'm sorry but I can't talk to you when your tits are out like that."

She glares at me mockingly. "You're such a pig."

"Oink."

"And don't change the subject."

"I'm not," I say, even though I guess I am. I clear my throat. "I got into marketing because I've always been interested in business."

"Was this before or after the NHL?"

"Before. Way before. I grew up in the frozen north, remember? I was in the middle of nowhere. All we had up there was hockey, and if you were lucky maybe your parents owned a tourist trap in Dawson City. We had that for a while. My father was straight off the boat from Lisbon, don't really know why he picked the Yukon but I guess he visited once when he was young and fell in love with the land."

"I heard it's beautiful up there," she says.

"You wouldn't like it," I tell her. "In the summer there are mosquitos the size of your hand."

She grimaces. "I'd have to up my game."

"You'd need a rifle. Anyway. My dad bought a bar of all places. He thought he could inject a little Portugal into the arctic. But he didn't have a clue about business, and throughout the years he lost more and more money and pretty soon we couldn't afford our shack in town. We were relegated to a trailer in the woods and while there are a lot of trailers in the woods up there, you want to be close to people when you're that isolated. The town is all dusty dirt roads and gritty can-can girls like they have in the Moulin Rouge, and either eternal darkness or the midnight sun." I close my eyes and I can see the sun in July, dipping over the breadth of the Yukon River but never setting behind those mountains. I sigh, missing home, or at least the memories of home before things fell apart.

I go on. "And less than two thousand people live there year-round. But those two thousand people count for a lot when you're in the middle of nowhere. My mother fell into a depression and she left when I was fourteen."

"I'm so sorry," she says softly.

"Don't be," I tell her. "I never blamed her. She needed to go. She didn't know it would be like that. And she wanted me to go with her, to start over again in Ohio. She was American, and wanted to be with her family. But as much as I loved her, I didn't want to go. I had just gotten into hockey in a major way. I couldn't fathom starting over." I reach out and brush a wayward strand of hair off Nova's face. "So I stayed and I trained. I knew that if I worked hard enough I could support my dad but I also knew that I had to have a business plan. I had to go to university, get a degree, get business smart, make the right choices. I knew that no matter what happened with hockey, I could never depend on it. And, well, you know the rest."

"No, I don't."

"I eventually moved down to Edmonton, then Vancouver. I was in junior hockey, then farm teams for the NHL.

My father moved back to Portugal. I never went to school, I was brought onto the King's as a defenseman. I got injured, couldn't play again. And I decided I would do whatever it would take to make sure I wasn't sitting on my ass and counting NHL checks. I applied for a job with a hotel and that was it."

"So where is your father now, still in Portugal?"

I nod.

"Do you talk to him?"

"Sometimes. I'll call him Christmas morning and on his birthday, but he was never really the same after all that. He has a new family now, I think he just likes to pretend that the Yukon never happened."

"And your mother?"

"She died a few years ago. Ovarian cancer. I made it to the funeral, at least. We were never that close either."

Nova studies me for a moment. I have to say, I rarely talk about my past because all it does is bring about pity and people feeling sorry for me when they shouldn't. It's just life and life happens to everyone. No one is immune.

But Nova doesn't seem to pity me, maybe because she understands this thing called life too. Maybe she knows that when you open up, you're not looking for anything more than for another person to understand you better. At least, I hope that's what she thinks.

"I'm glad you told me," Nova says. "I feel like a dick now."

"Why do you feel like a dick?"

"All those years of ribbing you over your motives. I just thought you were another guy trying to be a hot shot in the corporate world."

I laugh. "Well, I *am* trying to be a hot shot in the corporate world. But my motives are the same. I don't want to ever just rely on one thing. Hell, I don't even know if I'll stay in this corporate world forever."

She frowns. "What do you mean?"

I shrug with one shoulder. "I like the hotel world and I think I'm good at it. But I like hockey more. I'd like to get back into that side of things for a bit. Maybe open up a hockey school." I pause. "Here."

"Here? In Hawaii?"

"I went to that skating rink – they take their hockey pretty seriously. I was talking to the guy there for a long time and maybe there's a future there. It would take a lot of funding and time and I don't know if I'm ready for that at this stage of my life but it's there and it's nice to know that there's always another path to go down."

"Something tells me that you'll be great at whatever you decide to do."

"You're paying me compliments again. Is being nicer to me part of your resolution?"

"Maybe," she says slyly as she inches closer to me, sliding her hand down my chest and to my dick. I've been semi-hard just being in the same bed as her, naked. "I can be nicer."

I raise my brows, interested to see where this is going.

She smiles like a devilish angel as she moves down the length of my body and sticks my cock into her mouth. I watch, unwilling to take my eyes off her as she proceeds to give me head, sucking and licking with her perfect blow-job lips. Nova has never been one of those girls who sucks me off as a chore, she does it because she genuinely loves having my dick between her lips, loves what it does to me.

But I'm not coming again like this.

I need to come inside her.

"Hold on," I tell her. "Come up here."

As she moves up, I reach over and grab a condom from the stack on the bedside table. And yeah, they're Magnums, no piña colada dick for her anymore.

I open the foil and slide the condom on, then grab Nova by the shoulders and flip her over so she's on her back. She giggles as I attack her neck and my hands go under her ass, hiking her hips up. I slip a pillow underneath her for leverage and then in one swift motion, push inside of her.

Fuck. Me.

A lustful groan escapes me as she envelopes my cock, so hot and tight and slick. Her hips buck up into mine and I slowly start working myself in and out of her, biting and licking at her nipples. We have a rhythm together, something easy and fluid, our bodies working together in time. I know every inch of her as she knows every inch of me and it's kinetic, electric synergy.

I piston my hips into her harder, the headboard slamming back against the wall. My ass muscles flex as I pound and pound and pound, my cock deep inside, sweat dripping off of me and onto her, the air smelling like our decadent sex.

"Fuck yes," I growl, one hand gripping her hip, the other slipping over her swollen clit. She stares up at me in awe and wonder and pleasure and fear just before I stroke the right sensitive bundle of nerves and she's going over the edge.

This is raw. This her split right open.

She cries out and then she's coming hard, creaming all over my cock and I'm letting myself loose, fucking her harder in quick, sharp jabs until I'm letting out a hoarse cry.

"Fuck!"

I spill into the condom again and again and it's like the orgasm never ends and I can't stop coming until I've filled it to the brim. I wish I was inside her bare, filling up every cell inside her.

Then I'm drained, emptied, sated, and I collapse on top of her in a sweaty heap of pounding hearts and ragged breaths.

"Jesus," I swear, wondering when the world will stop spinning and if I'll ever come down off this god damn high. My heart is so loud in my head it sounds like someone knocking at the door.

Oh shit.

Someone *is* knocking at the door.

Room service.

I stare at Nova's sated eyes and smile.

"Hope you're still hungry."

God knows I'll always be starving for her.

CHAPTER FIFTEEN

"NOVA, WHAT DOES *WAHINE* MEAN?" Hunter asks, looking at me with his floppy sun hat all askew.

I do a double take at him, impressed that he's picking up Hawaiian.

"*Wahine* means woman," I tell him, adjusting his hat. "Like me. And *Kane* means man, like your dad." I gesture to Kessler who is lying on his back on a poolside lounger, soaking up the sun and looking ever so much a man.

Since it was my new year's resolution to be real and more open, Kessler's resolution was for the two of us to work less. That hasn't really happened. It's been four weeks since New Year's and with the year underway, both of us have been working late trying to get our projects pushed through for the summer ahead.

But we are making time for fun.

Every Saturday and Sunday, Loan gets time off from being a nanny, and Hunter and Kessler come out to see me on the North Shore. Sometimes they just stay the day, sometimes the night, sometimes the whole weekend. But whatever time we get, we make the most of it.

We're in the water a lot and I'm busy teaching both Hunter and Kessler to swim. Usually we're at the local pool like we are today, but sometimes we're at the beach. It's kind of funny teaching them both at once, but it's actually easier this way and it's making them bond like nothing else.

I think when it comes to Kessler, it teaches him humility, takes his rampant ego down a peg, and lets him shed any fear of not being "man enough." For Hunter, the fact that his daddy is learning with him makes him feel like a big boy and there's a lot of trust going around between the three of us that wasn't necessarily there before.

It's the best part of my week. I leave everything at the office, including the roles that Kessler and I have. At work we are strictly professional. Sure we have fun but I'm no different with him than I am with Kate or Teef and we make sure it stays that way. On the surface we are just work colleagues and nothing else.

But I'm often at Kessler's after work. We have a lot of dinner dates. We go out for drinks. We have a lot of sex in his car when it's too late to drive over to my house and we don't want to disturb Hunter or Loan at his.

I've even been with him to an ice hockey rink and done a few laps around while he checked out the hockey teams and talked to the administration, and he's been with me to the mental health center to do a shift of volunteer work with me.

It's been...complicated.

I don't even know what we are. We haven't had any kind of talk, though that's probably because I run the other way when it comes up. And we're careful not to show too much affection in front of Hunter in case he gets confused or if things go south between Kessler and I.

And it could go south. That's the thing that's always hovering in the back of my head.

I keep thinking to the past.

I keep fearing what was.

I keep thinking about my sister, of all people.

I think about that space in my heart that was filled with her when I was growing up. How she was my everything. Where she went, I followed. She was my best friend, and the kind of love I had for her was something I still can't really describe. I guess that's the way it is with sisters.

But then she broke my heart. And it sounds so fucking selfish to make it about me. That it was my heart she broke when she was so broken herself. But it's the truth. I loved her and I thought that my love would be enough to save her. I thought if I sat her down and told her that she was hurting me, hurting mom, hurting dad, that she would stop.

It never happened that way. I kept bringing her back and sitting her down and begging for her to be a part of our family again. I told her that I loved her and missed her and needed her.

And she would look me in the eye and tell me she loved me too.

She'd lie.

She took my love and she'd lie and she'd say she was on her meds and she'd say she wasn't on drugs and she'd say she was still at rehab. I know my parents got the worst of her lies and that pretty soon I was traveling up and down the west coast as a means of escape.

I started distancing myself from her because I was afraid of losing her.

I was cutting her out of my heart because I was afraid she'd keep hurting me.

I pretended everything was fine and put my feelings in a glass jar where I screwed the lid on tight and vowed to never open it, even though I could always see it.

But it didn't matter.

When I got the call that she died, the loss I'd felt was worse than anything I could have imagined. All this protection didn't help me at all. It didn't make me love her less, it just made it hurt even more when I lost her because of all the love I lost with it.

All that lost time, where I could have just loved her without fear.

Now there's Kessler in my life and I keep wanting to do the same thing with him. Every time my heart seems to spread wings, I try and clip them. Every time I come with him inside me and dream of doing this with him forever, I tell myself that we might only have one month. Every time I glance at him and he takes my breath away, I tell myself that I'm falling for his looks like last time.

I tell myself lies.

Over and over again.

I ignore the truth because it's safer to pretend, even though I know the truth, even though I know first-hand what it's like to put up walls. When it comes to love, they'll eventually come crashing down.

So much for my new year's resolution.

"What's *keiki*?" Hunter asks, snapping me back to the present. I blink at him.

"You're *keiki*," Kessler says, peering over his shades at him. "A kid."

Now I'm impressed with Kessler. Perhaps he's assimilating here after all. He's already a million shades browner now that he's been in the sun every weekend.

Still sweats a little, but we pass it off as a glisten.

"I think I'm going to get a drink," Kessler says, sitting up. Yup, just look at those abs glisten.

"Nova?" He practically waves his hand in front of my eyes. "You want anything?"

"Anything except a piña colada," I tell him, bringing my gaze off his body.

"I want a piña colada," Hunter says.

"Oh you do not, little buddy," Kessler says. "I'll bring you some POG."

Hunter makes a happy sound and I watch appreciatively as Kessler walks off over to the bar. We have a Kahuna Hotels property on the North Shore by Waimea Bay and so we've been using their pools a lot for the swimming lessons. We're done for the day, hence the booze, but I think in a few more sessions Kessler will be swimming like a fish.

While he's gone, my mind wanders and I feel like getting back to the book I was reading the other day, so I get up and start rummaging through my bag, trying to find my Kindle. That's the problem with e-readers these days, they're almost too slim and lightweight that they're hard to find.

I'm rummaging and rummaging with my back to Hunter when I hear him say, "No, no I think I want pineabble juice instead."

"I'm sure the POG will be just as good," I assure him.

But when I finally find my Kindle and turn back around, Hunter is no longer beside me.

He's gone.

He's running away from me, along the edge of the pool toward his father, yelling about pineapple juice.

And that's when everything happens in slow motion.

I'm yelling "Hunter!" for him to stop running, for him to turn around and come back.

He's running faster, his little feet stomping through the slick poolside.

Kessler is turning around at the sound of my voice.

He looks at me.

Looks at Hunter.

Just as Hunter's feet slide out from under him on the slippery tiles and he falls to the right.

SPLASH.

Into the deep end of the pool.

"Hunter!" I scream, scrambling to my feet as Hunter's arms flap on the surface for a few splashes in a desperate attempt to swim before he starts to sink.

He's gone under.

And Kessler is running at the pool full speed.

He jumps in, legs first.

SPLASH.

Sinks.

Now I'm trying to run after both of them.

I'm yelling for people to help, yelling that they can't swim, just as Kessler's head breaks the surface, gasping for air.

Hunter is in his hands and he's doing his best to hold him up, even though he's struggling to stay above water.

I'm close enough to dive right into the pool, swimming in a few strokes until I reach Kessler, trying to help him up. I see nothing but a flurry of whirlwind bubbles and feel the desperate, hard kick of Kessler's legs. They're so powerful I'm nearly knocked out.

When I manage to grab hold underneath Kessler's arms, we reach the surface and through the water in my eyes, I see that someone has grabbed Hunter already from Kessler's grasp and pulled his son to safety.

"Easy," I tell Kessler, though he can't look at me, his eyes are too wild. "Keep kicking but do it easy, don't tax yourself. You're almost there."

I help lead him over to the edge of the pool, just a few feet, and wrap his arms around the metal stair railings.

"Hunter," he cries out, coughing. "Hunter."

"He's fine," someone says from above, and we look up to see Hunter sitting just off to the side of the pool in the arms of an older gentleman. Hunter is crying his eyes out but other than that he doesn't seem hurt at all.

But Kessler does. He's staring at me through the wet lock of hair flopped across his face and his look says it all.

It says his son almost drowned.

It says he almost drowned.

It says it's all my fault.

And he's right. If I had kept my eyes on Hunter like I should have, if I hadn't turned my back for a minute, Hunter wouldn't have been able to run off like that. I would have helped him get his pineapple juice. He wouldn't have fallen in the pool and nearly drowned.

Kessler wouldn't have had to risk his own fucking life to jump in after him, knowing full well he can't swim yet either.

I could have lost them both.

And I would only have to blame myself.

"I'm so sorry," I tell him, feeling the hot prickle of tears at my eyes. "I'm so sorry Kess. I was watching him I swear, I just turned my back for a second and I'm so sorry."

But Kessler is breathing too hard to say anything.

Eventually a big Hawaiian guy standing by the pool helps haul Kessler out and I follow.

Hunter is wrapped up in a towel, his sobs quieting as someone hands him a small cup of pineapple juice.

We're ushered off to the side and the lifeguard looks us over, talking to us to make sure we're okay. It doesn't seem like anyone suffered any injuries, although my shins and thighs are going to have huge bruises tomorrow from Kessler's kicking. His hockey thighs are no joke.

I assure the lifeguard that I'm okay enough to drive us back to my house, even though I have a feeling I'm barely holding it together. I'm so shaken up inside that I feel the slightest knock might shatter me and I have to survive on autopilot as I drive us home, just going through the motions.

But the silence inside the car is killing me.

"I'm sorry," I say again, glancing at Kessler. He's looking out the window, avoiding my eyes, towel wrapped around his broad shoulders. When he doesn't say anything, I look in the rear-view mirror at Hunter in his car seat. "I'm so sorry Hunter."

"Don't talk to him," Kessler snaps at me quietly.

My eyes widen as I look over at him. "Why not? I'm sorry."

"He doesn't need your apology."

"Well do you need my apology?"

"You know, I was gone for *one* second."

I feel like I've just been poked with a pin and I'm slowly draining. I suppose it's better than shattering on the spot. "And I just turned my back for one second."

"You shouldn't be turning your back at all." He looks away and mutters under his breath, "But I guess that's what you do."

"*What?*"

We're going *there?*

"What were you doing?" he asks.

"I was looking for my book!"

He shakes his head. "Can't even trust you to put your own needs aside for one second."

Whoa, whoa.

Whoa.

"What the hell does that mean?"

"Don't swear in front of my child. I think you've done enough to him for one day."

"Why are you turning into a monster?" I cry out, my grip tightening on the wheel, my temper ready to fly off the handle. I take in a deep, sucking breath. "Look, I know you're upset. He almost drowned, you almost drowned. I know it's a lot to handle but please, I didn't do it on purpose. I would never do that to you, I would never hurt you, either of you, you know that."

"I don't think I know shit anymore."

"What does that mean?"

His eyes are blazing, sharp and dangerous, and I don't think I've ever seen him this angry, this vicious. It hurts to know how badly he can hurt me if he chooses.

Please don't hurt me, I think. *Please don't say anything to hurt me.*

"It means I have no idea what you want, what you're even doing with me. Maybe this is just some game to you, a fun way to pass the time. Today was just a prime example of you being selfish, of thinking of no one but yourself."

"Excuse me?!" I shriek.

"Mommy, Daddy, stop fighting!" Hunter yells from the backseat.

His words catch me off guard for a second but Kessler plows right on through.

"She's not your mother, Hunter," he says in a hard voice. "She's just a friend. Just your friend, just my friend. Nothing more. Isn't that right, Nova?"

I am fucking speechless. I can't even answer him and I don't know what I would even say.

So he does know how to hurt me and has no problems in doing so.

Fine.

As if I couldn't feel guilty enough for what happened, as if I haven't had to deal with enough guilt in my life. But hell, there I am making it all about me again.

Selfish, selfish Nova.

The air in the car is so thick with tension I'm surprised I can see out the windshield, surprised that I actually get us home.

I park in the driveway, ready to get out when Kessler says, "Sorry."

He's good at apologizing, but not this time.

He went too far.

And now, I feel myself being reeled back in like an empty fish hook.

Walls going up.

Brick by frozen brick.

I get out of the car and manage to hold it together enough to say goodbye to Hunter. Thank god the kid doesn't seem to harbor any grudges against me, nor does he seem that shaken up or traumatized.

But when it comes to Kessler, I keep my distance.

I watch as he puts the car seat in the back seat of the Audi and then goes around to his side.

He doesn't say anything to me and, with his sunglasses on, I can't read his expression.

But I can feel him.

All his cells and electricity inside him, I can feel how much he doesn't want me around, I can feel that I screwed up big time, not only by not paying enough attention today but by not paying enough attention to our relationship in general. Not giving him what he needs when I don't even know my own needs.

Kessler hesitates, hand on the open door, and takes his sunglasses off.

That's when I see the anger in his eyes has dissipated— all I see is pain.

Pain I caused. Pain we caused.

"I don't want to end it like this," he says.

"And yet that's what's happening," I tell him, crossing my arms, trying to hold my ground even though I don't know what I'm standing for anymore.

He swallows and nods.

Gets in the car.

Drives off.

I watch until he disappears around the corner and I look up at the mountains and wish I could bury my heart somewhere deep inside the green ridges, perhaps in a deep, secret cave. Keep it there until it feels safe to come out.

It's then that I realize it'll never be safe for me.

Whatever I was trying so hard to shield my heart from, happened anyway.

I think I'm still in love with him.

I think I love him more than before.

I think I might have just kicked that love to the curb.

And everything I think...I know.

CHAPTER SIXTEEN

KESSLER

"DADDY. DADDY. DADDY."

Hunter's cries enter my dream. For a moment I'm back in the ocean and he's drowning, slipping through my grasp.

No, no, no, no, no.

Not my son.

Not my love, my world.

I reach for him in the depths but soon I'm drowning too, swallowed into the darkness, seeing Hunter float away, getting smaller and smaller.

I wake up, covered in sweat, and see the shadow of Hunter by my bed.

"Daddy, Daddy, Daddy," he's crying out, tugging on the sheets.

"What is it? Did you have a nightmare?" I ask, my throat closed and words sluggish. I wipe the sweat off my face and peer at him, wondering if he's going to be scarred for life by what happened today, if he'll ever swim, if he'll need therapy. First he loses his mother to prison, then he nearly drowns.

Fuck, I don't know if *I*'ll ever get over it. I highly doubt it.

"I'm scared," he says in a small voice. "Can I come in bed with you?"

"Of course, little buddy," I say to him, picking him up by his waist and placing him in bed beside me, getting him under the sheets. "Tell me what you're scared of. It's the water isn't it?"

He shakes his head. "No. I'm scared of the Menehune."

I stare at him for a moment, figuring I heard him wrong. "Like...mermaids?"

"No, the Menehune," he says. "They're like Leprechauns."

Oh god. I sit up straighter and peer at the time. It's only ten thirty at night. I must have passed right out earlier after everything that happened today. "The cockroaches are back?"

"No," he says, getting impatient now. "The Menehune."

"I'm sorry Hunter, I don't know what the Menehune are."

"The Menehune are tiny people who live under your bed."

This isn't good. "By tiny people, do you mean insects? Like the cockroaches?"

Shit, maybe it's now a centipede infestation. I heard their bite can hurt for months.

He sighs. "Tiny people. They are this big." He gestures to the size of a Barbie doll. "They used to live in the forests but now because people are everywhere they can live in your house. That's what Nova said."

Oh shit. This explains everything. "Nova told you about them?"

He nods, his lower lip trembling. "Yes. The other day. She said they were chevious."

"Mischievous?" I say.

"Yes miss chevious," he says. "And they like to play tricks on you and hide things. I think there's one under my bed and he wants to eat my toes!"

I sigh loudly and pull him in for a hug. "Listen, Hunter. There are no Menehune."

"There are, I heard other people talking about them, too."

I'm not too sure about that but I have to do damage control.

"I think maybe you're just scared over what happened today. It's okay if you want to talk about it. You know what, I was scared too. I thought I couldn't save you and then I thought I couldn't save myself and it's like my whole world came crashing down on me."

Hunter is staring at me with big eyes, nodding. "You were like Maui."

"I was barely like Maui. I needed help."

"I wish I knew how to swim."

Fuck, this is breaking my heart. "You will. You just weren't ready and you took a tumble. It's not your fault."

"I want to be all powerful like you are."

I chuckle. "Oh, if you only knew the half of it. Tell you what, if you think I'm all powerful, then I will kill the Menehune under the bed for you. You said it's only one, right?"

"No," he cries out. "You can't kill it. Don't kill it Daddy."

"Okay, okay, I won't kill it. I'll just remove it and put it outside."

"You can't. Only the Hawaiian people can do that. You are what Nova calls a Nuck."

"A Nuck?" He must mean Canuck. "So Nova knows all about the removal of Menehune then?"

He nods thoughtfully. "I think so. You should call her."

I let out a dry laugh even though he has no idea why it's funny. I guess he doesn't even remember us fighting today, which is good. "It's late, buddy."

"I can call her."

"We aren't calling Nova right now, she's sleeping."

"But I can't sleep until the Menehune is gone!"

This back and forth literally goes on for another ten minutes before Hunter passes out in my arms.

I could kill Nova for doing this. She should have known how susceptible he is to these weird scary things after the whole leprechaun cockroach invasion.

I roll over and text her: **Thanks a lot for telling him about the Menehune. He's terrified and can't sleep and thinks he needs a Menehune hunter or they'll eat his toes.**

I know that's going to make her feel really bad, especially after today, but I can't help it. I guess I'm still mad at her, the way I knew she was shutting me out in the end.

Then again, I said some pretty shitty things to her. Things I didn't mean. Things I knew would hurt her, all because I've been so damn frustrated.

That's the thing about fighting with her now—it hurts. Before it was all fun and games where we could shoot arrows at each other and it would bounce off our armor. Every day was like going into battle when you never knew what the other person was going to do.

It was fun. A lot of fun. But it was shallow. When you

wear armor like that, you don't let anything in underneath and a lot of the stuff between us was just coasting on the surface, slipping right off.

But now the armor is down. At least it is for me. She might not know it yet, but she's got me, all of me. And I can only hope that with time I'll get all of her.

It's just, after today, I wonder if it's too late. There's not a lot of time these days and sometimes I feel like I have a pickaxe, just working away at her, hoping she'll let me in.

We said some things we shouldn't have and took two steps back. Maybe even three. I know it scared the hell out of both of us for many different reasons and we were jerks about it. And I really should have kept my temper under control in front of my son. That was a dad fail.

I squeeze Hunter tight and close my eyes, not bothering to see if Nova has responded or not, and try to drift off to sleep, try to train my mind to stop dwelling on all the should haves.

A knock at my door rouses me out of my half-asleep state.

I sit up and look at Hunter, who is rolling over and rubbing his eyes.

"Who is it?" Hunter asks, then his eyes widen. "Is it the Menehune?"

"No," I say quickly. "You stay here. Maybe Loan went for a late night walk and locked herself out."

But when I go downstairs and pass by Loan's bedroom, I can hear her snoring loudly through the closed door.

I'm not normally a paranoid person but I am in a strange state—literally and figuratively—and I don't know if I'm still shaken up over today or if I've angered an obsessed hockey fan or maybe this is the Menehune coming to look for my son, but I end up grabbing a hockey stick off the wall and creep forward to the front door.

The front door is frosted glass and I can see the shadow of weirdest fucking shape outside on the front steps. It's got like an extra head and extra long arms and, fucking hell, I must be hallucinating. Hunter did say the Menehune were small, right?

I grip the hockey stick and swing open the door.

Nova is standing outside.

In a damn wetsuit.

With her mosquito-fighting headlamp on her head.

A fly swatter in one hand.

And a jar in the other.

"Nova?" I ask her. "I think you've gone to the bad place."

"I'm here for Hunter," she says, raising her chin.

I shake my head, running my hand over my face. "Wh...what?"

"I'm a Menehune Exterminator, at your service."

I stare at her, nearly dropping the hockey stick.

She nods at it. "You can put that away. The Menehune can break your hockey stick in half. Is Hunter up? I can do a live removal right now."

This is blowing my ever-loving mind.

"It's midnight," I tell her, stepping outside and getting a better look at her. "Why are you here? In a wetsuit. What's with the jar..." I lean in close to take a look at it and then jerk back. "There's a fucking gecko in there!"

"It's Dwayne Johnson for your information," she says, walking up to me. "He'll keep the Menehune away." She stares expectantly at me and I can see an apology running through her eyes.

"You don't have to do this," I tell her. "It's fine. I shouldn't have texted you that, it was a dick move."

She adjusts her headlamp, getting me right in the eyes. "I do need to do this. But I don't want to disturb him if he happened to fall asleep."

"What's going on?" Hunter says from behind me. "Who are you?"

I turn around to see him in the doorway staring at Nova with big eyes.

With her hair pulled back the way it is and the wetsuit, I could see how he might be confused.

"I'm Supernova, your Menehune Exterminator. I heard you have an emergency."

He nods enthusiastically. "Yeah there's one under my bed and he wants to eat my toes."

"That's no good. May I come in and assess the situation?" she asks.

"Come, come," Hunter says, running back into the house, "follow me."

"Nova," I say to her, grabbing her by the arm before she goes inside. She stares up at me and in her eyes I see a woman who would do anything for my son and therefore a woman who owns my heart. "Thank you," I whisper.

She smiles shyly and then follows Hunter inside.

He leads her upstairs to his room and, after I lock back up, I go after them, grateful that Loan is still sleeping.

When I get to his room, Nova is on all fours on the carpet and poking her head under the bed. It can't be an accident that her luscious, wet-suit clad ass is pointed in my direction. She looks like a fucking superhero...but one of the crazy ones.

Hunter, meanwhile, is sitting on his bed staring at the gecko in the jar. The gecko is staring back at him. I have a really bad feeling about this, like they're about to be best friends.

"Is this really Dwayne Johnson?" Hunter asks, tapping on the glass.

"Yes," Nova says from under the bed, her voice muffled. For a moment I actually buy that she's looking for a Hawaiian goblin.

"I thought he was your favorite," I say, and Nova is so surprised to hear me she bumps her head on the bottom of the bed.

"He is, but he's best at Menehune guarding. Anyway, they're very territorial and he's been fighting with Jeff Geck-oblum lately so I figured he was needed here," she says as she climbs out.

"Did you get him?" Hunter asks her while she adjusts her headlamp.

"No, but that's because he left," she says. "He must have heard me coming and got out of here."

Hunter frowns, as if it's all too easy. "Are you sure?"

"I am absolutely sure," she says. "Remember that us Menehune Exterminators have a lifetime guarantee. He's not coming back, not as long as Dwayne Johnson stays here. Providing your father lets him."

I groan. She threw me right under the bus.

"Can he stay?" Hunter asks. "Please Daddy?"

Ah crap. The *please Daddy*. He knows I'm a sucker for that, ever since he first called me that word.

I cave in. "Only if he's outside. He's not a pet."

"No, of course he's not," Nova says, straightening up. The zipper of her wetsuit has come down just a little over her chest and it takes a lot to keep my eyes focused on her face. "He's a guardian of the house, a Menehune hunter," she goes on. "He'll be outside. But if you do happen to see him inside, it's only because he's protecting your son and it's best to leave him alone."

I want to be mad at her over this. The fact that I now have her fat gecko, which will probably spend all the time in the house because Loan thinks it's good luck and Hunter is probably going to capture him and bring him inside all the time.

But I'm already smiling. It's a tired, reluctant smile but a smile all the same.

I'm in fucking love with this woman.

That's really all there is to it now.

"All right, fine."

Nova grins.

Hunter lets out a squeal.

"But it's really late now and you have to go to bed, Hunter."

"What about the gecko?"

"How about we go downstairs and let him in the back-yard? He protects the whole house best from there." Nova takes Hunter's hand and grabs the gecko jar in the other and goes downstairs. I can hear the back door slide open and a few muffled words and then the two of them come back up.

"Better now?" I ask Hunter, arranging his bed for him.

He nods. "Yup. I'm safe now."

"Okay, well get into bed and go to sleep."

"Good night Daddy," he says, as I pull the blankets over him.

"Good night Hunter," I tell him.

"Good night Menehune Extra-irminator," he says to her.

She laughs. "Sweet dreams. Just remember, you're safe now. The gecko is protecting you and your daddy is too."

I have a feeling he's fallen asleep before we even leave the room.

I close the door halfway and then grab Nova's hand, pulling her toward my bedroom.

"I better go," she says, pulling back.

"No, we need to talk," I tell her, leading her to the room and closing the door. "We need to talk about today. And you need to take off that damn thing on your head."

She sighs, sitting on the edge of the bed and bringing the headlamp off and into her lap, switching off the light.

"Kess, I'm sorry," she says.

"And I'm sorry too," I tell her. "For a lot of things. I shouldn't have been so angry, it wasn't your fault."

"But you're right, I am too self-involved. I should have been watching him," she says quietly, voice soft as air. "I don't know what happened."

"I know what happened," I tell her, sitting next to her, hands clasped in my lap. "Shit got very real, very fast. That was the scariest thing to ever happen to me and I know it couldn't have been easy for you."

When she looks at me, her sweet eyes are brimming with tears. "I thought I lost you," she says. "When I saw you jump in the pool and you sank...I thought I lost both of you forever." She pauses, taking in a wavering breath. "I shut down inside. I thought about how risky all of this is, to be with someone when you could lose them. Again. And I just shut off...and I hate how I do that, Kess, I really do. I want to change. I want to be with you."

"You are with me, baby," I tell her, taking her hand and kissing her knuckles. "I've got you and I'm not letting go. It was just a fight. It was a scary fucking moment and a lot of shit came out because of it, shit that I should have been dealing with like an actual functioning human being. I talk a lot, Nova, but my actions don't always follow through and I'm sorry. I need to step it up too."

She chews on her lip, looking more crestfallen and vulnerable than I've ever seen her. "Nova," I say softly. "We're okay. None of this was your fault. I was scared shit-less when I sank but I wasn't thinking of you and how mad I was. When I ran to save Hunter, I wasn't even thinking about how I'd probably drown. All I thought about was that I would do anything for my son, no matter what, and tonight I learned that you'd do anything for him too. And now I'm thinking, you know what, he's a fucking lucky kid to have two bumbling adults in his life who would risk their life for him." I gesture at her outfit. "Or humiliation, as it were."

"This was nothing," she says, looking down at herself.

I grin. "Nova. I know you. You know I find you adorable with the headlamp and hot as sin in this wetsuit. What was something was the fact that you drove all the way here when we were both mad at each other and did this for Hunter. And, by way of that, you did this for me. You're a very proud stubborn woman. This sort of thing does not come easy to you and, believe me, I appreciate it."

I thought that would get a smile out of her but instead she gets up off the bed and starts pacing back and forth in front of me. I'm not sure what to do, if she's about to unload something awful on me, if she's going to put things back together. I watch in fear and awe, waiting.

When she finally stops pacing she looks at me again and it's like she's taken off a mask. Her eyes plead with me while her heart is on her sleeve.

"I know I'm difficult," she whispers hoarsely, hands flying to her sides. "I'm cynical and hard in places and too soft and sensitive in others. I'm running cold one second and then I'm a fiery volcano the next, with no way to turn me off. I'm ambitious and competitive and a little too focused. I should be more social. I should call more people and make more plans. Sometimes it feels like my head isn't on straight, some days I just want to stay in bed and cry. At night I get unbelievably afraid in the moments before I fall asleep, like I'm scared to let go and drift away, while in the mornings even three pots of coffee aren't enough to make me human. I want too much and I worry that I want too much. I want people to love me but I'm afraid to love them first. Most of all, I'm afraid that I'll lose the ones I do love because I was too much of something for them. Too much of me. Too broken and flawed and imperfect and selfish, with too much wrong in me and not enough right." She pauses, taking in a deep shaking breath that I feel to the very soul of me. "I wish I were easier to love."

And there it is.

Her truth offered to me on a fragile plate.

She's trusting me with it.

I've never wanted anything more.

"Nova," I manage to whisper. "It was just a fight. I'm not going anywhere." I get up, my legs shaking, maybe from the pool, maybe from what I'm about to say. I gently take her face between my hands, cupping it. "I love you. I love you so incredibly much it's like I'm seeing this world in color for the first time and it's nothing but the most beautiful sunrises and sunsets and even the stars make the night sky shine."

I kiss her and already things are brighter, lighter.

"Kessler," she whispers against my lips, almost whimpering

I pull back an inch, resting my forehead against her. "You don't have to say it. I know you didn't come here to tell me you love me and if you did, you did it without words. It's enough for me, just to have you here. Just to let me tell you that I love you."

"I can't believe you love me," she whispers.

"I do. Very much. So much. More than enough. I love you now in ways I never could have back then because I didn't understand what it meant. I didn't understand how much I wanted it, needed it. It took losing you once to know that I won't lose you again. Just...tell me that you at least Aloha me."

A wry smile creeps on her lips as she frowns. "Aloha you?"

"Yes. You don't have to say you love me, I get it, you need to do things in your own way and in your own time. But tell me you Aloha me, at least."

"Kess, no...that's not how the word works."

"No? That's totally how the word works. Aloha has a million different meetings. It's more than just hello or a greeting. It's a way of life. That's what all the postcards say. It's a spirit and you're my spirit. You're my Aloha."

"It's cheesy."

"Just because something is cheesy, doesn't mean it's not valid or good. I mean, what is cheesy but too much cheese and, honestly, how could you ever have too much cheese? Cheese is fucking awesome. Brie and pecorino and smoked applewood cheddar..."

"Kessler..."

"Aloha is everything," I go on. "It's the land and sea and sky and harmony. It's a way of life." I grab her by the shoulders. "Aloha means never having to say you're sorry."

"Stop."

"I'm just a boy standing in front of a girl, asking her to Aloha him."

She's laughing now. "Please."

"Nova, you...*Aloha* me," I say in my best Tom Cruise impression.

"You had me at Aloha?" she offers.

"Yes! You had me at Aloha."

"Can we stop saying the word Aloha now? It's starting to sound funny."

"Okay fine, but I had you at Aloha."

"Yes," she says with a reluctant sigh. "You did."

At least she admits it.

"Now come, let me get you out of this wetsuit. Where did you get this anyway?"

She pushes my roving hands away as I reach for her zipper. "Sometimes the water gets cold enough here."

"Well I wouldn't know because I am never going in the ocean again."

She gives me a sympathetic look. "Yes, you are. I know today was scary but I have no doubt that even if I didn't jump in after you, you would have made it out. I mean, fuck man, you have some powerful quads."

"I gave you a good wallop, didn't I?" I wince.

She shrugs. "I've had worse. But I'm being serious. I know it felt like you were drowning but you were keeping yourself afloat, not me. Like I could keep a man your size afloat like that. And you saved Hunter's life, so really, I think you're part fish already. I think you'll both be one with the ocean in no time."

"If you think I'm about to turn into Aquaman, you have another thing coming."

She grins at me. "All I know is that if you wanted to dress up as Jason Momoa, I wouldn't mind."

"That guy is Hawaiian isn't he?"

She nods.

"That fucker. All the women want him because he can swim."

She raises her brow. "Yeah," she says dryly. "That's totally the reason why."

"So about you taking off this wetsuit," I tell her. "Unless you have a hole somewhere, then you can keep it on."

"I'm going to go," she says, heading for the door.

"Why?"

"It's very late now and I just wanted to drop by."

"You can't just come here unannounced, exterminate a Hawaiian goblin, leave me a gecko, and then fuck off."

"I'll see you on Monday, Kess," she says.

I grumble in response as I see her out.

"See you Monday."

CHAPTER SEVENTEEN

NOVA

I NEVER THOUGHT I'd look forward to a Monday like this before.

I never thought I'd look forward to *any* day like this.

After the horrors of Saturday and the near drowning at the pool, after I showed up at his house, ready to fight the mythical Menehune, everything changed.

I unloaded on Kessler everything I'd felt about myself, all my fears, all my insecurities, all the things I'm strangely proud of too. I didn't want to hide anything from him anymore, didn't want to be a closed book.

I realized I was in love with him and I was past the point of no return.

There was no saving me from heartache.

If it happened, it happened.

I couldn't protect my heart from it even if I tried, and if I did try, I would miss out on all the joy there is in giving in and loving someone.

It's a surrender.

I was waving my flag.

And he waved his right back.

He loved me.

Loved me with all his ambition and brawn and ridiculousness and sweat.

Scratch that—*loves* me.

Present tense.

Because he does.

I left his house late Saturday night feeling his love beating in every corner of my body, like it had fused with my blood and infiltrated my veins and turned me into someone new, someone better.

Yeah, I know. That's the cheese I accused him of and I'm living it right now.

It's actually kind of hard not to be cheesy. I guess that's what love does to you, a minor drawback, if you will. All sense of cool has been compromised.

But I don't care.

Because it makes me happy, and if something makes you happy, what more do you want?

Of course, now all I want is to be with Kessler. I loved spending as much time as I could with him before but the whole love declaration pushed us to another level. Like, it's pulled back that lever I had deep in my gut, the one that caused me to lose my mind over Kessler in the first place, and I'm at level-ten obsession now.

This is what happens when you let go.

Thankfully, I think Kessler is down for it, to have me go all doting, gushing school girl crush on him.

After all, I still have to tell him I love him.

I guess I'm just not sure how.

Yesterday I spent the day at home, with only a few texts between us. He had promised Loan that he would take her and Hunter out to some Vietnamese festival thing and I decided it was probably a good thing to let them have their time together, especially since Loan does so much for them.

It was hard though, spending that one day away from him when all I wanted to do was just lie in his arms and stare at him like some damn fool.

And so, now it's Monday.

I'm at work.

He's at work.

And it's taking all of me not to go over to his office and say hello. I have a million excuses too, and yet I manage to keep my distance and put my head down and work.

Then, at four-thirty, it turns out I have a meeting with him, Desiree and George.

About twenty minutes prior I knock on Kessler's door.

"Come in," he says. He looks surprised to see me when I walk in, shutting the door behind me. "Where have you been all day?"

"Trying to be a good girl."

"I don't know if I like you as a good girl. Where's that nasty one who is usually hanging around?"

I laugh and come over to him, putting my arm around his shoulders and giving him a giddy kiss. "Oh, she's around." I pull back. "Hey, do you know what this meeting is about?"

He shrugs and that's when I notice his forehead is *glistening*. "I don't know," he says.

"But you're nervous."

"What makes you say that?"

"Because you're sweating and it's minus eleven million degrees in here." I usually have to put on a cardigan when I come in his office.

"Oh." He wipes at his forehead. "Well, then yes. I'm a bit nervous."

"Okay then I'm nervous."

"We shouldn't be though. We always have meetings with George."

"Not Desiree. Not HR. We haven't had a meeting with her since, well, your first day."

"God that feels so long ago," he says with a sigh.

"It kind of was. And a lot has happened since then."

Like the fact that I love you.

The words sweep through my mind like pink puffy clouds.

God, I'm pathetic.

"Do you think it has something to do with us?" he asks. "I mean, like you and me and all the sex?"

That's actually what I was afraid of. "I don't know. Should we have a game plan for when we go in there?"

"Well they can't actually fire us for it. I checked the guidelines."

"Did you?"

"Hey, a boss can get in some major trouble for screwing his employee. And vice versa. You know this. Of course I wanted to make sure it was okay."

"And is it?"

"It didn't say it was *not* okay."

I'm not sure if that's enough to stand on and it does nothing to make the nerves go away. When the meeting rolls around, I'm sweating as much as Kessler would in a sauna.

I knock on Desiree's door and go inside.

George is standing up and leaning against a table. Desiree is at her desk. Kessler is sitting across from her, giving me an uneasy smile. It's déjà vu all over again.

"Nova, you're here," George says with a pleasant smile. "Please, have a seat."

I nod at George and Desiree and sit down next to Kessler.

"You're probably wondering why we called you in here," Desiree says. "But it's getting close to your three-month probation and we need to discuss the next steps."

I swallow hard, wondering why I'm in the meeting if it's all about Kessler.

"Kessler, we've all been very happy with the work you've been producing and your ideas are top-notch. You really seem to have your finger on the pulse of our audience and that's great. And Nova, the same goes for you. Your hard work never goes unnoticed here and we know you're a big part of our ohana. And, as we know, ohana is everything and we would hate one day for you to leave our ohana because you don't feel appreciated. We all appreciate you, truly."

Damn. This is the nicest thing Desiree has ever said to me, even though I have no idea where this is all going.

"You see, Desiree and I had a heck of a predicament on our hands," George says, clasping his fingers in front of him. "Both of you are equally qualified for Kessler's role and both of you deserve it. We started thinking of maybe splitting the role in half, even though it would have become a logistical nightmare. You know how that is."

"And that's when Kessler called for a meeting with the two of us," Desiree fills in.

My head swivels to Kessler, brows raised.

What?

He held a secret meeting with them?

"Kessler, do you want to tell her what you proposed?" George asks.

Kessler turns slightly in his chair to face me. "You see, the other day I was at the skating rink and I was talking to them and out of the blue, I suddenly proposed a hockey school. Something I would get going through crowd-sourcing or fund-raising, something maybe the NHL would help support. I want to get into the game again in some shape or form and I know how much hockey helped me when I was young and things were rough. It's all about that ohana that Desiree was talking about. I thought it was just a line from Lilo and Stitch, but it turns out to be an actual thing."

I can't even form words. My lips come together and break apart as I stare at Kessler to go on.

"So," he says, "I decided that this was what I wanted to work towards. And I know it's risky and scary and I don't want to give up working at Kahuna Hotels either. So I decided to step down from my position as VP and, hopefully, take yours. I say take over yours, because you're going to be taking over mine." He pauses. "I wasn't sure if that was clear."

"Do you still want the job, Nova?" Desiree asks. "I know we all want you for it."

"Are you serious?" I manage to say after a few beats. "It's mine?"

George nods. "This worked out perfectly for us. Kessler will stay with us as long as he needs to and you'll be his boss now. Aren't role reversals fun? Heck, I live for this kind of stuff."

I am stunned.

Just...I can't believe Kessler would do that.

"Are you sure?" I whisper to him. "I know how much this all meant to you."

He nods, smiling. "It still means a lot. But I like to go where my life takes me and right now I think it's back to hockey. I really think you'd be amazing at this job. And you know it too."

I do know it. Doesn't mean I'm not surprised.

Doesn't mean I'm not scared.

But it also doesn't mean I'm not ready.

"Thank you," I tell Kessler. I look at Desiree and George. "Thank you guys. I won't let you down."

I shake their hands and I can't stop smiling.

I did it!

I got it.

And I have never been so turned on in my whole life.

The minute we get away from their office, I grab Kessler and drag him all the way to mine. It's late now anyway so everyone is gone and frankly I don't care who sees because I'm a big motherfucking boss now!

I yank him into my office, shut the door, and slam him back against my desk, immediately devouring him.

"My god, had I known this would happen I would have given up my job a long time ago," he manages to say.

I pause and look at him. "But you're not *giving* it up."

"Not in so many words," he says. "I'm stepping aside and handing it over."

"You're really sure about this? You're not going to resent me?"

"Baby, I love you. I could never resent you. Just as long as you don't think this is charity."

"Fuck no it's not. I earned it."

"Yes, you did. Now you're the boss. Who's Demi Moore now?"

"I thought it was always me," I grin at him.

And as Kessler stares back at me, I feel strength and courage where there wasn't before.

Courage of the heart.

I run my fingers down the side of his face, feeling his stubble. He turns his mouth toward my hand and kisses my palm.

"I...I love you," I whisper to him. "No Aloha. I *love* you."

He breaks into the sweetest grin. "I love you too, Nova." He kisses me softly and when he pulls away, he has a strange glint in his eye. "There. Now was that so fucking hard?"

"What?" I exclaim. "Telling you I love you?"

"Yeah."

Is he crazy?

"Fuck yes it was hard. My god, I never told you the first time, to gather the courage to do it the second time..."

He waves me away with his hand. "Nah." He grins. "You love someone, you feel it, you say it. I did it with you. I did it with you not knowing how you felt, just knowing that if you showed up at my house at midnight dressed in Menehune fighting gear and carrying a gecko all to help my son, I figured you might at least care about me a little bit."

I can't believe him. "You're taking this so lightly. Love is a big deal. You *know* it's a big deal with me. You even said so yourself."

"It is a big deal," he says, taking my hand and kissing my fingers. "But people also make it out to be more complicated than it already is. It doesn't need to be so hard. People just like to create problems for themselves."

I take my hand away and fold my arms. "Since when are you an expert in love all of a sudden?"

"Since I met Hunter," he says.

And that's when I know to shut up.

He shrugs. "I didn't think it would happen like it did. I was prepared to love him the moment I heard about him, you know? Like I was ready for him. That's why I wanted everything to do with his mother. I wanted everything to do with him. And when I got that call, as scary as it was to suddenly start being a father for the first time, I knew my heart was ready for it. It sounds cheesy as fuck but I don't care. I've become a total fucking cheesy sweaty beast since I've come here and I'm embracing that too. It's just...when you're ready for love, everything in your life changes. Doors open. Opportunities happen. You meet new people...and you reconnect with old ones."

I shake my head as I look him over. He's one hundred percent sincere. I can see it, I can hear it. All my preconceived notions I still had about this big lug have dissipated just like that.

"You really are a changed man," I muse.

He pulls me close to him, his hands going around my waist. "We all change when we're ready for it. You've changed."

I avert my eyes and look away. "I don't know about that."

"You have. You've changed from the woman I knew five years ago."

I snort dryly. "Yeah. For the worse."

"No, for the better. It took you a little while to find your footing but you're there now. You're no longer a girl with dreams. You're a woman who turned those dreams into goals. And you've got it. At least, you've got one hunk of a man with a giant dick and, really, what more can you want than that."

I grin at him, feeling saucy and sweet and a million emotions all at once.

"I really do love you," I tell him, and just as those words leave my mouth, I realize he's right.

I made it more difficult than it was.

I love him.

I *love* him.

He grabs my hand and places it on his erection. "How much do you love me?"

"Kessler," I say, biting my lip as I start tugging at his collar. "You know we have a rule."

"No falling in love with your boss? I'm afraid we both broke that one now."

"The rule where we don't fuck around in the office. Which means no acting like a couple and no fucking."

"That's a stupid rule," he says with a devilish grin as he leans forward and sucks my lower lip in between his teeth. "And as the new boss, your first order of action should be to disavow it."

My eyes close momentarily, my hand gripping his dick tighter.

I thought I wanted him badly before but now, after what he's done for me, after I know I truly have his love, my desire is ten-fold.

I want him inside me knowing that I'm his and he's mine and I'm safe.

I want him now.

"I won't tell a soul," he murmurs, kissing the corner of my mouth. I'm already getting breathless. "It might even help my year-end evaluation."

"Does the sexy boss talk work in reverse?"

"Mmmm," he says as he licks my earlobe, my weak spot. "It works for me. I can make it really work for you." His hand reaches over my ass and tugs me into him while pulling up my skirt. "Fuck, you little tease. You're not wearing underwear to work?"

I smile. "I forgot."

"Bullshit." He bites my lobe, tugging at it. "Bull*shit*."

Okay, let's throw that stupid rule out the window for today. It's not like anyone is here in the office, at least they shouldn't be.

"I can feel you giving in," he says to me, nibbling down my neck and collarbone. "I kind of like it when you argue back."

"Sorry," I tell him. "I can't be a cranky bitch all the time."

"That's too bad. I think we fight really well."

"But I think we might make love even better."

"We'll see," he says, stepping back from me. "Take off your clothes."

I do as he says, taking off my blouse and bra and skirt, kicking off my heels.

"Get on the desk," he says, undoing his shirt. Then he pauses, noticing all the shit scattered on my desk. So, I'm a bit cluttered. The whole clearing the desk to have sex scenario doesn't always work.

"What is this?" he asks, picking up a large figurine of a fat hula dancer that's meant to be for the dashboard of a truck. He peers at it closely. "Why does it say Bradah Ed on it?"

"Because it's a *guy*," I tell him, taking it from him.

"Does Bradah Ed know about it?"

"Bradah Ed gave it to me for Christmas," I tell him, as Kessler takes it back.

A wicked gleam comes across his eyes as he holds it in his hands.

"What?" I ask warily.

He shrugs. "I don't know, he's so much larger than a normal hula dancer, maybe he could join in the fun."

I shake my head in disbelief. "You're wanting to put that thing up my ass, aren't you?"

"Maybe."

I take Bradah Ed from his hands and put it back on the desk. "Bradah Ed isn't going anywhere near my asshole."

"Okay," he says with a grin, pulling me to him, running his hands down my naked back and giving my ass a squeeze. "As long as I'm allowed."

"We'll see," I say, as I start to strip him of his clothes.

But it's not long before my desk is cleared of all the clutter and I'm bent over it.

And it's not long after that, when Kessler is sitting in the chair and I'm riding his cock.

And then I'm slammed against the wall as he fucks me upright, pounding me as my legs wrap around his waist, riding out orgasm after orgasm as the walls shake so hard, more paintings fall down. Bradah Ed falls off the edge of the desk. My world is just sweat and skin and moans and cries and pineapples.

Somehow we end up on the floor at the end of it, breathing hard in each other's arms.

"Man, that was..." Kessler starts, but he's interrupted by a timid knock at my door.

"Hey guys," Teef's voice comes through from the other side. Oh god, please let him not barge in this time. "Are you done with your, uh, fun times yet or are you starting up again? Because I'm doing my podcast from my office and my microphone is super sensitive. It's picking up everything. I'm trying to keep it PG since it's a baking podcast and all."

Kessler and I stare at each other, wide-eyed.

"Uh, we're done!" Kessler yells at him.

"Mahalo, brah," Teef says.

Then we both burst out laughing.

"I can't believe we ruined his podcast," I say between giggles.

"I can't believe his podcast is about *baking*," Kessler says.

"You didn't wonder why he always had a tin of cookies with him?"

"I just assumed he was always high."

"You should try his cookies," I tell him. "They're amazing."

"Mahalo Nova!" I hear Teef say from outside the door. Obviously he hasn't moved an inch. "I like to have feedback on my creations."

"Teef, are you still standing outside the door?" Kessler asks.

Pause.

"Uh, yeah, sorry. I guess I should give you some privacy. *A hui hou.*"

And then he's gone.

Leaving Kessler and I in peace.

Still laughing our naked asses off on my office floor.

CHAPTER EIGHTEEN

IT'S JUST after dinner when the phone rings.

And not my cell phone.

The actual landline on the wall in the kitchen.

"Should I answer it?" Loan asks, even as she's picking up the phone and going, "Hello? Hello?" She frowns at the phone and hangs it back up. "That's strange, no one there. They hung up."

Suddenly there's a knock at the door.

"Who could that be?" I ask, getting up. I look over at Nova, who is sitting on the couch and watching *Finding Nemo* with Hunter. Her eyes widen. "Oh my god," she says. "This happened in a book I read once. The guy would call the house and then hang up and then he'd rob them."

"What book was that?"

"Claudia and the Phantom Phonecaller. But in the end they caught they robber and the guy calling her was just some dweeb who had a crush on her. You don't have anyone who has a crush on you, do you Loan?"

"Hey, why did you ask Loan and not me?" I ask, going down the hall to the door.

Through the frosted glass I see a shadowy figure of a man but because it's about seven at night, it probably doesn't warrant me grabbing a hockey stick from the wall.

I open the door.

My jaw drops when I see who it is.

"Holy shit," I say. "Mike, is that you?"

He nods. "It's me, in the flesh."

Somehow Mike Epson, the man whose house I live in, the man who gave me his job, who set me up with Loan, who made all of this happen, is standing right in front of me, looking like he never left at all.

I'm kind of speechless. "I didn't expect to see you for a long time," I tell him, blinking rapidly.

He gives me a bitter smile and picks up the two tattered duffel bags beside him. "I didn't either. There's been a change of plans."

Uh oh.

This isn't going to be good.

I open the door wider for him and follow him into the house.

His house.

"Hey everyone, I'm home," he says as he comes to the living room, looking all over the place. "Hey Nova! What are you doing here? Oh hey, you must be Hunter. Loan, good to see you. I got you some rice crackers from Bangkok."

Everyone, including Hunter, is staring up at Mike in his obnoxious pink and green Hawaiian shirt, questions on the tip of everyone's tongues.

Finally, Hunter goes, "Who are *you*?"

"Well, Hunter. My name is Mike Epson. And this is my house."

"Oh. You're the man who likes leprechauns."

Mike cocks a brow. "Come again?"

"What happened Mike?" I ask him. "Like, why are you here? Now. You said you wouldn't be back...at all. Ever."

He sighs and tugs at the collar of his shirt. "Yeah, I know what I said but...What can I say? The course of true love never runs smoothly." He plops down on the couch beside Nova and puts his hand on her bare knee, which immediately makes me step forward, wanting to punch him in the face.

Nova eyes his hand and gently lifts his hand off of her. "What's going on Mike? You could have called or something. Then again, you never gave any warning when you left before."

"Right, right," he says, wringing his hands awkwardly together. "Here's the thing. I'm an idiot, so let's get that out of the way. I met a woman, Patrice, and she was unlike any human I had ever met. I fell in love with her and I think she fell in love with me. I know, who can believe it, right? But it's true. And what do you do when cupid shoots its arrow into your heart? You follow the dance of love."

Fucking hell, I hope I don't sound like that.

"Well, anyhoo," he goes on. "As you know, I gave it all up to be with her. She was leaving the next day back to Thailand and I decided it was now or never. So I went." He sighs. "It was beautiful there. For weeks we traveled from place to place and she would visit her friends and I would stay in the hotel room and then after a while I realized her friends were in the movie business and she was acting with them."

I clear my throat, eyeing Hunter for a moment. "Uh, didn't you know about her, uh, occupation in the adult film world before?"

"Oh yes, that was part of the appeal!"

Nova makes a face.

"I just thought she was giving it up, you know? I mean, okay, I knew that's how she made her money but after a few weeks of filming I realized I was kind of jealous. Me! I know. I'm not a jealous guy and yet there I was. At one point I was feeling so left out that I asked to take part in the film and you know what role she gave me? Chinese takeout delivery man. I had to play the part of the guy who inter- rupts them. Now, I thought maybe I could have a speaking line and it would bring me one step closer to being union but that never happened."

"Mike, Mike, Mike," I mutter.

"I know. I really bungled that up! So, finally I told Patrice that I had enough. It was her or me. And I guess she chose all those other dicks instead of mine. Did you know that it's not actually acting in those movies? They're actu- ally having sex! Some of it I don't even think can be called sex." He shakes his head, looking disgusted and I'm so fucking grateful that Nova has her hands over Hunter's ears.

Then Mike slaps his knee. "Anyhoo, I left her and now I'm back here. As you can imagine, I'll be taking back the house and my old job."

"What?!" Me, Nova, and Loan all yell in unison.

He raises his brows at us, palms raised as he gets to his feet. "Sheesh. I guess I did kind of spring this on you."

"You can take your house back," I tell him. "The three of us can find somewhere else to live. But you can't just take your job back."

"Sure I can. I gave it away. Now I'm taking it back."

His smile is so happy and naïve and oblivious that I only want to punch him more.

I glance at Nova and back to him. "No, you don't under-stand. When you left, the job became mine."

"But the three months isn't up yet," he reminds me with a hokey wag of his finger. "It was all temporary."

"Be that as it may," I say carefully, so I'm not yelling. "We had a meeting today. Me, Nova, George, and Desiree. I gave up my job."

"What? Why would you do that?"

"Because I realized there are other things I want to do and more than that, there are other people who deserve the job more."

"People like who?"

Holy fuck he's dense.

"Me," Nova says to him boldly. "I deserved the job. I did from the start."

"You?" He gives her a dismissive shake of his head. "No offence my dear, but you're not cut out for it."

"Why not?" I ask, feeling defensive on her behalf, even though she doesn't need me to defend her.

"Because," he says to me now, not her. "She's...too emotional for it. You have to think sharp to be an executive. You have to know how to play in the big leagues, isn't that a good metaphor for you Kessler? And, hey, I am all for woman moving up in the world, I know the whole hashtag 'me too' thing, I know that women should probably get more pay and I especially know a woman like Nova should be paid more attention to."

Nova's face is nearly frozen with rage at literally every-thing he's just said. Actually, when I look at Loan, she looks the exact same way.

"What do you mean, a woman like *me*?" Nova asks, nearly spitting out the words.

Mike shrugs a bunch of times, all awkward as fuck. It's

like watching a car crash. "You know. You're, you know, not white. And I applaud that and all, you know, you go girl and raise the roof and such."

My head is in my hands. This is painful.

"But," he goes on. He fucking *goes on* when he needs to shut up. "I think equality means equal for all and it doesn't equal special treatment just because you're a woman or have a nice cappuccino skin tone."

Nova gasps and it's like the entire room is vacuumed of air.

This man is *dead*.

"I'll have you know that my skin tone is more than someone's coffee, first of all," she manages to say, and I don't know how she sounds so succinct and refined when I know she's a raging ball of fire inside. "And second of all, everything you've just said is not only completely inappropriate, but it's just plain wrong. I'm not asking to be given special treatment. I've worked my ass off extra hard to ensure that doesn't happen. I'm just asking to be looked at as an equal. You should have always given the job to me, it's what I've been working toward for so long. And I thought you, as my boss, knew that. I thought you respected me. Now I know it wouldn't have mattered as long as you were above me. You would just keep me down because that's where you think I belong."

She gets up and walks right up to him, looking him dead in the eyes with the kind of stare that would make any man's balls shrivel into prunes. "But let me tell you. Where I belong is miles above you. In the sun and the moon and the stars, motherfucker. I'm a Supernova."

And with that, she sashays past him, grabbing her purse and heading down the hall.

"Wait!" I call after her, grabbing her before she goes

outside. "Don't go. I mean, that was awesome what you just did, but don't go."

"I don't have to stand here and listen to this shit." She frowns. "Thanks for jumping in by the way."

"Baby, it's my turn to lay into him next. I just know you don't need an ounce of help in defending yourself."

She rolls her eyes. "I doubt he gets it."

"It doesn't matter."

"Yeah, well this is all sorts of fucked up, Kessler. What are you going to do now? What am I going to do? You're out of a house, I'm out of a job."

"You're not out of a job, Mike is fucked in the head. I think he has syphilis or something now because he's not making any sense at all."

"What are you going to do then, kick him out of his own house?"

"I'll take the couch or double up with Hunter."

"You know you can stay with me."

"I know. I will if it gets weird." I look back down the hall to the living room where Mike is watching the movie with Hunter and I can hear Loan swearing in Vietnamese. "It might get weird."

"Good luck, Kess."

I exhale and kiss her on the lips. "I'm so proud of you baby. It had to feel good to stand up to him like that."

But she looks a little sad. "It did. I just wish I didn't have to do it to begin with. I always thought he was on my side."

"I know. But it was pretty obvious he wasn't when he gave the job to a lug like me."

She smiles. "You're not a lug. You're a hunk. And you're mine." She pulls me into a deep hug. "I love you."

"I love you," I tell her, holding her tight until she's

breathless. Then I reluctantly let her go. "See you at work tomorrow. Wear your armor. We're going into battle."

She gives me a small wave. "I'll bring my headlamp."

I BARELY SLEPT LAST NIGHT.

Not only because I had to sleep on the couch and give up the bedroom to Mike, who was doing all sorts of weird things in there. I don't know if he was watching porn and crying over it or what, but that's exactly what it sounded like.

But because, well, my life turned upside down in the snap of Mike's greasy fingers.

One minute I had a house, the next minute I didn't.

One minute I had stepped aside and given Nova my role, the role she deserves, the next minute *Mike* thinks he's my boss. I didn't give up the motherfucking job for him. I still like the role. I gave it up because Nova was more deserving and it would give me more motivation to concentrate on the hockey school.

Now everything's all fucked up and I had the most awkward ride into work ever with Mike, who insisted I drive because he'd sold his car when he packed up and left.

"And you haven't told anyone at work that you're back?" I ask Mike as we step into the elevator. He's wearing an orange and red Hawaiian shirt today, which makes my eyes burn.

"It's always better when it's a surprise," he says all happy-go-lucky. "Hey Kessler, when you played for the Kings, how close were you to Wayne Gretzky?"

I give him a look. "Gretzky played for them in 1989. Just how old do you think I am?"

The elevator doors ding open before he can answer.

"What the shit?" Kate says, as we walk in the lobby. "Mike. You're back?"

He holds his arms out. "I'm back, baby" and starts walking down the hall, probably to my office.

"This is a surprise," Kate says, looking to me.

"Yes, it is," I tell her. I lean in close to her desk. "Did Nova already come in?"

She shakes her head. "Not yet. But hey, that was pretty big of you man to give her your job. That takes balls. It's all that Big Dick Energy."

"She deserves it more and I'm ready for other things," I tell her. "But Mike is taking her job back. So he says."

"Oh shit," she swears. "That's my one motto in life! No takesies backsies." She pauses. "And never have sex with a guy with a man bun." She reads the expression on my face. "What? I had some weird experiences."

I'm shaking my head at her when suddenly Desiree appears looking flustered. "Kessler," she hisses. "Is Nova here?"

"I don't know if she's coming in today," I admit. "I texted her this morning but no response."

"Yeah well I just saw Mike sitting down in your office," she says. "I might need some help with him."

"You want me to throw him out? Because after what he said to Nova last night, I wouldn't mind that at fucking all."

"It depends," she says. "I really wish Nova—"

Just then the elevator dings and Nova steps out. Shoulders back, head raised, walking tall in her white blouse and black pencil skirt. She walks in like she owns the damn place, a small smile curved on her lips.

"Good morning Desiree," she says. "Good morning Kessler."

"Hey what about me? You think you're too good for me now that you're promoted!" Kate yells.

Nova rolls her eyes. "Good morning, Kate." She looks back to Desiree, brows raised. "But I guess it remains to see whether I'm still promoted or not."

Desiree's jaw wiggles. "I was waiting for you, Nova. Come with me. Both of you."

Nova and I exchange a look of *what the fuck is going to happen?* and follow Desiree as she marches down the hall.

She marches all the way to my office where Mike is sitting at my desk, already rearranging things and trying to deal with the influx of condoms in all the drawers. "Kessler, you the man," he says to me, or maybe to himself, as we all step inside.

He looks up at us in calm surprise. "What do I owe the pleasure of having all three of you lovely people here?"

"Mike," Desiree says, and she licks her lips and I can tell she's trying to find the right words. It's rare to see her flustered like this. "What are you doing here?"

"Surprised to see me? I know. I was surprised too. But when you gotta go, you gotta go. That's the way it was with Patrice. Both ways, in fact."

"What are you doing *here*," she says, pointing at the desk. "At work. In Kessler's office, which is soon to be Nova's office."

He coughs, frowning. "Well, I'm back. Ta-da. Here I am. Ready for business."

"But you quit," she says. "You quit without even giving your two weeks-notice. You just left and you left us scrambling to fill your position. Which we did. With *two* very talented people." She gestures to Nova and I.

"Aw shucks, I know," Mike says, taking my pineapple stress ball off the desk and squeezing it. He has no idea that

Nova had to bite on that thing to keep from screaming as I screwed her on the desk. "I feel bad for making you come all this way, Kessler, but surely the company can find a place for you. I'll probably need an assistant. And there's always the mail room."

"Mike," Desiree says in a warning tone. I've heard rumors that she's good at martial arts and now I'm waiting to see if she's going to bust out some unsuspecting moves. "You can't just waltz back in here and get your job back. I'm sorry, but you quit."

"Kessler was supposed to be temporary."

"He was temporary because George and I didn't want to commit to someone *you* picked, someone we had no prior knowledge of. Now we know he's done an excellent job but if it had been up to us before you went ahead and filled his position and contacted the poor man and made him and his son move all the way out here, we would have gone another way."

Mike looks at Nova who just gives him a cold stare.

"We would have picked Nova," Desiree informs him. "And, as of yesterday, that's what we settled on. Kessler is taking Nova's position for a while until we find someone else and he's ready to move on to other things, and Nova is now the Senior VP of Sales, Marketing and Revenue. So if you want your job back, well I'm sorry, it's not available. But if you want to apply for a position in the mail room, well, we have your resume on file."

Boom.

Mic drop, Desiree.

Mike stares up at us, blinking. Poor guy. From what I heard, he was never this stupid. I really think the porn star did something to his brain, or who knows what was going down in Thailand with crazy drugs and shit. But right now, well he's a big fucking idiot that just got himself served. I mean, what did he expect?

But of course, now Mike is staring at me, forehead furrowed. "Does this mean I don't get my house back?"

Oh brother. "Mike," I explain. "It's *your* house. Hunter and I will move elsewhere and I've already secured Loan for the next few years out of my own pocket. I really appreciate every single thing you did for me. You changed my life. But now that my life has changed," I glance at Nova and give her a knowing smile, "I want to keep it that way."

After that, Mike seems pretty despondent and out of it. Desiree leads him out of my office and over to hers, where they sit down with George and have a talk.

Nova leans back against my desk, arms folded across her chest. "Is it wrong that I feel sorry for him?" she asks.

"Wrong? No," I say, turning on the AC. "It just means you have a heart, that's all. But don't go giving your job away."

"Phhfff are you crazy? I barely pried it out of your hands, I'm not going to hand it over to him."

"You know, you didn't quite pry it from my hands, I gave it to you," I remind her.

"Yes, in a grand sweeping gesture of love, I know." She grins. "Are you ever going to let me forget it?"

"Hell no. I'll be living with you and I'll be reminding you of it the first thing in the morning and the last thing at night."

"Wait a minute," she says. "Who said you'll be living with me?"

I go around the desk and press up against her, wrapping my arms around her waist. "You did. Last night. You said we could stay with you."

"I meant last night."

"Mmmm," I say into her neck, kissing her softly. "I think you owe me."

"Oh I see, it was all a ruse." She laughs. "Part of your elaborate plan."

"I don't know how elaborate it was but you were always part of the plan. Even if I didn't know it yet." I kiss her earlobe, making her shiver.

"Even when it seemed impossible."

I pull away and gaze into her eyes. "Everything seems impossible until it's not."

She looks up at me through her long lashes. "I guess that's true." She then sighs, burying her head into the crook of my neck. "Poor, poor Mike. I wonder if we'll see him in the copy room. It would be even better if he ended up *my* assistant. Can you imagine?"

I laugh and she goes on. "He was obviously living in some delusion that his life could go back to normal after all the heartbreak he had to endure but that's never the case." She studies my face, pausing at my lips, my nose, my eyes. She smiles. "You're never the same after you get your heart broken. But if you're just lucky enough, maybe you'll find someone to help you pick up the pieces."

"Even if he's your level-ten heartbreaker?"

She kisses me. "Even if."

EPILOGUE

Nova
Two years later

HOLY SHIT.

I am a ball of nerves.

Who knew a beach wedding could be so damn stressful?

Actually, *everyone.*

I kept thinking that a beach wedding in Hawaii would be easy and low-key, especially since we live here, but everyone from Desiree to my mother to Loan told me that weddings were a handful, no matter where you planned it, no matter when you planned it.

And technically I've been planning this wedding since the day Kessler proposed, a year ago. It's just that I've been so busy with work—being an executive is no joke—and so wedding planning was the last thing on my mind. I just wanted it at the beach up from my house (well, our house now), with our closest family and friends.

But then I had to factor in the fact that getting my parents and family in from the mainland and Kessler's family from Portugal was a logistical nightmare, then there was dealing with the press (because with Kessler's hockey school, he's back in the NHL picture) and then all the other nitty gritty things like the dress and hair and makeup and food and permits and flowers and vows.

God, the vows. That's what I'm the most nervous over.

I wrote mine a year ago.

Then proceeded to rewrite it.

And rewrite it.

And rewrite it.

And it's literally the day of the wedding and I'm trying to rewrite it again.

"Nova, stop," my mother says, looking over my shoulder. Mahina is doing my hair (yeah, she's a pro surfer *and* awesome at hair) and just finishing putting it up, pinning plumeria in places, while I'm trying to edit my vows on my phone's note section.

"I just want it to be perfect," I tell my mother.

"Honey, look at me."

I glance up over my shoulder at her, Mahina stepping to the side and pinning another flower above my ear.

"Just relax, honey," my mother says. "Have faith. Deep faith. You know everything is going to be fine."

I nod, taking in a deep breath, as if to conjure my faith from within.

My mom looks absolutely gorgeous. She always does. She's ageless. She has the best skin, so flawless, no wrinkles, her hair is short and natural with a few highlights at the tips from being in the sun. She also has a flower in her hair, a giant coral hibiscus that Mahina clipped in, which matches her lipstick.

She and my father have been in Hawaii for a month now. Once they knew I was getting married, well they couldn't object to my buying their tickets, and my father put his fear of flying aside. But they decided if they were going to come all this way, they wanted to do it in style so they've spent their time on a cruise visiting all the different islands.

I don't want to jinx anything, but I feel like they're falling in love with the state. For years I have been begging them to move out here. With the motel sold and Rubina gone, there's nothing to hold them to Washington except for guilt and memories. I want them to break out of the rain and gloom and spend their days in a place where you feel Aloha in every single part of you.

Selfishly, I want them here for me. I want them to be with me and Kessler and Hunter.

I want them to spend their days on the beach with their new grandchild.

Well, grandchild-to-be.

That's right.

I'm pregnant.

In fact, I'm almost ready to explode. I'm at seven months and my dress has had to be taken out a lot, even though it's empire-waisted. I look like someone's lost beach ball got wedged under here.

I know that we probably should have held off on the whole preggo thing until after the wedding but I'm just going to blame a wild night where I'd been lazy with the pill and Kessler had reached for a piña colada condom and well, surprise. Baby on the way!

Not that we aren't overjoyed. I wasn't sure how badly I wanted to be the mother of Kessler's children until I saw that positive test and then I was smiling through morning sickness.

Okay, that's a bit of a stretch. Morning sickness was absolutely horrendous and it was a lot of Kessler holding my hair back in the bathroom, at the beach, at the pool, etc. But Kessler has been a trooper. He's taken to this pregnancy like nothing else. I think he's finally making up for lost time when he couldn't be there for Hunter.

Speaking of Hunter, he's pretty darn cute about the whole thing and is super protective of the bump, speaking to it already like a big brother. He's five now and, though he's still quiet, he's an active, curious little guy who calls me mom so freely and with so much love that it breaks my heart a little to hear it.

I wasn't aware of how much love I had inside me until I met Kessler.

Until I met Hunter.

Until they asked me to be a part of their lives forever.

Until I learned I was going to bring another soul to love into this world.

Now I feel like a star about to implode in the most beautiful way.

I exhale slowly, letting any fear and worry leave me. It's something I've been working on these last few years, especially after I went into therapy. There were some things to do with Rubina that I hadn't quite dealt with that I needed to deal with. The guilt. The fear. The loss.

My mom massages my shoulders. "There you go. Let it go. All that worry. Honey, you're going to marry the man of your dreams today, the father of your child. That's the only thing that matters right now, nothing else."

I give her a sad smile. "I wish Rubina were here."

She sighs lightly. "I know. You know I do too. But she's around us, she always is. You know that, don't you?"

I nod. I do. I feel it growing in my chest in a place I kept barren until Kessler convinced me otherwise.

"I hate to interrupt," Mahina says quietly. "But I think it's time."

She gestures to the doorway of my bedroom where Kate and Desiree are, dressed in the same teal flowy bridesmaid dress Mahina is wearing. Because we're just blocks from the beach where the wedding is, we figured my house made as good a staging place as any. Plus, there's a lot of POG and champagne here and I'm looking forward to finishing it all off when this is over.

When this is over, Kessler will be my husband.

I wonder if I'll ever stop marveling over that word.

Husband.

I hope I never do.

While Kate squeals over how good I look, my mother picks up my long train and we head out of the house and down the road. Since Mike, who, yes, is my assistant at Kahuna Hotels, picked up the photography hobby out in Thailand (which he insists had nothing to do with porn) he's our wedding photographer and taking pictures, running ahead of us all and making us pose. Occasionally, a flock of chickens get in the shot and I think about Kessler's reaction if it makes the final wedding photos.

And then...it's time.

The beach has been taken over by guests in white chairs flanked by plumeria and orchid blooms, a shell-lined aisle leading up to the altar where Kessler stands with the officiant, and Bradah Ed and Teef as his best man and groomsman, with my bridesmaids on the other side. I know Hunter would have come up the aisle earlier as the ring bearer and I can only imagine how cute that was.

When I start going down the aisle with my father on my arm, I feel all my cares and worries drift away.

"You've never looked more beautiful," my father whispers in my ear, and I see tears glistening in his eyes. I swallow my own tears down and try to keep it together for everyone's sake. I look forward as we walk, my eyes locked on Kessler's. Both he and my father are giving me strength and love every step of the way.

Once at the altar, everything becomes a blur. We went for the shortest ceremony because we didn't want to bore people but it goes way too fast and before I know it, it's time for our vows.

Kessler goes first and I'm holding my breath at how gorgeous he looks, dressed in his tuxedo, reminding me of that New Years when I realized I was in love with him again, even if I didn't know it.

"Nova," Kessler says to me, holding out a wrinkled piece of paper with shaking hands. It's practically see-through. "When people talk about your name, they say you are a new star in the sky. That you suddenly appear where there wasn't a star before, bringing light into the darkness. I couldn't agree with that more. But the truth of what a Nova really is, is that you're not just a star alone. You're part of another star. You're the result of two stars that come together, becoming so much brighter than what those stars were before."

He takes in a deep breath, looks across the crowd, and keeps reading. "That's how I feel with you. That you shine so bright it blinds me but when we're together, we become something else. We transcend the people that we were. We become something greater together, a bright force in an ever darkening sky. Nova when I'm with you, I..."

He trails off, stares at me and I see wetness forming in the corners of his eyes and I really hope that it's sweat because if he starts crying I'm going to break the fuck down.

"Nova, I..." He goes back to reading from the paper.

Frowns.

Looks up at me.

Looks at our officiant and gives him a sheepish smile.

Looks at the crowd.

Crumples up the paper and flicks it to the side.

"I can't even read what I've written now," he admits to me. "I wrote it before I even proposed to you and the rest of the words have all faded away."

"You know you probably should have double-checked that before the wedding," I tell him but I'm laughing because honestly, now that we're standing here like this, the vows aren't the most important thing. The important thing is that I'm here with him and we're pledging to be together forever.

"I'm just going to wing it," Kessler says. He grabs my hands and squeezes them tight. "Nova, baby, I love you. That's really all I can say and it isn't enough. It will never be enough. Maybe I'm better off not having those vows because all of those words couldn't describe the way that I feel about you. I tried and I did my best. You know how I like to try and market anything, and yet I knew I would fail when it comes to telling you how I feel. I'm trying to be a romantic but it's hard when maybe the best thing to say is the easiest. So here it goes. Nova, I can't wait to love you forever, to sit on the lanai and name geckos and grow old with you. With Hunter, with our baby, with nothing else but our love. That's all I need. That's all I need for the rest of my life."

I'm not sure if he's crying or sweating but I know I am, big fat tears running down my cheeks. I can't stop staring at him, at my husband-to-be, at the beautiful ocean behind him and the sun coming through the clouds and everything is just too big for this moment, too grand to contain.

Words won't do it for me either.

I glance at the crowd, at my parents, at Hunter and Loan, at Kate and Desiree and everyone from work. Everyone I care about, my closest friends and loved ones and I think how lucky I am.

Like Kessler, I need to keep it simple.

"Baby," I say to him. "I had written my vows a long time ago too. I had written them and rewritten them and rewritten them because I could never get it quite right. I was rewriting them this afternoon, thinking I finally found the right words, but you made me realize no amount of words will do. I love you Kessler Rocha. I am honored to become your wife, to be the mother of your children. I am filled with Aloha for you, my spirit and yours will be together until we're all just stars in the sky."

I barely hear the reverend say the rest of his speech.

I just say "I do" and then Kessler is kissing me and everyone is clapping and cheering and I am lost in his orbit, two stars and spirits circling around and around into infinity.

We're brighter than the sun.

We walk, hand in hand, cheering down the aisle as the ukulele gets louder, playing "Somewhere Over the Rainbow," and we're heading to the waves to dip our toes in the purifying salt water and—

Suddenly, Kessler stops walking.

His eyes are sharply focused in the distance.

"What?" I ask, wondering what's going on. We're barefoot, maybe he stepped on a stick.

"It's him," he whispers to me, leaning in close, never taking his eagle eyes away.

"Who?" I ask, looking around. "Do we have a party crasher?"

He nods toward a bush, looking grim. "We do."

A rooster steps out of the bush.

"It's that motherfucking chicken."

The chicken stares at Kessler.

Kessler stares at the chicken.

"Oh no. No. Kess, that's not the same chicken. It was two years ago, I—"

But Kessler doesn't hear me.

"This time it's personal," he says, before he starts running.

The chicken runs down the beach, squawking and flapping his wings.

My husband follows.

My husband.

THE END

THANK you so much for coming on this journey with me, Kessler, Nova and the gang! If you want to read some of my books in a similar vein, check out my romantic comedy: SMUT - an enemies-to-lovers romance about two opposites who fall in bed (and into trouble) when they start to write anonymous smutty romances together.

Also check out the ultimate friends-to-lovers romance BAD AT LOVE, about two best friends who are bad at love and decide to "date" each other in order to figured out why their love lives are so screwed up!

If you want another office romance, I have that in BEFORE I EVER MET YOU, about a single mom who falls for her new boss - who also happens to be her father's best friend.

You can also find all my books on Amazon HERE.

THANK YOU

Thank you so much for reading Nothing Personal! I really appreciate it and I hope the book made you laugh and swoon. I wrote it after a difficult time in my life, one of those purely selfish "for me" books and I ended up falling in love with the story and characters, as well as the act of writing again, which is no small feat.

Even though I wrote this book to bring joy back into my life, I really hope it does the same for you. The world seems awfully dark sometimes and I truly believe laughter, hope and love can be the best medicine.

BY THE WAY if you loved the book and end up leaving a review, write to me at karinahalleank@gmail.com between December 27th and February 1st 2019. If you send me a link to your review along with your mailing address, I will send you a signed postcard from Hawaii! (Please allow a month to arrive). This is open internationally but reviews must be posted to Amazon.com.

Mahalo and thanks for reading!

Ahi Poke diced raw tuna and onions tossed in a sesame soy sauce marinade.

A Hui Hou a phrase that means "until we meet again" or "see you later."

Aloha greeting used to say hello or goodbye. Aloha can also mean love. According to Kessler, you can use Aloha in many different ways, i.e. "You Aloha me."

Aloha Kakahiaka good morning.

Hula Hawaiian form of communication using dance

Kane man

Keiki kid

Kālua Pork super tasty shredded pork cooked in a traditional Hawaiian cooking method that utilizes an *imu*, a type of underground oven. The word kālua, which literally means "to cook in an underground oven," can be used to describe various foods.

Lanai porch, veranda

Laulau meat or fish wrapped in taro leaves and steamed in a ti leaf packet

Lei garland of flowers, leaves, nuts, or shells

Lomi Lomi Salmon a side dish in Hawaiian cuisine. It is a fresh tomato and salmon salad, and was introduced to Hawaiians by early Western sailors.

Luau feast

Mahalo thank you

Mahimahi dolphin fish

Mai Tai very strong boozy rum drink. Cut yourself off after three of them.

Malihini newcomer, visitor

Mele Kalikimaka Merry Christmas....also a very catchy song (in a good way, unlike that *other* song we shall not speak of)

Menehune mythical small people who are rumored to have inhabited the Hawaiian islands before Polynesians

POG stands for Pineapple Orange Guava and according to Nova, if you mix it with Veuve Cliquot it becomes a "POG Cliquot" and it's extremely tasty.

Ukulele stringed instrument, small guitar

Wahine woman

ACKNOWLEDGMENTS

For Scott, always and forever. All my thanks belong to you this time. Thank you for helping me, loving me, living this life with me.

    I Aloha you.
    You Aloha me.

ABOUT THE AUTHOR

Karina Halle is a former travel writer and music journalist and The New York Times, Wall Street Journal and USA Today Bestselling author of The Pact, Bad at Love, The Swedish Prince, Sins & Needles, and over 46 other wild and romantic reads. She lives on an island off the coast of British Columbia with her husband and her rescue pitbull, where she drinks a lot of wine, hikes a lot of trails and devours a lot of books.

Halle is represented by Root Literary and is both self-published and published by Simon & Schuster and Hachette in North America and in the UK.

Hit her up on Instagram at @authorHalle, on Twitter at @MetalBlonde and on Facebook (join her reader group "Karina Halle's Anti-Heroes" for extra fun and connect with her!). You can also visit www.authorkarinahalle.com and sign up for the newsletter for news, excerpts, previews, private book signing sales and more.

ALSO BY KARINA HALLE

A Nordic King

Nothing Personal

Made in the USA
Columbia, SC
26 January 2022

54805805R00174